THE EYES OF NIGHT

DAVID C. SMITH

AVON BOOKS • NEW YORK

If you purchased this book without a cover, you should be aware that this book is stolen property. It was reported as "unsold and destroyed" to the publisher, and neither the author nor the publisher has received any payment for this "stripped book."

THE EYES OF NIGHT is an original publication of Avon Books. This work has never before appeared in book form. This work is a novel. Any similarity to actual persons or events is purely coincidental.

AVON BOOKS
A division of
The Hearst Corporation
1350 Avenue of the Americas
New York, New York 10019

Copyright © 1991 by David C. Smith
Cover art by Tim O'Brien
Published by arrangement with the author
Library of Congress Catalog Card Number: 91-91767
ISBN: 0-380-76011-8

All rights reserved, which includes the right to reproduce this book or portions thereof in any form whatsoever except as provided by the U.S. Copyright Law. For information address Donald Maass Literary Agency, 64 West 84th Street, New York, New York 10024.

First Avon Books Printing: July 1991

AVON TRADEMARK REG. U.S. PAT. OFF. AND IN OTHER COUNTRIES, MARCA REGISTRADA, HECHO EN U.S.A.

Printed in the U.S.A.

RA 10 9 8 7 6 5 4 3 2 1

He kept fingernail clippings, pieces of hair, dried skin from old blisters—something personal from everyone, just to keep people in line. He'd pull out the piece of dead skin and start stoking the demon fires. And then you'd wake up in the middle of the night some night shrieking like a terrified little girl because the bottom half of your body was gone—stripped clean—just the leg bones there. Or you'd wake up and be alive just long enough to see something dark and sharp jumping at your face. Or you'd see your heart being torn out and dangled in front of you, the blood squirting up and blinding you, splashing in your face...

Welcome to hell...

Other Avon Books by
David C. Smith

THE FAIR RULES OF EVIL

Avon Books are available at special quantity discounts for bulk purchases for sales promotions, premiums, fund raising or educational use. Special books, or book excerpts, can also be created to fit specific needs.

For details write or telephone the office of the Director of Special Markets, Avon Books, Dept. FP, 1350 Avenue of the Americas, New York, New York 10019.

**This book is for
Stuart McLean,
in friendship**

With thanks to
Judy Milkovich
and
Bob Morrison

> The fiend in his own shape is
> less hideous than
> when he rages in the breast of man.
>
> —NATHANIEL HAWTHORNE,
> "Young Goodman Brown"

THE EYES OF NIGHT

1

In the twilight, the house looked like some wounded animal that had stumbled in midstride and died there, lopsided. Half burnt, the back porch twisted and broken, the roof covered with a whispery dusting of snow and ice that shimmered in the last cold light of the sun.

Jack shifted the van into first gear to make it up the final steep turn of the driveway. The wheels spun for a second and whined before catching and pulling forward. He and Dragomir lurched in their seats. Then Jack let the van roll to a stop.

Dragomir stared at the house. His breath fogged the passenger-side window.

Jack said, "So this is it."

Dragomir said nothing.

Seven hundred miles, all the way from Cincinnati, in just under fourteen hours. They hadn't eaten a thing the whole time, had stopped only for gas. Jack was tired and hungry, but Dragomir, silent for the entire trip, living off whatever had been going through his mind all day long, seemed fine, composed and intense and focused. Normal, for him.

Grunting, Dragomir opened the passenger-side door and got out. He moved slowly.

Jack got out, too, closed his door, and looked around. He'd never been up here before, in the Adirondacks. Mountains. Endless walls of trees. The last of the sun was gone, his breath was steaming, and he was cold. He buttoned his coat and walked around the front of the van.

Dragomir was leaning on his walking stick, still watching the house. Looking at him, Jack realized for the first time since he'd met him that Dragomir seemed old. Bent and tired and old. Like any other old man, needing assistance, needing others to help him.

Jack wondered if the feeling were a trick Dragomir was playing on him.

"So this is it," he said again.

"Go inside. Look around. Find something."

Jack leaned inside the van and got the flashlight out of the glove compartment. He closed Dragomir's door and flicked on the flashlight. He played the beam around the back porch and saw clearly the black streaks on the wood, as if left by lightning, and one whole side of the porch smashed down.

"Fry."

"Yes, most likely," Dragomir agreed, moving away, leaning on his stick.

Does he really need the fucking cane? Jack wondered. Isn't this all just a show, so that the rest of us think he's helpless?

He walked onto the porch and with the flashlight found the handle to the screen door and pulled it open. The back door was locked, so he kicked it in. The whole porch trembled when he did it, and snow and ice drifted down on him, slipping under the collar of his coat and tickling him.

Jack found a light switch and flicked it on and off. No electricity. He wasn't surprised. Whoever'd locked the place up last would no doubt have notified the utilities companies that Emma Daedalus had wanted the power turned off. Cover your tracks, all of them. If Dragomir was right, then that had only been a month ago, maybe less.

Jack wasn't picking up anything, he didn't *sense* anything, but Dragomir no doubt was, sniffing around, his antennae out, sucking up psychic juices everywhere.

He went through the kitchen, shined the flashlight all around, tried to ignore his gurgling stomach. Minutes went by as he sorted through drawers, looked into all of the cupboards, leafed through books. He found some mail— advertising fliers and other junk. Either she got no personal mail or she'd hidden it all or had destroyed it.

THE EYES OF NIGHT

A sitting room, a spare room of some kind, a storage room. More books, tons of books, odds and ends. He went through everything, holding books open so that any papers stuck between the leaves would fall out, checking behind paintings on the walls for anything hidden there, kicking his damp shoes on the floorboards for sounds of a hollow spot.

Find something.

Find fucking *what*?

He took the stairs that led to the second floor. Bedrooms. More time wasted. Jack was beginning to feel angry. This was pointless, there was nothing here.

The last room on the second floor was small, and Jack promised himself that he'd have something to eat before he checked out the basement.

The room was little more than a closet—a bed, a small desk and a chair, an armoire.

He sifted through the drawers of the desk, then got down on his belly and shined the light underneath it. He twisted his head the other way and shined the light under the bed. There was a piece of paper on the floor.

Wriggling like a snake, Jack lodged himself between the floor and box spring, blinked away the dust he kicked up, and grabbed the paper.

It was an envelope.

He stood up and brushed himself off, then shined the light on the return address.

"Ho-ly shit..."

He pulled out the letter and scanned both of its pages under the glare of the flashlight.

"Ho-ly fucking shit..."

Dragomir was not in the van. Jack saw him standing on the other side of the driveway, leaning on his cane before a tall, deeply sloped hill.

"Mr. Dragomir!"

He didn't turn around. He waited until Jack was beside him before he lifted his cane and waved it, indicating the hill.

"Graves. Two of them are buried here. What did you find?"

"A letter. It's from Ginny Trevisan to her brother, David."

"Who is Ginny Trevisan and her brother, David?"

"Mr. Dragomir, it's addressed to David when he was at the seminary. At Saint Luke's. I knew David when I was at Saint Luke's."

"The same man?"

"There was only one person there with that name. And the fucking wimp was here. He was here with Emma Daedalus."

"No doubt he could tell us something about what happened."

"But we don't know if he knew Fry, though."

"Anyone who knew Emma Daedalus knew Theodore Fry."

"Well, okay."

"Find him." Dragomir looked him in the eyes, and if Jack had wondered earlier about Dragomir's being ill, playing games, putting on an act—

The eyes, the eyes that could burn right through you.

"You are to find him, Jack."

"Yes, sir."

"Find him and tell him . . . impress upon him how important it is that I speak with him."

"I'll find him."

"I leave this to you."

"Yes, sir."

Not a request—it was an order.

2

It was a little after two in the afternoon, so Pat's, the restaurant Sister Mary had chosen, was relatively quiet, which was fine with her because she had the impression that the woman she was to meet would prefer some privacy. She took a booth near the back and asked the waitress for a cup of coffee.

"There'll be two of us."

"All right, ma'am."

Over the phone, the woman had sounded young. Young and—what? Frightened? Anxious?

"I asked around and they told me that, you know, you'd be a good person to talk to. I just need to talk to someone."

"Could you give me an idea of what this is about, Miss—?"

"Look, I really can't give you my name right now, is that okay? I just need to—" And she'd started crying.

The bell above the door jangled, Sister Mary looked up, and the woman who came in met her gaze and didn't smile but walked down the aisle between the booths and the stools at the counter.

She was pregnant.

Twenty-two? Twenty-one? And at least six months pregnant.

"Sister Mary Francisco?"

"Yes."

She slid into the seat opposite Sister Mary, moving awkwardly, settling herself, not looking up.

The waitress came over with Sister Mary's coffee and the young woman said, "I'll have a cup, too. With cream?"

"Cream's right there on the table."

"Oh, yes. Thank-you."

Finally, she met Sister Mary's uncertain stare. "Thank-you for agreeing—for coming here." She was slender and dark-haired and quite pretty.

"You sounded so serious on the phone."

"Well, this is kind of serious. This is very serious, for me, at least."

"Does it have to do with . . ."

Absently, the young woman touched her swollen belly. "Well, yes, in a way. Yes, it does."

"Why don't we start with your name?"

The waitress returned and set her coffee on the table. The young woman waited.

When the waitress left: "Nora."

"Just—'Nora'?"

She thought about it. The bell above the door jangled and someone else came in. Nora twisted in her seat, turning around to look. It was a big man in a heavy winter coat; he sat on a stool near the cash register at the front of the restaurant and he didn't notice Nora, didn't even look at her, so he must not be following her.

She and Sister Mary were pretty much alone here in this booth, no one in the seats behind either of them, but that might change pretty soon, so she'd better just come right out with it.

"I asked—I made some phone calls. Called the church. I've never been to that church but I said that I needed to talk to someone, a woman, and they told me, whoever it was, they recommended you."

"Okay."

"I'm Nora Dragomir."

There was no way for Sister Mary to hide her surprise. "His daughter?"

"He only has one child and I'm it. I'm her."

"Well, why did you call—why would you want to see me?"

"It's his baby."

"Dear God."

"Sister Mary, there's more to it. There's a lot more to it." Nora glanced around and she lowered her voice almost to a whisper. "Do you think it's safe to talk here?"

"Why wouldn't it be?"

Nora looked at her coffee but didn't sip it. "I have to make sure that I wasn't followed. My father—he has people who watch me. I mean, spy on me. He has people everywhere."

Sister Mary was cautious. "Your father's a very powerful man."

"I'm not exaggerating when I call them spies. I'm not— Am I frightening you?"

"Not really."

"Sister Mary, *I'm* frightened. I want you to understand why I'm so frightened."

"The baby is his."

"Yes, but—"

"Was it rape? Did your father rape you?"

Nora sipped her coffee. The cup shook visibly as it hovered at her lips. She set it in its saucer with both hands. "Dear God," she said, whispering again. "I've been trying for weeks to do this, to talk to someone, to get out of the house..."

"You live with your father?"

Nora nodded. "He's out of town. I don't know when he'll be back because he makes sure I never know things like that. I had to sneak out of the house, and I still think somebody might've seen me."

"Nora... take your time. Tell me exactly—"

"He raped me. It's... the reason *why* he raped me. He's—"

"Nora..."

"He's *evil*, Sister Mary."

Sister Mary told her, "I'm sure you must think—"

Nora interrupted her by lifting her purse onto the table and removing from it a white legal-sized envelope. She shoved the purse aside and from the envelope took out a number of newspaper clippings. Some of them were yellowed, some were photostats.

All were stories about murders or bizarre deaths.

"This one was a state senator," Nora told Sister Mary, sorting through them. "This woman was a reporter. This woman was a cocktail waitress. A cocktail waitress! There are two more. . . . This man here owned a television station and a radio station. This one published—"

Sister Mary put a hand on one of Nora's.

Nora looked her in the eyes. "He had these people murdered."

"I can't believe that."

"Sister Mary . . ." Her voice fell quiet again. "I'm not lying to you. My father is a very evil man. He—Sister, he does evil . . . rituals. Ceremonies. I'm serious! He practices black magic. He has people who help him, who protect him. He—"

"Nora, please."

"He uses black magic to kill people and for power. That's why he's as powerful as he is, it's why he knows so many people. He *owns* people."

"What do you—"

"And that's why he got me pregnant, too. He's dying. My father is *dying*," she whispered. "Do you understand what he's trying to do? He wants to put his soul inside my baby, and that's—Sister Mary, it's possible!—and that's why he got me—pregnant. . . ."

Sister Mary watched her.

"Dear God," Nora moaned. "You're a nun, you're a religious person, you *understand*, don't you?"

"I didn't say that I don't believe you."

"But you have to *help* me!" There were tears in her eyes and she was shivering, trembling.

"I'm not sure what—"

Nora moaned and looked around again, paranoid. She'd made a mistake and she was ashamed of herself, she felt stupid and alone. "I have to go, it's getting late."

"Please—"

The waitress came back. "Anything else? More coffee?"

Nora looked away and wiped her cheeks with the edge of her hand.

Sister Mary said, "No. Thank-you. I'll take that." She reached for the check as the waitress left.

"I have to go," Nora said again, moving.

"Just sit right there for one minute."

She was a little surprised at the abrupt tone of authority in Sister Mary's voice.

Sister Mary pulled out her own purse and placed two dollar bills on top of the check.

She said to Nora, "I didn't say that I don't believe you. And I didn't say that I don't want to help you. Do you need these?"—the newspaper clippings.

"They're mine, I don't know... No. Take them if you want them."

"You understand that they don't prove anything about what you've said."

"I know that, I just... Can you *help* me?"

"I can talk to some people who can. What do you think we should do?"

"I don't know. I—don't—*know*! I'm just so—so scared, he's got me trapped in the house, he has people watching me all the time, I can't—"

"Calm down. Calm down, now."

"Dear God..."

"Are you thinking of having an abortion? Do you want counseling?"

"I just want to get away from him! From all of these people he has!"

The bell above the door jangled again and Nora turned her head frantically. The man by the cash register had left. When she faced Sister Mary again, there was an expression of utter fear on her face.

"I don't know what to tell you," Sister Mary said. "That's the truth. Let me speak to Father Kendrick, maybe a few other people. I'll do what I can. But Father will ask to talk with you. Can you give me a phone number?"

"Oh, God, you can't call me!"

"Give me something. How am I supposed to get hold of you?"

Nora whined, "I don't know. Can't we—can we just meet someplace in a few days?"

"All right. Tell me where."

"Promise me, please, Sister, that you won't try to call me, I mean at my father's house."

"I promise."

"And tell Father Kerrick—"

"Kendrick."

"Please don't have him or anyone talk to my father about this."

"You're over eighteen, aren't you?"

"I'm twenty-one."

"You're an adult. There's no reason to talk to anyone else. But I'm not in a position to decide."

"I have to do something *soon*," Nora insisted. "I'm seven and a half months pregnant. He *wants* this baby!"

"And you don't?"

"Just—get me away from him!"

"All right. . . . All right. Where should we meet?"

"You tell me. Anywhere."

"You're sure you can get out of the house?"

"I'll manage, I'll do it somehow."

"What about . . . what about the Big Boy out in Madison? By Red Bank Road?"

"That's good. Nobody'd think of looking for me there."

"Is that all right?

"Yes, yes."

"Would it be better in the afternoon? In the evening?"

"It doesn't matter. Just tell me, I'll be there. I'll get there."

"Today's . . . Tuesday. Tuesday. Thursday evening? Seven o'clock."

"Okay."

"You'll meet me there then."

"Yes, yes. Dear god. . . . You *are* going to try to do something, aren't you?"

"I told you I would."

"Sister Mary . . . you be careful, too. He has people everywhere. They're always watching. I'm not lying to you when I tell you how *evil* he is. He *does* things—"

"I'm not afraid. And I do want to help you."

Nora stared at her for a long minute, wanting to believe that Sister Mary could, indeed, do something to help her. But now she wasn't certain any longer. She wasn't sure that anyone could save her.

She said, "There *is* evil in the world, Sister Mary."

"I've given my life to Christ, Nora. I believe that through His love and through His Father's strength, evil can be vanquished. I'm not afraid."

"I am," Nora admitted. "I am afraid. Sister Mary . . . there's so much to be afraid of. . . ."

3

The phone call came early Friday evening. Father Kendrick was in his office, sorting through memos, reviewing next week's schedules. A tape of Handel's *Messiah* played in the background.

Christmas, two weeks away.

He answered on the second ring. "Father Kendrick."

"You be careful and keep away or you'll find out what it feels like, too."

That was all. Kendrick sat there for a moment listening to the dial tone, half expecting the caller to come back on the line.

Was it a mistake of some kind? Some sort of prank? It had to be some sort of prank.

He cradled the receiver and reached across his desk and wrote as well as he could remember it on one of his notepads:

You be careful, too—keep away or you'll know what it feels like, too.

The words of the threat, written out, read, and reread, sounded ridiculous.

He'd identified himself, he was sure. It was a habit, whenever he picked up the phone. So the threat was actually meant for him. The voice had seemed vaguely familiar, but he didn't know anyone who made threats. Who would say something like that to him?

Kendrick sat back and ran through his mind the names and faces of the young men he'd spoken with in the past few days. None clicked. It was a ridiculous thing to do anyway. He was a priest in a seminary; he was surrounded by male voices.

THE EYES OF NIGHT

"You be careful, too—keep away or you'll know what it feels like, too."

Mistake or prank or bona fide threat, Kendrick decided that he ought at least to let someone know about it. He dialed the police department downtown and asked for Bud Pomeroy. They'd known each other for twenty years; Bud wouldn't think that he was overreacting or being alarmist.

"Sergeant Pomeroy."

"Bud, this is Mike Kendrick out here at Saint Luke's."

"Hey, it's been a while. What's up?"

"I just had a strange phone call and I don't know whether to take it seriously or not."

"What'd they say?"

Kendrick read it to him.

"You recognize the voice or anything?"

"I don't know. That's hard to say."

"Male?"

"Yes."

"It doesn't mean anything to you?"

"No. I think it's some kind of prank, myself."

"Yeah, maybe."

"Well, I thought it wouldn't hurt to tell you, I guess, but I don't know what else we can do about it."

"Wait and see if he calls back. That's about it."

But when he hung up and returned to his paperwork, Kendrick couldn't concentrate. The voice bothered him, and the threat itself, the very idea that anyone would threaten him.

Face it, he told himself. It was someone's idea of a dumb stunt. You can't do anything about it anyway, so forget it. File it away. It was a mistake.

He went back to work. He listened to Handel, he jotted notes on his desk calendar, he scribbled his initials on memos and added them to the growing pile in his Out tray.

The phone rang again at seven-thirty. Kendrick waited a second before answering, trying to decide what he'd say if it were the prankster calling him back.

But it was Bud Pomeroy. "Mike. I was hoping you might still be there."

"What's wrong?"

"We found her."

"Found who?"

"You, uh, don't want to hear this over the phone, do you?"

"Bud, what's happened?"

"It's a very nasty one, Mike. There's been a murder. I've got to tell you that right now."

"Who?"

"You have a Sister Mary Francisco—'Francisco,' right, Glenn? As in 'San'?—a Sister Mary—"

"I know her."

"Mike, I'm sorry."

"Tell me what's happened."

"We're still trying to sort that out. Right after you phoned me, we got another call. Somebody found her in a warehouse."

"What was she doing in a warehouse?"

"Mike, this is not pleasant for me, it is not. Are you all right? Because I'd like you to—"

"Bud, I'm . . . What does this have to do with the phone call?"

"I don't know. I don't know if it has anything to do with the phone call or not."

"Dear God. Give me . . . Did you call anyone else? Monsignor Pantik? He's the rector."

"You're the first besides us."

"Can I—Where is this? Where are you?"

"Where we found her. Mike—this is brutal."

"What does 'brutal' mean?"

"Look, I want to go at it this way. Tell me what you know about—and I'm serious, now—anything you know about Satanism or black magic or voodoo or whatever they call it. What about that stuff?"

Kendrick's mouth went dry. "I don't know anything about voodoo. Satanism. Why?"

"Because this was a very brutal ritual killing of some kind, and it looks to us a lot like voodoo or something like that, I kid you not."

"Tell me where you are. I want to see her."

"No, Mike, you don't."

"Just tell me—"

"Wait until—"

"Damn it, Bud! Tell me where you are!"

"All right. Shit. All right. Look, let me send a car."

"No, because you won't do it. You think I'm—"

"I'll send it. I will send the car. Okay?"

Kendrick was quiet for a long moment. "What did they do to her?"

"I'm going to wait until you get down here before we get into that. I'm sending an officer now. Okay, Mike?"

"Yeah."

"Mike, you gotta be strong about this."

"Dear Christ."

"Mike?"

"Dear Christ. . . ." He tried to put down the receiver but it dropped from his hand and fell lopsided on the desk. He picked it up and furiously slammed it down. "Jesus—dear—*Christ*!"

As he did, his eyes fell on the note. The threat.

You be careful, too—keep away or you'll know what it feels like, too.

Kendrick went cold and his stomach tightened, it bunched up inside him, he went nauseous.

He remembered the voice.

The warehouse was down by the railroad tracks along Mill Creek. There were police officers and detectives and technicians there. The building, inside and out, was lit with portable arc lights. A drizzle was falling, cold, chill, creating a haze. The warehouse building, the flat gravel lot in front of it, the dark railroad tracks just beyond—it was a surreal image, darkly poetic, strange and sad, almost beautiful.

Kendrick got out of the patrol car and Pomeroy was there, ambling over with one hand thrust out. Kendrick, shivering, took it.

"Hello, Mike."

"Bud."

"This way."

Pomeroy led him across the gravel lot, helped him move under the plastic yellow ribbon, the POLICE LINE—DO NOT CROSS barricade that had been strung up, and walked him into the warehouse.

It was a large building and, except for some old wooden crates and broken pallets in one corner, vacant. The whole structure was of wood and had obviously been abandoned; Kendrick was surprised that it hadn't been razed long ago as a fire hazard.

The middle of one wall looked as if it had been splashed with red paint. Kendrick could see the shape of an upside-down human body there, a silhouette outlined by the blood.

Pomeroy told him, "They, uh, nailed her to the wall, Mike, is what they did."

On either side of the silhouette, blood had been used to paint symbols on the wall. Kendrick recognized some of them; he remembered them from encyclopedia articles. Other symbols he did not understand at all. Inverted stars and words written in Latin and other alphabets, and odd signs drawn with lines and circles.

In front of the silhouette, on the bare earth floor, was a large circle. It, too, had been drawn in blood, in Sister Mary's blood. The circle enclosed a large, red pentagram, an inverted star. And there were candles, black candles, or what was left of them. Pools of melted wax.

"Oh, God," Kendrick whispered.

"Does any of this mean anything?" Pomeroy asked him. "Or is it just garbage?"

"I don't know if I know enough about it. The marks on the wall, there—I've seen things like that. In books, I mean. They go back to the Middle Ages."

"They're Satanic, aren't they?"

"Bunch of goddamn kids," called one of the detectives in his Kentrucky drawl, kneeling on the ground on the other side of the warehouse. "Bunch of goddamn drug addicts is what they are. Listen to that rock and roll music, that heavy

THE EYES OF NIGHT

metal, whatever you want to call it. That and what they put up their noses."

The body was about to be driven to the morgue. Kendrick, turning away from the wall, saw the white-sheeted gurney and the paramedics getting ready to lift it up. He told Pomeroy, "I want to see her."

"Not the best idea, Mike."

But Kendrick walked past him. Pomeroy followed and, behind Kendrick's back, high-signed the medics. They waited.

"Please," Kendrick said, looking at one of the young men.

"Go ahead," Pomeroy told him.

The medic lifted the sheet, revealing Sister Mary's head and shoulders.

Kendrick gasped. His right hand flew to his mouth. Pomeroy gripped his shoulders and turned him away and the medic covered the body again.

"Mike?"

"What did they do to her *eyes*?"

"Take some deep breaths."

Kendrick swallowed air, did it until he began to feel dizzy. Then he faced Pomeroy. "Why did they do that?"

"They cut her eyelids off. We don't know why."

"Bud—" But he couldn't say anything. He turned away, moved away. He looked back at the wall, the circle on the ground and the star inside the circle, the candles. He started walking toward the candles and the blood, but stopped.

It was as if he sensed something. He could almost feel the evil of it in the air, could almost see the shadows moving on the wall, shadows lit by the light of the burning black candles. He could almost hear the screams.

He felt cold, then. Kendrick felt as if he were standing in a tunnel of cold, a world of cold. Evil cold.

He whispered, "Oh, Mary, I'm so *sorry*. . . ."

Pomeroy stepped up beside him and kept a respectful distance but said, "Let's get you home now, all right?"

Kendrick nodded but didn't move. He told Pomeroy, "A year ago, maybe a little more than a year, we expelled a student from the seminary. I found him in the church doing a ceremony like this. This kind of thing. The symbols, I mean. The candles, the star.''

''You remember his name?''

''Starkis. Jack Starkis. I think—I *think*—he was the person who called me tonight.''

''You know where he is now?''

''I have no idea. But you can call Monsignor Pantik's office in the morning. They'll have the records.''

''You think maybe he has something against you or against Saint Luke's because of that, because of being kicked out?''

''I don't know. But if he does—'' Kendrick's voice was very quiet, very sad. ''If he does, why would he hurt Mary? Why not just hurt me? Why hurt her?''

''Come on.'' Pomeroy clapped him on the shoulder. ''Let's get you out of here.''

4

Monsignor Pantik did not have a pleasant Saturday.

He and his staff spent several hours helping the police, answering their questions about Sister Mary, reviewing her files and her appointment book, and photostating for investigators everything in Jack Starkis's folder. Afterward, Pantik spoke with his people, consoling them, asking them to continue cooperating with the police, and doing what he could to allay fears that had already begun to make some of them apprehensive. What if everyone at St. Luke's were a potential victim? There were a lot of crazies out there. How could they be sure that Sister Mary wasn't only the first of several victims?

By the time the Monsignor met privately with Father Kendrick, early in the afternoon, his nerves were frayed. Pantik asked Kendrick into his office and closed the door. He did his best to begin on a cordial note.

"I'm very sorry," he said. "I know that you and Sister Mary were close."

"Thank you, Father."

"Phillip."

"Phillip."

"Did you get any sleep last night?"

"Not a wink."

"I'll make this brief but, Mike, I want to have a few things clear in my own mind. I think we know each other well enough. I think we respect each other."

"True."

"So I'm going to be blunt."

"Go ahead."

"You know what I'm going to say."

"Sister Mary and me."

"Was there anything between the two of you, ever, at any time, that could lead to the embarrassment of Saint Luke's, or that could be behind some sort of blackmail threat or . . . or this murder?"

"No."

"You two were very good friends."

"We were. We were, Phillip. And we never did anything to hurt either one of us or the church or—anything else."

"All right, then. I believe you."

"Thank you."

"How strongly . . . I must tell you, I'm glad to have that out of the way. How strongly do you feel that Jack Starkis is involved in this?"

"I don't know. I'd like to be absolutely certain that it was his voice on the phone, but in all honesty—"

"It's been a long time."

"It's been a long time."

"Did he threaten you last year? At any time during that whole incident?"

"No."

"Not at all?"

"I got the impression that he was actually kind of relieved to be out of here."

"Yes. Yes." Pantik was thoughtful. "All right. We have a very serious problem here. I want you to be careful. You particularly, Mike. If Jack Starkis is involved in this, he may do something more than just make a phone call next time. If there is a next time."

"I know that."

"I'm taking this very seriously where you're concerned. I think we ought to vary your schedule a bit. I've already asked Ernest to look into that for me. And I want you to think about taking some time off. Or staying someplace else for a while."

"I'm not a coward, Phillip."

"It's not a question of being a coward. It's simply being smart. You know that."

THE EYES OF NIGHT

"You're right." Kendrick admitted it.

"I guess that's all. I simply wanted to clarify that issue, some issues."

"Understood."

"We'll be going through Sister Mary's personal effects. We'll take care of that."

"All right."

Pantik sighed. "Maybe we'll find more clues for the police. Dear God. This is insane."

"I'm going to take it upon myself to write a few letters. Let some people know. Some of our old students."

"I guess you'd better do that."

Kendrick stood up and went to the door.

"You don't have any idea, do you," Pantik asked him, "why Sister Mary went to that warehouse last night?"

"No."

"Assuming that she went there on her own, of course."

"I can't see that happening."

"Neither can I. Neither can I."

"But whatever it was," Kendrick told him, "it was a trick of some kind. Someone tricked her. Because she was good. She was a good soul, and someone took advantage of that."

"It happens too often in this world."

"Personally, I'm getting sick and tired of all the filth in this world, and everybody making excuses for it, as if it has to be that way and nobody can really do anything about it. I'm getting damned tired, Phillip, of standing there with my finger in the dike. I'd like to walk away and let the whole sick mess collapse."

"You're tired. You're—"

"I'm tired and I'm heartbroken and I'm heartsick and I'm disgusted. And if some animal like Jack Starkis is behind this and I find that out and I know I had the chance to do something about it a year ago and I didn't—"

"Calm down, Mike."

Kendrick stood there, his whole body clenched like a fist. He told Pantik, "I even tried praying last night. Do you believe that?"

"And?"

"It wasn't a nice prayer."

In his room, Father Kendrick poured himself a cup of coffee and, from the bottle he kept in the bottom drawer of his desk, added some whiskey to it.

And he wrote letters.

Letters to friends of his in other parts of the country, letters to friends of Sister Mary's.

Because they had, indeed, loved each other, and they had wondered occasionally how things might have been had they met under different circumstances. They had wondered and they had spoken of it, always carefully and always with an undercurrent of humor, of understanding.

"We've done the best thing," she'd said to him once. *"We have our boys."*

Our "boys." The seminarians at St. Luke's. She'd been a surrogate mother to them, and the best of them—some of them going back twenty years at least—had stayed in touch with her with Christmas cards and notes and letters and occasional photos.

Kendrick knew them, too, and had their addresses in his file. He wrote each of them a brief, sad note. *I'm sorry to have to tell you* . . . He did not use the word *murder*; he said that Sister Mary had been killed and referred to it as "the tragedy," as "the shock that has stunned all of us."

Late in the morning, he came to the *T*s. Trevisan . . .

David Trevisan.

It was his parents' address—David's address, now, Kendrick assumed, since he'd gone back home. How long had it been since David Trevisan had left? September, October, November . . .

"I don't think I really wanted to become a priest. I think I just wanted to hide for a while."

Kendrick honestly wondered what had become of him. David Trevisan had been one of Mary's favorites; she'd always tended to prefer the bright ones, and the ones who seemed a little lonely, and David had certainly fulfilled both those qualities. Was he all right? What had he done with himself since leaving St. Luke's? He would probably have made a fine priest. A little too sensitive, perhaps, but he could have managed that, in time.

"I want you to feel that Christ is with you, David. Don't you feel that Christ is with you?"

"This is . . . very uncomfortable for me, Father."

Kendrick poured himself another generous cup of coffee—his third since coming back from Monsignor Pantik's office—and wrote a letter to David Trevisan.

He didn't refer to "the tragedy" or to "the shock." The David Trevisan whom Kendrick remembered would have appreciated the facts.

He did not, however, go into detail about the circumstances of the murder, for he really saw no good reason to tell David Trevisan that Sister Mary's death seemed to have something to do with Satanism or black magic.

5

David Trevisan was in his backyard, dressed only in a white robe, standing barefoot in the hard crust of snow. It was noon; a cool, almost transparent sun hung in the winter sky. David faced the sun, crossed his arms over his chest, and prayed:

"In nomine Sabaoth, Spiritus Magnus, suscipe me, o omnipotens aeterne, Spiritus..."

When he finished his prayer to the sun, to the life force, to the universal spirit, he sat down in the snow, crossed his legs, held his head straight, and meditated for an hour.

Then, not in the least cold, he went into his house, took off the robe and folded it carefully, and placed it in the wooden chest where he kept a number of other robes in a variety of colors, and bowls and incenses, and his knives and swords and wands. He pulled on his jeans and a sweater and went downstairs to make himself lunch, a sandwich and some coffee.

The house was one he'd bought six weeks earlier through the real estate office Cheryl worked for. He'd sold his parents' home and had looked for something secluded, something with some land around it, trees. This cottage, a story and a half, was twenty miles outside Noland in farm country, and David had appreciated it instantly. It reminded him of Emma's house in the Adirondacks. He liked that; but that was precisely one of the things about it that unnerved Cheryl.

She'd moved in with him, thinking that what they'd been through made that sensible—inevitable, maybe—but she wasn't happy now.

David knew that. He'd tried to convince her to learn some meditation techniques. He'd asked her to perform a ceremony with him sometime, a modest ceremony. She would get such insight from it. She'd feel so content and complete afterward, at peace.

"But I don't want to be at peace, David."

"Cheryl—"

"Don't you understand? I want a normal life, a normal relationship with a normal man. I want to be dull and average and normal."

"Look, I know this isn't what you'd call run of the mill. I know that what I do isn't—"

"David, it isn't what you do. It's what you *are*."

It's what you are.

It was her denial that got to him, Cheryl's taking what they'd gone through, what had happened to Ginny, Fry, what she herself had suffered, her taking it and pretending that it was something it wasn't.

Was I—? I was really . . . dead?

Dead . . .

Nothing ever really dies. It just changes, it moves on, it becomes more of whatever it's supposed to become.

Dead.

Yes, Cheryl, you were really dead. Yes, Fry killed you. Yes, I brought you back to life. Yes, yes, yes. That's where the headaches come from. That's why your eyes are fucked up, it's why you need glasses, contact lenses. It's why sunlight, bright light, hurts your eyes. You were dead, Cheryl. Like Fry. And you came back. I brought you back because I didn't want you to die.

She told him and she told herself, now, that that was ridiculous, it wasn't possible, she'd only been knocked unconscious or something, she'd gone into shock, no one dies and comes back to life, it's not possible.

Was I—? I was really . . . dead?
Nothing ever really dies.
Wrong.
Love dies.

* * *

After lunch he went out into the woods, dressed now in his winter coat and hat and gloves, scouting for a Christmas tree. He was determined that they'd have a nice Christmas. He'd already bought Cheryl the gold necklace that he knew she wanted, and he was going to buy her mother the good set of china that she'd made a comment about last week. They were going to have a nice Christmas, even if it meant that David would be pleasant to her mother.

He found his tree, one that was a good eight feet tall, and tied a piece of twine around it so that he'd know it when he came back later to saw it down. Returning to the house, he decided to get his mail and continued on down the long gravel driveway.

He felt good as he walked down the drive. He was home. He hadn't really had a home since his parents' deaths, he hadn't felt comfortable anywhere, not with Ginny, not at the seminary, not with Emma and Gray. But now he'd bought his own place and he was home.

He felt very pleased with himself.

In the mail were a May Company bill, an envelope full of sales coupons for rug cleaning and pizza parlors, and a letter from St. Luke's seminary in Cincinnati. It was from Father Kendrick. He'd typed his name below the return address and the envelope had one of those yellow Postal Service forwarding address labels.

David tore it open and began reading it as he walked back up the driveway, happy to hear from Father. But in a moment he stopped cold.

. . . with great hurt that I must tell you, David, that Sister Mary Francisco has been killed. She was found murdered last night under mysterious circumstances. The police are now looking for the perpetrator or perpetrators and, as you can imagine, all of us here are in deep shock. I thought it best to . . .

He ran back to the house. He left his coat on as he hurried into the living room and pulled his address book out of the desk and carried it with him into the kitchen. He misdialed the first time, swore out loud, told himself to calm down—Get a grip, Mr. Wizard—and dialed again.

"St. Luke's."

"Father Kendrick, please."

"Hold, please."

"Wait. Would you tell him, tell him that it's David Trevisan. Long distance."

Father came on quickly. "David?"

"Father Kendrick. I just got your letter, it just came in the mail."

"It's good to hear from you. I'm sorry I had to be the bearer of such bad news."

Kendrick told him that nothing more had been learned about the murder. Sister Mary had been buried yesterday and the shock was beginning to wear off, of course, although there was a heaviness hanging over everything, over everyone.

"And the police don't know how it happened?"

"Apparently not."

"Look, Father, I'd like to come down there."

"I appreciate that, David, I really do, but it's not necessary. I don't think this should upset your holiday."

"But I want to. I'd like to see you again."

"Yes. I'd like to see you again, too."

David told him that he'd pack tonight and plan on leaving tomorrow morning. He could be in Cincinnati in four or five hours, depending on how the roads were. Get a room and stay for a day or two. See some of his friends at the seminary.

"If you'd like to do that, why, it'd be nice to have you come down, it really would. Call me here when you get into town, can you do that?"

"I'll be happy to, Father."

He sawed down his tree and dragged it to the house, propped it up on the back porch. It gave him something to do, a shot at taking his mind off what had happened to Sister Mary.

Cheryl phoned him a little before five. She didn't sound

as if she were in a particularly pleasant mood. "David, I'm going to be a little late."

"Tell me when. I'll have supper ready."

"Oh, God, I don't know."

"Six? Six-thirty? Seven?"

"Shoot for six-thirty."

"We've got stuff for chili. I'll make us some chili."

"Fine. David?"

"Yeah."

"I'd like us to have a talk when I get home. Could we do that? Could we have a talk?"

"Yeah."

"I think we need to talk."

"Sure. We can talk."

We can talk.

It isn't what you do. It's what you are.

He started the chili, feeling angry and resentful. There was nothing to talk about. They'd talked about, around, inside, and outside everything. The only reason she talked was to—

Stop it, asshole.

You fucked up her life. Whatever you do, whatever you say, it's not quite going to be enough, because she was willing to do whatever it took, and you fucked up her life.

"You have the gift," Emma had told him. *"In your soul. It is your soul. You were born to it. None of us knows why."*

I sure as hell don't know why, David thought.

I want to have a normal life.

There are no normal lives, he wanted to tell Cheryl. There never were any normal lives. We just think so; we just pretend so. With me, it's a little more obvious. I was born fucking weird. Other people, they have to learn how, it takes them a little longer. But everything's fucking weird.

Dear God, he thought. I'm losing it. I'm scared.

I want to have a normal life.

I'm scared. I fucked up her life, he thought, and I'm going to lose her.

* * *

"Chili's good."

"Yeah, it'll put hair on your chest."

"Groan."

"Groan."

After supper, as he rinsed out the dishes and stacked them in the dishwasher, Cheryl said to him, "Remember this guy I told you about at work? Frank?"

"Frankly, no."

"He wants to take me out."

"And?"

"I told him yes, David."

He turned from the sink and looked at her, wiping his hands on a dishtowel. "What does he do, make passes at girls who wear glasses?"

"I hate these fucking glasses," Cheryl told him, leaving, going into the living room.

He gave her about fifteen minutes. She'd scrunched herself into a corner of the couch and had started *Out of Africa*. Again.

"I got a letter today from Father Kendrick. At the seminary. One of the nuns, Sister Mary, I knew her ... She was killed."

Cheryl stared at him. "Oh, God, David, I'm sorry."

"They buried her yesterday, Father said. But I told him I'd like to come down to see him. Talk to him."

"I am so sorry."

"Leave tomorrow morning."

That night, as they lay together in bed, neither of them able to sleep, David said to her, "I know you're so damned unhappy. If you want out of this, if you want out of here, look, do it, okay?"

She was silent for a long time, so long that he wondered if she'd fallen asleep and not heard him. Finally, in the darkness, Cheryl told him, "I've been thinking of going back to stay with my mom. I called her today."

"Then do it. Do whatever's going to be good for you, okay?"

She was quiet again for a while. "Okay."

"If you think it'll make you more comfortable, you could move your stuff out while I'm in Cincinnati. I'll probably be gone three or four days. Three days. Okay? Would that make things easier?"

She got up, got out of bed and went into the bathroom, and David could hear her crying. It sounded hollow and alone, her crying, her pain, in the middle of the night.

He packed the next morning, after Cheryl had gone to work. He'd left her her Christmas present, the necklace, on the kitchen table. She'd left him a letter folded up inside an envelope. He read it and didn't know how he felt about it, because what she said was sincere and it hurt.

He showered, threw some clothes into his suitcase, and took the suitcase out to his car. He was just about to lock the front door and leave when the phone rang.

"David?"

"Yeah."

"This is Jack Starkis."

"Jack Starkis?"

"From St. Luke's."

"Jesus! Jackass?"

"Please, please."

"Sorry."

"I'm calling because I have some bad news."

"I think I've heard already, Jack."

"Sister Mary."

"Father Kendrick wrote to me. I was just on my way out the door. I'm heading for Cincinnati for a few days."

"No shit? David, I'm living in Cincinnati now."

"Jack—Christ, this is weird. What the hell happened to you? Did you ever get that letter I sent you?"

"I got it. David, it's a long, involved, complex, very interesting story. You're coming down here, you're going to be here this afternoon?"

"Yeah . . ."

"We've got to get together. Tell me where you're going to be staying."

"I don't know yet. I was going to find a motel."

"Stay with me."

"No, no, no."

"David, I've got a nice place down here. Look, I'll meet you when you get here."

"I'll call you."

"You'll be down here around... five-thirty, six o'clock?"

"At the latest."

"I can be in Saint Luke's parking lot, how's that?"

"If you want to. Jack, I can call you when I—"

"Between five-thirty, six o'clock. Saint Luke's."

"Okay. You got it."

"It's going to be good to see you again," Jack said.

6

The drive to Cincinnati went smoothly. It didn't snow, and though the freeways were slushy for the first hour, once past Akron David found the roads only slightly wet. And once he reached 270 around Columbus, everything was dry.

He stopped for a cup of coffee in the middle of the afternoon, to break up the monotony of the low, flat land that went on forever in southern Ohio. By four-thirty he'd reached the outskirts of Cincinnati but driving through rush hour traffic took him the better part of the next hour to arrive at St. Luke's.

The seminary was isolated, sitting by itself at the end of a long driveway in low rolling hills way out on the west side. As David pulled up the drive, he was gripped by a feeling of nostalgia. He felt once more, freshly, the serenity that St. Luke's had promised, the dignity, the sense of purpose.

You considered entering the seminary because you felt—confused after the accident?

I don't really think I really wanted to become a priest. I think I just wanted to hide for a while. Not a good reason for becoming a priest, is it?

No . . . But your instincts were right.

Yeah, well, your instincts were right about something.

You were born to it, David.

He walked up the wide steps and pulled open the outside doors and walked into the lobby. He didn't see anyone around.

The lobby had been decorated for Christmas. There was a big tree and the perennial golden crucifix high on the wall and the wreaths and the pine roping, good scents in the air, warmth and the aroma of stone and wood.

Directly ahead of him was the chapel, and off to the right was the stairwell that led down to the cafeteria and up to the dorms on the third floor. David took the stairs to the left, the other stairwell that led to the administrative offices on the third floor.

He remembered Father Kendrick's office being the third or fourth door. And now David wished that he'd phoned first instead of barging in like this.

But the door was open. As David approached, he was mildly surprised to hear Kendrick in conversation with someone.

It sounded like Jack Starkis's voice.

David rapped lightly on the open door and stepped in. He saw Father Kendrick seated at his desk, the dark window behind him, and Jack Starkis, as tall and gaunt as David remembered him, standing in front.

Kendrick looked up.

Jack turned around and nearly yelled his name—"David!"—and moved toward him, all smiles, acting as if they were twins separated at birth and at long last reunited. He threw out a hand and when David, feeling awkward, didn't rush to grab it, Jack slapped him on the back.

"I'm glad you made it!"

"Hello, Jack. Father."

Kendrick nodded to him but didn't smile and didn't seem at all pleased to see him.

There was an uneasy silence. Kendrick looked away, glanced back at David, and met his eyes. There was odd look in his eyes, a disturbing look of anxiety, almost of pain.

What the hell was going on here?

Jack, still acting as enthusiastic as a used-car salesman on a roll, said, "David, I'll meet you downstairs. Father"—He threw out an arm in a good-bye gesture, a frozen wave, as if the two were old friends who communicated in shorthand.

His retreat, footsteps clattering down the stairs, echoed behind them and fell quiet.

"What is it, Father Kendrick?"

"Maybe I'm in the middle of a misunderstanding here," he said, turning away, moving sideways in his chair.

"What's going on?"

"Jack tells me that you two are having dinner together."

"It's news to me."

Kendrick eyed him sharply. "Did you know he'd be here?"

"He called me this morning, said something about meeting me here. Father—what's going on?"

"It's . . . it's very difficult to explain. Are you going to have dinner with him?"

"Not unless you had other plans."

"No."

"Father . . . I don't understand. You and Jack weren't exactly on the best of—"

"Go ahead, have some dinner," Kendrick told him. "Get yourself something to eat. You're going to be here for a few days, aren't you?"

"Certainly."

"I don't mean to be rude, David, but I'm a little upset, that's all. You'll have to bear with me. Did you get a room at a motel or something?"

"Not yet. I thought I'd stop in to see you first."

"Will you phone me here?"

"Tonight?"

"Call me at the rectory."

"All right."

"Will you do it, David?"

"Of course! Father . . ." He stepped up to the desk and leaned on it with both hands. Something was terribly wrong. "Does this have anything to do with Sister Mary? I've walked into the middle of something, haven't I?"

"I would say," Kendrick told him, "that, yes, you've walked into the middle of something."

* * *

On their way out to the parking lot, David asked Jack, "What the hell's going on here?"

"Nothing's going on."

"Father Kendrick's all bent out of shape, I walk in and find you talking to him, and you two didn't exactly part on the—"

"All will be revealed, David."

"What's that supposed to mean?"

"Here we are." He took his car keys out of his pocket. It was a new Ferrari, a black Ferrari.

"Who're you trying to impress, Jack?"

"Hey, just myself."

"Maybe I should follow you."

"Will you please relax? We're going out to Le Chateau. You like lobster bisque?"

"Let me lock up my car."

He felt Jack watching him as he did so. What kind of game was he playing? David knew he wasn't going to get any straight answers. Jack was going to dance around all night long, because that's the way he'd been at the seminary, all Mr. Innocence with his hand in the cookie jar. I didn't say that; someone must have misunderstood. That wasn't me; someone must be mistaken. No, no, you have it all wrong, let me explain. Salesman. Jackass.

David locked his car and walked back to the Ferrari. Jack was in the driver's seat and ready to go as David got in.

"A Toyota?" he grinned. "Who're you trying to impress, David?"

"Hey, nobody, Jack."

The restaurant was very nice. Jack acted as if he owned the place, waved to some gents at the bar, flirted with the waitresses. The lobster bisque was excellent. And through it all he chatted on and on, spinning this story, giving David meaningless details but not saying anything of substance.

He'd gotten tied in with a local guy, very big, very very big. Stefan Dragomir. *Stefan* with an *f*. An *f*. He owns the city, he knows fucking everybody. Sucker buys pol-uh-tish-uns, Da-vid. Bucks. Money. Right here. Comes from some *village* in *Europe*, is that a hoot? He's buying up businesses, he's flying all over the world, fucker's magnetized, the stuff clings to him, it jumps on him."

"So what do you do for him, Jack?"

"He's teaching me the ropes. I'm learning from a pro. I can't believe I ever thought I wanted to be in the seminary, like I'm really cut out to be a priest, right?"

"Yeah, well, life's funny."

"Yeah, it's funny, but it's not ha-ha funny."

"So will you tell me what was going on with you and Father Kendrick?"

"Calm down, relax! You want dessert?"

"No."

"You gotta have some dessert."

"Jack, how come you called me out of the blue to tell me that Sister Mary had been killed, and when I come down here, you're talking with Father Kendrick? The man does not like you, and you probably hate his guts."

"All will be revealed."

"Why'd he kick you out of the seminary, Jack?"

"Yeah . . . Bad attitude. He's got a real chip on his shoulder. Irish thing, I guess."

"Thanks for dinner, Jack." David pushed back his chair and stood up.

"Whoa, whoa."

He dropped his napkin on the table. "If I ever need any—"

"Calm down, sit down."

"Damn it, Jack, you're jerking me around!"

"I'm just having fun!"

"Go to a fucking amusement park, you want some fun."

"Sit down. Please." He acted petulant.

"I hate this kind of crap."

"Yeah, I know. Come on. You ready to go? I thought we'd have a nice meal, talk about old times—"

"We didn't have any old times, Jack! I knew you for maybe three months!"

"We'll go. I can see that you're upset. I want you to see my place and I want you to meet some people."

"I came down here to talk with Father Kendrick."

"I know that, I know." He downed the last of his coffee and stood up, took out his billfold and dropped a ten on the table. "And I didn't mean to barge in."

"That's exactly what you meant."

"Come on." Jack walked him to the front desk. "I want you to meet some people, I have some ideas, I want us to talk. Take it easy." He gave David his most winning smile. "Trust me. All will be revealed."

7

The house was new and modern and big, all the way across town, out in Indian Hill. Turn at the hand-carved wooden plaque, drive past the acres of wide lawns in the dark with their guardian hedgerows, their iron grillwork fences, big homes hidden and exclusive, cool, distant.

The front door was actually a pair of double doors. Jack threw them open and David followed, stepping into a large, hollow foyer. A staircase led off to the right, a tall, dimly lit hallway to the left. Directly in front was a great room or a living room, its entrance open. Jack closed the front door and led the way in, David behind him.

"Take your coat?"

"Oh, I guess I'll hold on to it."

The living room was large and severe, with an arched cathedral ceiling, a fireplace the size of a medieval oven, sofas and tables and rugs not quite filling up the vastness. A balcony on the second floor looked down on it.

"These are some of the folks I wanted you to meet," Jack said, taking off his jacket and throwing it over the back of a chair.

David stood still, just inside the room, as three pairs of eyes surveyed him. No one stood up; no one smiled or offered a hello.

Two men and a woman. One young man, white, small and slight and looking rather bookish in his corduroy pants, white shirt, tweed jacket, wire-rimmed glasses. One middle-aged man who hadn't shaved for three or four days, tall and overweight, Hispanic as far as David could tell, in an old sweater and jeans. One young black woman, as large as the

Hispanic man, her head shaved on one side with dreadlocks hanging down the other, dressed in well-worn camo jacket and pants. She must have practiced her I'm-bad scowl for hours in front of the mirror; she had it down.

"Please . . ."

Jack tapped David on the shoulder and led him to one of the sofas. He didn't introduce the men and woman. David sat down, facing the three of them on the other side of the wide room, and he left his coat on.

Jack went to the bar that stood along one wall and poured himself a tall glass of something.

"Anyone? David?"

None of the three said anything. David shook his head and said, "No, Jack, thanks."

Jack carried his drink with him and sat in a chair cattycorner to David. "Here's to," he smiled, and took a long swallow.

Here's to *what*?

David looked at him and glanced at the other three, who continued staring at him, silent and cold and judgmental. He felt as if he were being observed under a microscope.

Maybe he was.

He resisted an impulse to look over his shoulder, to look behind him at the balcony, where he felt that more eyes were watching him.

But he shifted his position in the couch and said, "Okay, Jack."

"Okay . . ." He leaned forward, rested his elbows on his knees, tipped his glass for another sip. "I'm here to make you a business offer, a kind of a business proposition."

"What kind of 'business proposition'?"

"Mr. Dragomir's heard about you and he'd like to meet you, he'd like to talk to you. He'd like to have you on his team."

"Jack, this is stupid. I'm not a businessman. I don't have any desire whatsoever to go into business with Stefan Dragomir and you."

"David, he has a wide range of business interests."

"I'm sure he does. Only I'm not interested."

"He can make it worthwhile. You're bright, you're—"

"Is this why you've been acting so mysterious all night? Jack, is it? Is this why See-No-Evil, Hear-No-Evil, and Do-No-Evil over there are staring at me like I'm some kind of fascinating new species?"

"There's a little more to it."

"Jack, I'm tired. I'm tired. Take me back to the seminary."

"Look. Mr. Dragomir's been interested in you ever since he heard about what happened to Emma Daedalus."

David went cold. *"What?"*

"You're a very interesting man."

"What did you say?"

"I didn't think you had it in you. Maybe you don't. I always thought you were kind of nerdy, myself."

David stared at him.

Jack set his drink down on the floor, stood up, and walked over to the couch.

David didn't move; he was sweating, he was nervous. The room was suddenly underwater, shifting and cloudy.

Jack smiled down at him and, timing it for the full dramatic effect, crossed his arms at the wrists and held them up for David to see.

The universal symbol of magical self-defense.

"You've been a naughty boy, David Trevisan."

For a moment, his breathing seemed to stop. David very nearly jumped up and almost crossed his own arms, expecting an attack or challenge.

"David, did you kill Ted Fry?"

Jack was staring at him from behind his clenched fists, crossed wrists, and he must have realized then that he'd done enough, pushed it just far enough, because he lowered his arms and laughed out loud, laughed at David, at his surprise, and backed away, fell into his chair, and took up his drink again.

David got control of himself. He breathed. He carefully looked at the three on the other side of the living room.

They hadn't moved.

They didn't make any kind of threatening motion.

THE EYES OF NIGHT

"How . . . How do you know about Emma Daedalus?"

"We went up there. Dragomir and I did. Steverino."

"To Emma's house?"

"Right-o."

"And you found out about me? How?"

"Pure luck—if you believe in luck. Found an old letter from your sister. It was under the bed, old buddy."

"I'll be damned."

"Won't we all be, though? Won't we all."

"And you killed Sister Mary."

"Now, now, now. That's called jumping to conclusions."

"Did you?"

"Be a pro, David! We have our own secret recipe! You can't expect us to—"

"You motherfucking son of a bitch!" David jumped to his feet. *"Did you kill Mary Francisco?"* His hands automatically balled into fists.

The three on the other side of the room got to their feet, too. They didn't move and they didn't make a sound, but they watched David.

Jack giggled and swallowed the last of his drink.

"Did you, Jack?"

"No! Yes! No! Oh, don't be such a stickler for details! You don't have any right to be so high and mighty, anyway! *You* killed Ted Fry, *didn't* you? Don't lie to your Uncle Jack, now."

"He murdered my sister!"

"Life's tough when you're stupid."

"Jack—!"

"All right. Chill out, calm down." He stood up and took his glass to the bar and filled it again. "Anyone? David? No? Why am I not surprised?" He walked back to his chair and sat in it and told David to sit down.

David did so, tingling, his face flushed.

Jack said to him, "Dragomir knew Fry. They were friends or something. Whatever these people are. Professional acquaintances. They had an appointment in Toronto or someplace and Fry didn't show." He sipped thoughtfully. "Well.

Where's Ted Fry? So we started looking. We started asking around, David." Jack flipped the fingers of his left hand in the air and accompanied the gesture with sound effects. "Bdoop bdee bdee. Ghosties and hobgoblins and all kinds of nasty things. And *none of them knew.* Where's Ted? We can't find him. Not a sign. Now, somebody like Ted Fry sends out signals of some kind. But it was all warped and fuzzy. It was nothing but static. Noise. Aha, we say. Something's rotten in the state of Ted Fry. So we drive to New York, because those of us in the know, as it were—and you've got to be included in the loop in this, David—knew all about this torrid love affair between Fry and Emma Daedalus. Emma will know. Guess what? Emma's dead."

He stopped for a moment, sipped some more, and eyed David over the rim of his glass.

David didn't say anything, so Jack continued. "They're *all gone*! Who could've done such a horrible thing? Bodies all over the place, buried in the backyard. Goodness. But somebody tidied up. We even called the electric company. We called the phone company. 'We're sorry, but she's no longer at that address.' Very sharp, David. We ask ourselves, is it entirely possible that this wimp who was at Saint Luke's could somehow have managed to wrestle from Theodore Fry the very secrets of the universe, the great and ancient and ominous words of power, and delved into the heart of darkness itself? Well, now, David. Is it possible? You can tell me, Clark. Are you really Superman?"

"Why did you kill Sister Mary?"

"That wasn't planned. She started poking her nose into places where she shouldn't—"

"Why?"

"Hm?"

"Why'd she'd start 'poking around'?"

"Well, we're going to save that bit of hermetic wisdom for when you're formally initiated into our little club here."

"I'm not joining any fucking 'club.'"

"Don't you understand what you *are*?" Jack asked him, suddenly becoming agitated, setting his drink on the floor again and spilling some of it onto the rug. "Jesus Christ,

David! Nobody knows we exist! And we're the people who run the show! Don't you know how things get done in this world?"

"I know how things get done."

"If you killed Fry—Let's be frank now. You killed Theodore Fry. We don't know how, but we want to know how, and even more than that, Mr. Dragomir wants to meet you. He *likes* you, David. You've impressed him, young man."

"Be still my heart."

"We're talking about the big leagues, D.T."

"I don't want to play in the big leagues."

"Don't be an asshole! He asked me to get hold of you and I, faithful servant, have gotten hold of you. So now you're invited to stay here in this nice house, you're going to be Mr. Dragomir's guest, and we're going to have such fun together that I just can't stand the excitement."

"Wrong. Take me back to the seminary. Now."

Jack became sincerely angry. The mask dropped. "Listen, you stupid fucker! When're you going to stop acting like an old lady? We're offering you the chance to be part of something remarkable! We're the fucking people who run the show! People are *scared* of people like us! They just fucking look the other way, and they kiss our asses, because they *know*, David! What the fuck are you going to do about it?"

"Nothing," he answered in a cold voice and stood up.

"That's right," Jack smirked. "Nothing. Because you're outnumbered."

David turned his back on him and walked out of the living room, into the foyer.

"Wait a minute!"

David turned around. He saw Jack waving to the other three, waving them back, as he came toward him.

"David, David, David. Maybe I've gone about this the wrong way." Jack threw an arm over his shoulder. "Look, now. Listen to me. It takes a very special kind of person to become an all-powerful sorcerer in this day and age. It's not everyone's cup of tea. David, you and I and Stefan

Dragomir *are* those very special kinds of people. And people like us have to stick together."

They walked toward the front door, Jack leaning close, his arm heavy on David's shoulder.

David said, "Get your damned arm off—"

Jack shoved him. Surprised and off-balance, David slammed into the front door, smashing his face. His nose clogged up instantly and he felt pain erupt in his cheek, and then he felt Jack's strong hand grip him by one shoulder and haul him back.

"Jesus Christ, Jack!"

"I apologize from the bottom of my wicked little heart."

David wiped the blood from his nose and mouth, the sticky red coating his fingertips.

"Here, here, here . . ." Jack took out a handkerchief and quickly wiped David's nose and mouth.

David glared at him and made a grab for the handkerchief.

Jack was faster, pulling back before David could catch it.

"Nyet! Nein!"

"Give me the handkerchief, Jack!"

"Da-vid. All I'm doing is—"

He brought up his left hand and gripped the wrist of Jack's right, where the handkerchief was balled up in his fist.

"Give it to me, Jack!"

They stared at one another. Stared. David began trembling, and Jack's arm started shaking.

"You're—"

"Give it to me!"

"—fucking—"

"Jack!"

"—*hurting me, David!*"

Heat. Heat radiating from David's grip, heat rippling like liquid down Jack's arm, into his hand.

"My fucking wrist is on fire!"

Smoke seeped from between Jack's fingers. Instantly David yanked the arm down, not strongly enough to wrench it from its socket, but so suddenly that Jack's hot fingers spread open. The handkerchief, charred and smoking,

THE EYES OF NIGHT 45

dropped and landed on the wood floor of the foyer.

It continued to smolder for another minute, until all of it was reduced to black ashes.

They still stared at each other, until Jack turned away and leaned back against the front door, grimacing, rubbing his hurting wrist with his left hand.

"Je-sus, David!"

"I've had it with these fucking stunts of yours! I've had it with these—"

Footsteps.

He looked up, looked at the entrance leading into the living room.

The three stood there, the black woman and the young white man in front, the Hispanic in the back, like a trio of zombies from some old movie.

Jack shook his head at them. "It's okay. It's... all right..."

But they stayed right there.

David was panting. He wiped the last of the blood that still seeped from his nose. "Move, Jack." He tapped him on the foot with the toe of his shoe.

"What?"

"I'm leaving now, Jack! Thanks for a pleasant evening! Loved the lobster bisque! Now will you please *move*?"

Jack grunted and lurched away from the door.

David threw it open.

"You can't walk back."

"Why not?"

"It's over ten miles!"

"Fresh air'll do me good." He stepped onto the porch and was stunned for a second by the chilly air.

"Wait! Just wait!" Jack yelled to the others, "one of you get my jacket! On the fucking chair!" He came out onto the porch.

"Leave me alone, Jack."

"I never pegged you for a troublemaker."

"Yeah, well, life's funny, but it's not ha-ha funny."

"Jack." The black woman handed him his jacket.

He pulled it on and closed the front door. David was already walking down the steps.

"Will you let me drive you?" Jack said to him. "Goddamn it! I will fucking drive you, David!"

David turned around and looked at him.

Jack was still rubbing his wrist underneath the sleeve of his jacket.

8

They were quiet for a long time during the drive back. Jack didn't push David any harder about joining the "club." Maybe David would construe the silence as an unspoken threat and become restless. Maybe after a while David would start to get edgy, ask some questions, give Jack a sign that he'd come over.

But it didn't happen.

Instead, as they got closer to St. Luke's, David asked Jack why he'd been kicked out of the seminary.

"I wanted to know. I wanted to really know. So I tried it, to see for myself."

"Tried *what*, Jack?"

"A ritual. In the church."

"This is bullshit. You're lying."

"Ask Kendrick yourself."

"But *why*?"

"Because I didn't know, David. You're... Fuck it. Look. I wasn't in a good place back then. Haven't you ever been so depressed that you just wanted to get it over with? I mean, not even take it seriously anymore? Just jump out the window, pull the trigger, maybe give the steering wheel one good yank?"

David glanced at Jack's hands on the Ferrari's steering wheel.

"That's an excuse," he said. "Everybody gets tired of the bullshit. Everybody gets depressed sometimes."

"I don't mean that. I mean... the ultimate. You're not just hurting because your life's fucked up. You hurting because you know something's going on and you can't figure out what the hell it is. We're human beings, for chrissake. So what the fuck is this? What the hell is going on?"

"That's what brought me to Saint Luke's in the first place."

"Well, that's why I came here, too. La-de-da. Priests have to know, right? They've got the hotline to God, right? I ought to give them a chance, right? What a bunch of shit."

"This still doesn't explain—"

"Don't you get it?" Jack nearly yelled at him. "You don't fucking get it, do you? This is what it is, David! I had to find out, I had to make sure. Go into a goddamn seminary, they don't know shit, they don't know anything more than anybody else does, it's all a bunch of fucking lies for the dipshits and the losers. I want the fucking truth! I want to know, I want the fucking *truth!*" His hands were tight on the steering wheel. "So the priests can't tell me, they don't know, so I decided to find out for myself. Push it to the limit."

"You did some bullshit ritual in the church."

"I desecrated that church and I did the best fucking ritual I could, the best ritual anyone could if they hadn't consecrated themselves yet."

That remark chilled David.

"And I found out the truth. Are you listening to me? Life is pain, David. It's as bad as it could be. Life is fear. And terror. That's the only stuff that keeps us alive. That's the only stuff that keeps us on our toes. It keeps us aware. Why do you think the Aztecs used to tear the hearts out of their enemies, and show those fuckers their hearts before they ate them?"

He pulled into St. Luke's parking lot.

"So Father walked into the middle of it and kicked you out."

"Father Kendrick walked into it when it was all over and done with. 'Oh, my, I hear mice making noise in the chapel! Oh, my, I had better investigate! Oh, my, what have we here?' Welcome to hell, Father."

Jack kept the car running but didn't say anything else.

THE EYES OF NIGHT

He looked straight ahead, out the windshield and not at David.

"When you did your ritual," David asked him, "—not in the church, but your consecration—what did you see?"

"What do you think I saw? I saw puke and vomit and pus and all the shit that ever existed. I saw life. I saw reality." Jack looked over at him. "Why? What the fuck do you care?"

"I wanted to know."

"You've done it, too."

"Yes. With Emma's help."

"So what did you see?"

"Nothing like that."

"Well, la-de-da. What'd you see? Jesus? Angels? Let me guess. You saw your parents, right? Or your grandmother. Grandmothers are good. Sweetness and light."

"Go to hell, Jack."

"I've been to hell."

David opened his door and stepped out.

"Hold it." Jack reached over, grabbed hold of the door handle, and looked up at him. "This isn't over."

"I know that."

"The offer still stands."

"Where'd you meet him, Jack? Did you find him? Did he find you?"

"When the student's ready, the teacher appears. Isn't that how it works?"

"That's how it works."

"David—we're brothers now, you and me."

"We're not brothers."

"You've got to take responsibility for what you are! Get rid of this middle-class morality act. You're one of *us*."

"No, I am not one of you, Jack."

"You're trying to hide! You're not *normal* anymore! What do you fucking want?"

"I just want to be left alone."

"People like us don't get left alone."

"Jack, go home."

"I'm telling you right now, if you don't get down off

your high horse, somebody's gonna push you. People are going to get hurt."

"Don't threaten me. Do not fucking threaten me, Jack!"

"David, listen! You've got an important decision to make. You don't get left alone. After what you did to Fry, you're too important to leave alone. You're part of it."

"Good-night, now."

"Do you hear me?"

"Jack, the only problem you've got is explaining to your boss why you couldn't baffle me with your bullshit."

David leaned on the door; Jack let him close it. David turned and walked across the parking lot to his Toyota.

Behind him, he heard the Ferrari roar and squeal as Jack drove away.

He was frightened.

He took his keys out of his coat and they shook in his hands as he opened his car door.

He was mildly surprised that the Toyota was fine, that no one had tried to do anything to it while he was with Jack.

He didn't call Father Kendrick; he simply drove over to talk to him, right then.

The rectory was a small square building that sat by itself behind the church. A long blacktop driveway led to it, out of St. Luke's parking lot and over a low hill and through some trees.

David parked in the front and got out. As he took the steps he pulled back the sleeve of his coat and looked at his watch. Eleven o'clock, a little after.

The front door was unlocked. He opened it quietly and stood for a moment in the flagstone foyer. Everything was quiet. The place smelled warm and old and masculine, dense. There was a well-lit room to his right. David approached and saw someone he didn't recognize, a novitiate, sitting under a lamp in the library, reading. The face looked up.

"Father Kendrick?"

"Hallway behind you. Third—no, second on your left."

"Thanks."

THE EYES OF NIGHT

"Uh-huh."

Kendrick's door was ajar. David knocked lightly and pushed the door open wider and looked in.

There were two small rooms, this one, unlit, apparently an entryway of some kind with a hall tree and a table and a chair and Kendrick's boots in the corner, and the bedroom farther back. Light came from the bedroom, and voices.

David closed the door behind him.

"Father?"

He heard feet shuffle, then Kendrick approaching, and he saw Father's silhouette filling up the open doorway. "Turn the light on. Right behind you, there."

David turned around and saw the switch and turned on the light in the small room.

Kendrick stepped in, closing the door that led to his bedroom, looked at David and said, "What happened to you?"

"We had a little difference of opinion."

"You and Jack Starkis."

"Yes. Is there someplace where I can clean up?"

"Down the hall, here." He led him to a small lavatory and watched as David washed his face, scrubbing away the dried blood on his nose and mouth, and examined his one eye, which had swollen and turned purple.

"Well?" Kendrick asked him, after a few minutes of this.

"You and I are going to have to have a long talk."

"No doubt."

"What did Jack tell you about me?"

"Let's go back, shall we?"

Kendrick led the way, making sure, once they were in his little front room, to close the door behind David. He gravitated toward the door leading to his bedroom, as if protective of that room, or protective of whoever was in there.

"What did Jack tell you, Father?"

"That . . . you're like him. You did what he did."

"Not quite true."

"What *is* the truth, then?"

"There are good guys and bad guys. I'm one of the good guys."

"I don't think there are any good guys anymore."

"I'm inclined to agree with you." David walked over to him then and stood in front of Father Kendrick, looked him in the eyes. "It's what I came here for, Father, why I came here, to Saint Luke's. Only I found it in a different way. I'm not going to apologize for it, but I want you to know about it because I respect you."

"Go on."

"But for right now, I don't think you're safe, you or me. Jack set all this up so I'd walk into a dumb trap. That's what this was tonight."

"What happened?"

"Not what he thought. But he murdered Sister Mary, he and some other people did."

"Jack's wanted by the police."

"Then you're going to have plenty to tell the police."

"He told me not to. He threatened my life."

"He's getting pretty good at that."

"He's a dangerous man. I think he's mentally ill."

David said, "Whatever else he told you, Father—lies, half truths—he's real smooth. What I've gone through—"

"You *are* one like him."

David crossed his arms upon his chest, palms flat on his breast, and bowed slightly. "I'm called a magus. A magician."

"A sorcerer."

"Yes."

"That's why they wanted you."

"We know our own kind, Father. We're like cats in the dark. They found me."

"Why you?"

"Because I killed a man. I killed the man who killed my sister. If you could call it a man."

Kendrick said, "I'm not up to this."

"Jack's tied in with someone named Dragomir. Stefan Dragomir. Real big guy around here? That's what I get for not paying attention. I think Sister Mary was just the start

THE EYES OF NIGHT 53

of it. And I'm sure your life's in danger. Mine certainly is. I'm serious, Father. I've got to ask you—please—to trust me." He tried to read Father's expression. "Trust me."

"Trust you . . ." It took Kendrick a while. He seemed to make an important decision, then, standing there in his small room. He stepped back from the doorway and said to David, "Come in here."

David followed him inside.

There was a young woman sitting in an easy chair on one side of the room. Opposite her, Father Kendrick sat down in the chair of his old rolltop desk and turned the chair around so that he could face both of them.

"David Trevisan, meet Nora Dragomir. The daughter."

9

She was slender, pretty, quite pregnant, and her face was flushed; she seemed very frightened.

Kendrick said, "When Nora talked to Sister Mary last week, that's what started all this—hell breaking loose." He told Nora, "David can be trusted."

"You're the one my father was trying to find, aren't you?"

"Yes."

"You killed Theodore Fry." There was a tone almost of awe in her voice.

David grabbed the chair that stood at the foot of Father's bed and dragged it toward Nora and sat down. "I was at Jack Starkis's house tonight—"

"It's not his house."

"Well, does he use it as his address?"

"I don't know. I doubt it."

David turned around to look at Father Kendrick. "The police are looking for Jack and they haven't found him yet?"

"As far as I know."

"Then he's playing games. He's moving around or using aliases or something."

"My father owns a million buildings. Jack could hide anywhere."

"Were you there tonight?" David asked her. "Did you see me there?"

"No. No. I was at my father's. See . . . I sneaked out."

"Nora, is your father here? In town?"

"No. He comes and goes. He's always going different places."

"All right. All right. . . ." David stood up, wiped his face, yawned, and fought his tiredness. "How soon before anyone knows you're gone?"

"They probably know by now."

"How soon before they guess. . . . That's stupid. Jack will figure it out in a second."

"Then we can't stay here?" Nora asked him.

"David," Kendrick told him, "no one would dare—"

"We're in serious trouble, Father!" He nearly yelled it, not meaning to. "I'm sorry. I apologize." He sat down again beside Nora. "From the beginning. Who, what, when, where . . . Where does Sister Mary come into this?"

Nora told him about getting hold of Sister Mary, about needing help, help from anyone, because of her father, because of the baby. "My father is dying of cancer. This is his baby! He wants to put his soul into my *baby!*"

"Did you tell this to Sister Mary?"

"Yes. Only I don't think she believed me."

"Did she—"

"I showed her—"

"Go on."

"I showed her newspaper clippings about the people my father's had murdered. Because he's done that. That's how he's gotten to be so powerful and so rich." Nora told them that she'd been raised in Chicago by relatives. "Only I don't know if they were really relatives or not." Dragomir had sent for her about a year ago, and when she got to Cincinnati, he raped her and kept her in his house as a prisoner. "I didn't know what he was! I didn't know!" She'd escaped once, to meet Sister Mary, but her father always had people watching her, always knowing where she was, always following her. Jack, especially. But she'd had to find someone. She needed help. "I didn't know who else to talk to! I don't know anyone here!"

"Tell me about—"

"David," Kendrick interrupted. "If Stefan Dragomir is supposed to be a sorcerer, how come he's dying of cancer?"

"Nobody lives forever, Father. I'm a sorcerer and I've still got allergies. It doesn't work that way."

Nora told Kendrick, "Sister Mary mentioned your name. She said that she was going to show you the newspaper clippings."

Father shook his head. "She never did."

"Did those newspaper stories mention your father?" David asked her.

"No, of course not. Sister Mary told me that they don't mean anything."

"David," Kendrick asked him, "did Jack tell you about *how* Sister Mary was killed?"

"No." He turned around in his chair.

"She was nailed upside down to a wall. They mutilated her! They cut her eyelids off!"

Nora moaned.

"Why, David? Do you know why?"

"So that the demon could see into this world."

"What?"

"It's an old way of doing it. Of making a sacrifice, a compact with the spirit. It's deliberately sadistic. A warning, Father. Whatever they conjured, they wanted it to see into this world."

"A demon?"

"It can . . . use . . . the victim for as long as she remains alive. It would have allowed the spirit to witness—"

"And what happens to her *soul*?"

"Her soul is fine, Father. Sister Mary is fine." He told Kendrick, very carefully. "Probably they were conjuring Bezemoth. That was the name of the creature that—"

"This is insane."

In a small voice full of dread, Nora said, "Fry. That was what Fry did."

"Yes." David kept his attention on Kendrick. "Fry killed himself first. He committed suicide in a ceremony and conjured Bezemoth. I . . . reversed that."

Nora said, "I brought a tape."

David and Kendrick both stared at her.

"Sister Mary told me that the newspaper clippings weren't enough."

"What kind of—"

THE EYES OF NIGHT

"So I stole a videotape."

"What kind of videotape?" David asked her.

"A party. My father has parties for all of his friends."

"A ceremony?" David asked her.

"I don't know!" Nora said. "Only nobody believes me, and he wants to hurt me and my baby!"

"Nora, where's the tape?"

She took it out of her purse.

Father Kendrick retrieved the TV monitor and VCR from the closet down the hall and wheeled them into his room. He closed the outer door and locked it and closed the inner door leading into his bedroom.

David looked at his watch. It was nearly midnight.

"I can never... Why did someone disconnect it?"

"Here." David crouched behind the cart, connected the VCR to the television, and turned both of them on. "The tape, Nora."

She handed it to him. David fed it into the VCR and pushed play.

Nora and Kendrick stood side by side, staring. David hovered near the television.

The screen flickered. Horizontal lines of static waved up and down and cleared themselves. The first pictures appeared suddenly. Some kind of party.

David turned up the sound. Occasional voices came in, very loud, near the microphone. Whoever had been operating the camera had simply walked around Dragomir's home and photographed a large number of well-dressed people gathered for a party.

"I recognize some of these people," Kendrick said. "That's the Vernons, there. The Troys... William O'Connell... Dear God, that's Iva Daugherty...."

"This is a party for rich people," David said.

They stood around, businesspeople, executives, socialites, politicians, the movers and doers and the owners, sipping drinks, laughing, waving at the camera. A middle-aged wife stuck her tongue out while her husband grinned. A bosomy young woman in a low-cut dress leaned close to the camera and shook her breasts.

"This is just a—"

A tall, slender man, somewhere in his fifties, was caught off-guard by the camera. He turned to face it, did not smile, stared at it with an almost sinister glare. The picture jumped abruptly to other faces.

Nora made a low sound.

David looked at her.

"Stefan Dragomir," Kendrick said.

They watched for another minute. David considered the possibility that Nora was wrong, or mistaken, or under some kind of mental stress. There was nothing here to prove that her father was a sorcerer. Absolutely no indication that—

"Oh, Jesus," Nora said.

The picture went dark, but something was going on. The image was blurred.

It came into focus.

Kendrick whispered, "What on earth . . . ?"

It was a large room, cavernous looking, of stone or cement block. There was a long altar draped in a sheet and around it stood a crowd of people, perhaps a dozen or more. They were dressed in red robes. Brilliant lines moved like flares on the screen, obscuring much of the activity—candle flames caught by the video camera.

The picture jumped. Now the people standing around the altar were naked. Their bodies were glistening with oil or perspiration. Still, the image was dim, lit only by candlelight, and it was impossible to see around these people or over their shoulders, see what was happening at the altar.

The picture jumped again. The image was completely steady, now, as though the camera had been mounted on a tripod. The naked bodies, shiny and heavily shadowed, moved and swayed, the brilliant orange backs of the men and women moving in unison.

David tried to turn up the sound, but there was no sound, or very little. Only a low hum. Human voices, all of those people humming one note. No individual voices.

The brilliant orange backs moved, people parted out of

THE EYES OF NIGHT

the way, and Stefan Dragomir came into focus in the distance, at one end of the cavern or cellar. He was dressed in a black robe and standing over a smoking bowl, which sat on the altar. Fumes from the bowl spilled upward and spread a thick haze. Dragomir gestured over the bowl, waving his hands. He crossed his arms on his chest, said something that was muffled by the low humming sound of everyone else there. He lifted his arms as if in prayer.

Once more the picture jumped, and now it was obvious that the naked celebrants were involved in some kind of group sex. The lighting was very dim, candlelight, still, but enough could be seen of the shadowy, orange bodies moving on the floor to understand what was happening. Two of them on the altar, a woman sitting on top of a man—

"Turn it off, David."

He kneeled down and pressed Stop on the VCR.

Kendrick was obviously disgusted. "Staged," he told Nora. "Posed."

"Dear God, no!"

"I don't think so," David told him. "Is there anymore?" he asked Nora.

"I don't know! I've never seen these before. I only heard about them from Jack."

"I'm going to jump ahead a little bit." David hit the fast forward button. The VCR whirred. He hit Stop, then Play.

In a moment the picture flared up on the television screen.

"Dear Christ!" Kendrick yelled.

It was Sister Mary in the warehouse, upside down on the wall, covered with blood. Somebody moved in front of her, somebody in a robe—

"David, turn it off!"

—and the picture cut suddenly to a close-up of Sister Mary, her face upside down, her breasts hanging awkwardly and covered with blood. She tried to speak.

Nora moaned and made a sick sound.

It was not Sister Mary's voice. It was a heavy voice, very deep, a beautiful deep voice—not human—

David whispered, "Defende me contra nequitiam..."

"Turn it *off!*" Kendrick yelled. He was holding Nora,

who was breathing heavily, gasping and shivering in his arms.

"Turn it—"

The picture vanished.

David reached for the VCR.

The picture came back on, unclear behind lines of static—

And the lights in Father's room went dim, came back on, dimmed again.

Kendrick said, "What—"

"Damn it!" David yelled.

He moved past Father and Nora, went to the one window in the room. The shade was down, the curtains drawn. He stood to one side and pulled back the curtain and looked out.

"Shit," he said. "They're here, they've found us."

10

"Jack Starkis?" Kendrick asked.

"Yes."

David didn't see Jack but he saw the big one, the Hispanic man, crouching behind one of the trees that surrounded the rectory. He was leaning forward with his arms crossed on his chest. It was dark and David didn't see him so much as sense him there, a shadow hidden in other shadows, but his presence, his will, his energy was obvious enough.

He sensed the others, too, Jack and the woman and the guy with the glasses. They'd surrounded the building.

David turned from the window and moved quickly to the center of the room. "Move that chair," he ordered Kendrick. "Throw it on the bed, push it against the wall."

He himself wheeled the television back a foot or two, into a corner, where it continued to flicker off and on and glow with lines of static.

"Pick up the rug, Father. Will that rug come up?"

"It's just a throw rug."

"What're you doing?" Nora asked him.

The lights continued to flicker on and off, and now David heard the wind coming, beginning to bump against the window.

"Saving our lives. I need some water, Father Kendrick. And something—"

"Down the hall."

"Something to draw with. Anything. Anything liquid."

Kendrick went to his desk and pulled out the bottom drawer; he handed David the bottle of whiskey.

"Listen to the wind!" Nora said.

"That's not the wind. Father—chalk, a pencil, anything."

Kendrick opened the top drawer of his desk and pulled out a felttip marker.

"A Magic Marker." David grinned. "How appropriate. Father, stand over there. Nora—you, too."

"Where? Here?"

"That's fine."

He joined them and placed the whiskey bottle on the wooden floor at Father Kendrick's feet. There wasn't a great deal of space for the three of them. David got down on his hands and knees.

"Both of you, quiet now, please."

Nora moved close to Kendrick; Kendrick held both of her hands in his.

David crawled around them, describing an imperfect circle on the floor, drawing it with the Magic Marker. As he did, he began his invocation, his prayer.

"In nomine Sabaoth Elohim, suscipe oratio mea, o Agla Elohim."

He stood up, handed Father the Magic Marker, quickly opened the whiskey bottle, and tipped some of the whiskey into his hands. With his wet fingers he inscribed a five-pointed star in the air in front of him.

"Veni, Gabrilis."

He stepped around Father Kendrick, then behind Kendrick and Nora, then beside Nora.

"Veni, Urielis . . . Oriensis . . . Astralis . . ."

The flickering lights went out. The television died. Wind pounded louder at the window.

Nora whispered to Father Kendrick, "I'm frightened, I'm scared."

He held her hands, tightening his grip on them, but said nothing, only watched David, frightened himself and fascinated.

David faced the window again and spread out his arms. "In nomine Sabaoth Elohim." He bowed his head. "Elion." He crossed his arms over his chest. "Amathia."

He lifted his head again and once more spread his arms wide. "On."

Kendrick whispered to Nora, "Those are the names of God."

He crossed his arms over his chest, hands tightened into fists, and said out loud, "Defende nos in proelio, Agla Sabaoth Elohim. Contra nequitiam esto praesidium. Spiritus malignos! Ite! Ite! Aeior!"

Thunder boomed.

"Aeior!"

Nora groaned.

"Aeior!"

Kendrick pulled her closer to him.

"*Aeior!*"

Thunder boomed again. The glass of the window rattled. They saw smoke, green smoke, boiling up against the outside of the window.

"Aeior!"

The green smoke crawled against the glass, trying to get in, as if it were some kind of animal.

"What *is* that?" Kendrick asked.

It seemed to become solid, a gluey green mass, as it pushed against the glass.

"*Aeior!* Ite!"

Nora screamed.

Lights, lights, burning lights grew within the green smoke, lights like eyes, moving in one direction, then looking in the other, peering into the room—

More thunder boomed, tremendous, right over their heads, rocking the building. Rain began to sweep down, coming in solid curtains, pounding on the roof, beating against the window.

Nora screamed again.

The window shattered, bits of glass flying into the room. Kendrick pushed her face into his shoulder.

"David!"

"Ite! Aeior! *Aeior!*"

The thick, foaming green smoke moved into the room. It swayed like the stalk of a plant, a long snaking line of burning green, its two eyes floating at the front of it, looking at them, the three of them inside David's circle.

"My God!"

It bobbed and swayed until it reached the outline David had drawn on the floor, the circle, his wall.

Only inches from David's face, the green snake of smoke pushed against the air, tried to spread, tried to reach in—

"Dear *God*!" Kendrick yelled.

—and could not.

"*Aeior!*"

Kendrick saw another color, he saw blue light, like a pane of glass or a translucent sheet, form in the air in front of David and resist the green smoke—

"Stop it, stop it!" Nora moaned, lifting her head from Kendrick's shoulder.

Kendrick held her. "Shhh . . . Nora, Our Father, Who art in heaven, hallowed be Thy Name . . ."

"Ite! In nomine Sabaoth Elohim! *Aeior!*"

There was a scratching sound, like stone on glass, a fingernail on a blackboard, as the green tendril tried to push through David's wall, weaken it, break it, break in and reach the three of them—

"*Aeior!*"

The green mist pulled back. The tendril of it, snaking, pulled away, reached back across the room and through the window, and vanished, as if suddenly sucked out by a fan or a vaccum.

Thunder boomed again.

The wind died down.

The rain fell and they could hear it on the roof, a welcome sound, a clean sound.

The lights flickered, came on, blinked out, came on again, and stayed on.

David was panting.

Kendrick said, "Dear Christ in Heaven . . ."

"Don't—move—" David warned him. "I'm not—done yet—"

From outside they heard the loud sound of car doors

slamming, then the gunning of a car engine and the car driving away.

"What—?"

"They gave up," David said, breathing heavily. "They gave up. It was—a stalemate...."

Kendrick said, "I want Nora to lie down."

"Don't move!" David warned him sharply. "Don't—"

He shook his head, wiped his face, swallowed several deep breaths of air. He crossed his arms over his chest and bowed toward the window.

"Gabrilis..."

He moved around Father Kendrick, then behind him and Nora, then around Nora, banishing, cleansing, reversing.

"... Urielis ... Oriensis ..."

Finally he walked from the circle, stepping over the ink on the floor, and sank into the chair of Father Kendrick's desk.

"Now?" Kendrick asked him.

David nodded, exhausted.

Nora was shivering and moaning. Kendrick walked her to the bed and helped her lie down.

There was a knock from the hallway.

David looked quickly at Kendrick.

Father left the bedroom, closing the door behind him. He turned on the light in the outer room before opening the door to the seminarian whom David had seen in the library.

"Do you believe that storm coming up like that?"

"Freak weather. It happens."

"Did your lights go out for a while?"

"Just for a minute or two."

"Bet your visitors were scared."

"Just a little."

"Well, I just wanted to make sure that everything was okay."

When Kendrick came back into the bedroom, he noticed that cardboard—the back of his desk blotter—had been taped over the broken windowpane. He saw David standing over Nora, hands on either side of her neck, massaging her. Nora was asleep.

"She'll be all right now."

"Uh-huh." Kendrick replaced the rug on the floor, doing his best to cover up the circle David had drawn. He looked out the window, wondering. The night was dark. It was still drizzling. He saw the wide lawn behind the rectory, and the trees, misty.

David went to the television and pushed Play on the VCR.

"I thought so."

Kendrick looked at him; David's silhouette was outlined by the flickering, shimmering lines on the television.

"What?"

"It's gone," David said.

"What's gone?" Kendrick stood up. "The tape?"

"Yes. Erased."

"That was evidence! That was proof, that was—"

"Proof of what?" David took the cassette out of the VCR and turned it off, and the television. "Proof that rich people throw wild parties?"

"How did it get erased?"

"Power surge," David told him. "Or the energy in this room when that thing came through the window. Electromagnetic energy, Father. That's what it is. That's what we all are. Electromagnetic energy." He put the cassette on the desk.

"And . . . what was that . . . thing?"

"An elemental of some kind. A mental creation, an energy creation. An . . . attack dog, Father."

Kendrick glanced at Nora lying on the bed.

"Will she sleep for a while?"

"Yes."

"You need some rest, too, don't you?"

"I can get by without sleep."

"Good." Kendrick grabbed the chair that had been at the foot of his bed and dragged it toward David and sat down. "Because now you and I are going to have our talk."

11

Kendrick wanted to know, and so David told him.

Told him everything that had happened since leaving the seminary last September.

He told Kendrick about going home when he learned that his sister, Ginny, had put herself into some kind of coma. She'd tried to perform a magical ritual.

"She was trying to contact our parents, Father. The same thing that brought me to the seminary—it pushed her in the same direction. I mean in a spiritual direction. Only Fry found her, and Fry twisted her around."

David told Kendrick about Fry, the magician, and about Long, the detective from New York, who had even tried to learn magic himself in order to find Fry and kill him.

"Because Fry had this long trail of bodies behind him. He killed people, hired himself out as a killer. An assassin. Only what I found out was that it wasn't really Fry. It was a demon, a spiritual being, in the shape of Fry, in Fry's body. The ceremonies, the power, the life of it, for Fry... I think it became like a drug for him, and he needed it more and more. Finally he cut himself off from this world entirely and gave himself up to a spirit named Bezemoth."

"And you, David? What have you given yourself up to?"

"Father, Jack... Dragomir... me... We've done something to ourselves on purpose. It's a ritual, a ceremony. It's very old and most people have been taught not to believe in it anymore. But what happens is... true sight, true seeing. Everything is in focus, everything fits together and makes sense. It's as if I got a second chance at everything. It's like dying and coming back, only knowing everything this time, knowing it already, because you *see* underneath everything, you see behind things, you feel the things and see the things other people don't feel, the things they don't see. It's just one big . . . life force, energy, the whole universe—trying to stay in balance."

"This contradicts everything I've been raised and trained to believe in. And you, too."

"Father Kendrick, there's religion, and then there's the truth. Religion is what they want you to believe and how they want you to behave. The truth is always something else. Father . . ." David spoke carefully. "Religion—faith—has limits, has boundaries. It has to, because it's social, a social agreement. Religious faith has boundaries. But where those boundaries end, that's where the path to something else begins. And that's where I am. Beyond that boundary."

"What I saw tonight—what you and Jack have forced me to believe—to see—"

"Father Kendrick, the remarkable thing isn't what I'm telling you. It's not remarkable that the universe is full of life, full of energy, and that people like me realize that and use it. The remarkable thing is that we've blinded ourselves to the truth. The scary thing isn't that there are demons; the scary thing is that we won't *admit* there are demons."

He told Kendrick about Cheryl D'Angelo, his girlfriend, almost his fiancée, because before David came to Cincinnati they were going to get married. He told Kendrick about how Fry had broken her neck that night in the field, and about how David had brought her back to life afterward, using the sorcery he had mastered.

"She was dead, Father. Dead. It doesn't matter, because in a way they're both the same thing, life and death. Hide and seek. Now you see it, now you don't. But she's alive now, what we call life, and she was dead for a little bit, and it affected her. It's affected her vision. Only she won't admit it."

"What do you mean? Did she see a doctor?"

"Doctors . . . They're going to look for everything from sinus infections to brain tumors. That's not what it was. I know that. Cheryl knows that. Only now she won't admit it. Father, what I'm getting at is—it's the same thing that scares Nora so much about her father."

"He's evil, an evil man. He is a sorcerer and he wants to kill her."

"No. That's the easy part. People can live with that. What scares her is that everyone else in this city looks at her father and doesn't see what she sees. People will look something right in the eye and not see it. They'll deny it, they'll lie to themselves, they'll call it something else. People will look right at something and not see it. That, Father, is the scary part."

It was nearly three in the morning, and still neither of them slept, still they continued to talk. It was as if both of them were afraid that this would be the last time they'd ever get to talk, both of them afraid that, for whatever reason, things were going out of control, and they were going to get caught up in them, and they might not see each other again.

Certainly not if Jack Starkis tried pulling that stunt with the green smoke when David wouldn't be around to do whatever it was he did to stop it. . . .

"Jack fired a bullet, Father. I gave us a bulletproof vest."

"That's not what it looked like to me."

"Well, that's all it was. You have to talk the same language. That's where the ritual comes in.

"I'll tell you what I think happened," he told Kendrick. "I think Jack found out, from Dragomir or somebody else, that Nora stole the videotape. I think they figured out that she was here. They followed her or something. Jack had to screw up the tape, get it back or ruin it, and he had to try to get to Nora. If he'd been able to hurt you and me, he could've gotten her."

"You're saying that he came here to do as much damage as he could, whatever he could do."

"Absolutely. If he couldn't get us, get Nora, then at least he screwed up the tape. That's important."

"But what about Nora?"

"She's very important. I think Dragomir and Jack and whoever else is involved in all this is engaged in what politicians would call damage control. That's what I think. And we've got to try to stay one step ahead of them."

Kendrick told him, "I want to do everything I can to hurt them, to drag this out into the daylight and expose them."

"Okay. But in the meantime we've got to make sure that Nora stays safe."

"I know that, I understand that. . . ." Thoughtful, Kendrick looked over at her. "How big could this be? How many people could be involved in something like this?"

"You mean, those people at Dragomir's house?"

"Yes."

David shrugged his shoulders. "Rich people . . . Dragomir's probably using them, too. Exploiting them. Giving them candy. There's probably only him, Jack—just a few others." David said, with obvious contempt in his voice, "We saw a bunch of drunken people rolling around on the floor. That doesn't make them sorcerers. Just because some kid draws swastikas on his notebook doesn't mean he's a Nazi. Most of the time most people are mostly stupid, not evil."

"And these people are being stupid."

"Yes. Dragomir's the one to be afraid of. And the reason to be afraid of him is because of Nora." David looked at her over there on the bed. "If she's right, and—"

"Can she be?"

"Certainly. For Dragomir to work it so that he slips into her baby, his soul taking over? Certainly. It's a matter of lining up the right path, that's all."

"It sounds incredible."

"See, Father, you're used to thinking of things in terms of God's will, and the rest of us putting up with that. Only that's not the way it works. The way it works is that everything has a will, a will to be alive, to move, to take over. Willpower. Life energy. Channel it, direct it, you can do whatever you want. That's what Dragomir's doing."

"And . . . to stop him?"

"Get her as far away from him as possible, for starters."

"Could you do that, David?"

"Could *I*? Yes. . . . I mean, I'm capable of it. But what about you?"

"What about me?"

"Father, we're all in this together."

"All the more reason, don't you think, for us to split up? Move in different directions?"

"So where will you go? For how long?"

"David, I want to get this out into the open. Even if the tape's no good, maybe somebody can do something with it. Anyhow, I want to talk to Bud Pomeroy—to the police—and I want to give it to a reporter I know, too. Then I can take a leave of absence. Monsignor Pantik's already offered. Fly out to Phoenix for a few days, even for a week."

"Meanwhile—"

"You do whatever you can to keep Nora safe."

"I'd feel best taking her back to Noland. My stuff's there. At the very least, if this turns into something like Fry—" He shook his head. "Jesus . . . I didn't plan on making this my career," he said.

"You've got to do what you can to save her. Keep her away from her father, and from Jack."

"But you and I have got to stay in touch."

"I can phone you as soon as I get to Phoenix."

"Maybe we ought to head out there, too."

"Whatever it takes. I could have Phillip arrange it."

"I've got money," David said. He was thinking. "First things first. Because I have the feeling that . . . Stefan Dragomir looks like a very powerful man, and you and I and Nora are going to have to work real hard to stay away, to get away from him."

Kendrick asked him, "That thing that came through the window—what did you call it?"

"The attack dog? The elemental?"

"The elemental. What would it have done to us, if it had touched us? Say, if it had touched me?"

"Killed you."

"Just like that?"

"Yes. Certainly."

He glanced at Nora. "Is he going to kill her, too?"

"He can't afford to kill her. Not until she has her baby, anyway. At least, I hope that's the way Dragomir feels about it."

"Let her sleep, but you'd better plan on leaving in a few hours," Kendrick told him.

"Yeah. I don't want to wait too long. They're not going to waste any time. You know they're pulling an all-nighter tonight. Either they're trying to decide what to tell Dragomir when he gets home, or they're putting up with whatever it is he does to people who screw up."

Kendrick was looking at Nora.

David sensed something. "What is it, Father?"

"Nothing."

"Tell me."

"What time is it?"

"Three-forty-five. Heading for four."

"Daylight, soon."

"What is it, Father?"

He didn't look at David but he told him, "Within the past few days—the last week—it feels like just a few hours—everything I've ever believed in for my entire life has been shattered. All of it—gone. Sister Mary—Jack—you—Nora—her father—everything I ever knew or trusted or seemed to . . . to know instinctively—all gone."

"The widening gyre," David said. " 'The center cannot hold.' " He wasn't being flippant.

Kendrick said, "It's unbelievable that so much could happen so quickly. And I'm a fifty-five-year-old man. This must be what it's like when there's a flood or a tornado or something. This must be what it's like living in Lebanon or someplace." He made a sound. "Do you have any idea what this feels like?"

"Yes," David told him. "I do."

Kendrick turned around in his chair and looked at him. "Of course," he said. "Of course you do. . . ."

12

David tried phoning Cheryl a little before seven, hoping that she hadn't left for work yet. But there was no answer. Maybe, he decided, she'd spent the night at her mom's.

"Are you going to be all right?" Father asked him.

"Yeah. Sure. I'm fine. I just need to get going."

Nora came in. She'd washed up in the lavatory at the end of the hall.

"You ready to hit the road?"

"I . . . I guess so. Only I wish I had some other clothes, some of my other things."

"As soon as the stores open, we'll get you whatever you need," David promised her. "Father, you have everything?"

"Jack's black Ferrari . . . the license number . . . the address of that house . . . I can't think of anything else."

"It should give the police something to get started with, anyway."

"You don't think the police can do anything, do you, David? You don't think they can handle this."

"I don't think they're prepared for it, that's all. I don't think they're going to like what they find. I think they're going to bury it. Or get buried. That's all. One more thing." He reached behind his neck and undid the chain he wore, handed it and the talisman attached to it to Kendrick. "Keep it."

"Dear God."

"You don't have to like it. You don't have to understand it. Just—please—keep it in your pocket. Please, Father."

They shared a look and Kendrick nodded.

Nora went to Father and took his hands. "Thank-you."

"I'll call you tomorrow or next day." He glanced at David. "All right? We've got to stay in touch, now."

"Agreed." Nora nodded.

David pulled on his coat and helped Nora with hers. Kendrick followed them out, down the hallway, and across the lobby and outside, and he watched them as they got into David's car.

Cool morning. Cold morning. David closed the door for Nora. It was a heavy, hollow sound, lonely. As he came around to his door, he saw Kendrick watching him from the front steps of the rectory, and David waved good-bye.

Kendrick nodded and smiled. Lonely smile.

David got in and started the car and didn't waste much time getting out of the parking lot, moving down the driveway past the seminary and out onto the road.

Nora was quiet until they were out of sight of the seminary and heading for I–275. Escaping. Then she said to him, "You know last night? When I was asleep?"

"Uh-huh."

"When you did whatever that was that you did? That massage?"

"Just to get you relaxed. Calm you down."

"I wasn't asleep the whole time."

"Oh, no?"

"I woke up once or twice. I overheard some of what you and Father Kendrick said."

"What'd you hear?"

"Nothing that important. Only—"

She made a sound in her throat; it startled David and he glanced at her, momentarily alarmed.

"Only," Nora said, "I thought it was interesting, the *way* you talked. I never heard two people talking quite like that before."

"What do you mean?"

"I just think it's nice that you two are such good friends, you and Father Kendrick. You must've known each other for a long time. You two mean a lot to each other, don't you?"

"I don't know," David told her. He'd never thought of it in quite that way before, him and Father Kendrick.

"Well, you do," Nora told him, smiling a little, pleased with herself for being so insightful. "You two really talk the same language. I think you mean a lot to each other. And I want you to know something else, too."

"What's that?"

"However this works out... I appreciate what you're trying to do. I want you to know that."

"Nora..."

"My father's liable to kill us both, David. Father Kendrick, too."

"I doubt it."

"Anyway... So I just want you to know that I—I do thank you."

"What do you think this is all about?" David asked her. "What do you really think's going to happen here?"

"I think my father and Glen and Jack and his people are going to find Father Kendrick and kill him, and then find us and kill you, and kill me, eventually. Me, too."

"Wait a while. Who's Glen?"

"He's my father's... I don't what you'd call him. Vice-president."

"Major domo. Right-hand man."

"Yeah."

"Jack gave me the impression that *he* was real tight with your father."

"He probably likes to think he is, but for as long as I've known anything about it, my father treats Glen Dennison as if he were his own son. Not Jack, that's for sure."

"Okay. That's interesting, that's good to know."

Nora said, "I'm afraid because I don't want to die. Not that way."

David reached for her hand on the seat and found it and gripped it for a minute, and tried to be reassuring.

"Nobody's going to die," he told her, as he watched out for traffic. "Nobody's going to die...."

* * *

Kendrick phoned Bud Pomeroy and told him that an old student of his had been visiting for the holidays and that Jack Starkis had threatened his life, this ex-student's life, and that Jack had said something to him, to this old student, about the murder of Sister Mary Francisco.

"Where's this 'ex-student' now, Mike?"

"On his way back home. He's trustworthy, Bud, believe me. He just walked into the middle of this and got taken by surprise, is what I think. But he gave me a license number for a car Jack was driving, a black Ferrari."

"I think we're looking for that one already."

"And he gave me an address, too."

"Let me have it."

Kendrick read it to him. "It's one of those houses back there. I couldn't find Jack's name in the phone book, but this ex-student of mine, David, told me that you could no doubt check with Stefan Dragomir, because Jack works for him."

"Oh, brother. You're kidding."

"No."

"Do we really want to lift up that rock? Find out what's going on behind the scenes with that guy?"

"I'm not saying he's involved in this, I'm just saying—"

"I know, Mike. I know. It's just that—all right. One step at a time. Dragomir sits on top of about a dozen businesses. Which one does Jack Starkis work for?"

"That I don't know."

"So be it. We're the police, right? All right, thanks. Mike, we're going to use this, though I'm telling you this connection with Dragomir makes me nervous."

"Me, too, believe me."

Believe me, indeed, Bud. You don't know how nervous.

Kendrick dialed the paper next and asked to speak with Wayne Beck.

"Wayne, you're the only reporter I can trust."

"Father, I'm probably the only reporter you *know*."

"So I'm going to give you some strange information I've

gotten hold of and let you do whatever it is that reporters do."

"How strange?"

"Real strange. Real—scary."

"I like it. Does it name names? Does it trash the high and mighty?"

"Well, Wayne, it does, yes."

"I love it. Let her rip, I'm writing it all down."

"Could we get coffee somewhere?"

"Now? Immediately?"

"Yes. Is that—?"

"Let me see. Yeah, okay. I can do that. Yeah. Where?"

Kendrick named a place near the seminary. "Twenty minutes?"

"I'll be there."

"I just hope you can use some of this. But it's liable to get you into trouble, so I want you to be careful."

"Trouble's my middle name."

"I'd kind of hoped that 'careful' would be your middle name."

Jack had just finished his shower and was toweling his hair dry when Lona, the black woman, knocked on the door and said to him, "Glen."

"Great," Jack muttered. "Fucking great. Tell him to give me a minute."

He heard Lona say, "You got it," and start to walk away, and then he heard Glen's voice and he heard the doorknob rattle. The door opened and cool air blew in, swirling the steam.

"I like it," Jack said. "It's bold, it's provocative. Catch a man with his pants down. Very daring."

"Dragomir's pissed and I'm here to haul your ass in for the official reaming."

"And you're such a poet with words, too. Truly a master of *le mot juste, le bon*—"

"Get dressed, Jack."

"Would you mind turning around? I'm a tad shy about—"

"Today, Jack."

And on the way to Stefan Dragomir's house, Glen, driving, told him, "I'd advise you not to try anything funny. Don't be cute. Just take your lumps. He's getting sicker."

"Meaning?"

"Meaning, don't piss him off, give him something, throw him something, convince him that even though you're an asshole, Jack, you're a well-meaning asshole. Admit that you fucked up."

"Like your parents did, you mean."

"Funny guy."

"Look, I'll do what I can to assure him of my deep and profound humility and ineptitude."

Glen said to him, "You'd better. Because if somebody doesn't come up with Nora soon, meaning you, then somebody's going to be in real big trouble."

"She's not that hard to find, Glen."

"Finding her isn't the problem. Even you could find her. Doing something about her—that's what you seem to have a problem with. Doing something about her and about David Trevanson."

"Trevisan."

"Yeah. Him, too," Glen said. "There's going to be some fireworks."

13

"What I have," Father Kendrick told Wayne Beck, "isn't proof. I can't prove this. But you tell me if it's worth doing anything about."

"Okay."

"It has to do with the murder of Sister Mary Francisco."

"Yeah, that nun."

"Stefan Dragomir seems to be involved."

"Holy shit."

"Does—"

"Sorry, Father."

"Does it make sense to you that Stefan Dragomir would be involved in something very dirty like this?"

"You don't know the half of it. We got scuttlebutt on him going back three, four years. But prove it, right? I think he's lined more pockets than, you tell me, half the cotton plants in the world or something."

Kendrick said to him, "Start writing," and took a sip of coffee and then told Beck about Dragomir's daughter, Nora, who had been raped by her father because Dragomir was dying of cancer and he believed that he could put his soul into his daughter's baby by some kind of black magic ritual he'd learned.

Beck's mouth fell open.

"I saw a videotape," Kendrick told him. "Dragomir and a whole party of rich people, acting as if they were at a black mass or something." He took the cassette out of an inside pocket of his coat and put it on the table. "His daughter stole that, Wayne. Nora stole that from Stefan Dragomir."

"Jesus H. Christ."

"But it's been erased."

"*What?*"

Kendrick told him about the storm. "Some kind of power surge."

"Fuck it to—sorry, Father."

"My life's been threatened, too, just as Sister Mary's was. She spoke with Nora and a couple of nights later she was murdered. Then I was threatened."

"So I've got to get hold of Nora. I've got to talk to the daughter."

"A friend of mine's taken her out of town for a few days. This is heating up real fast, Wayne."

"I guess so. Daughter blows the lid on rich daddy and trashy friends. He really raped her?"

"Somebody did. She's seven months pregnant."

"Jesus H. Christ."

"But that's all I have. Hearsay from her, from Nora. The videotape. I saw about ten minutes of it, fifteen minutes of it, but then it was erased. And it's stolen property, it belongs to Dragomir. And that's all I have."

"But it's more than *I* had before, Father. Look—if I need to talk to you, you're gonna be at the seminary, right?"

"For about one more day. The rector thinks that maybe I should take a brief vacation, too. I'll let you know."

"Please do."

"But all I have, everything I know . . . Wayne, that's it."

"I appreciate it, Father."

Kendrick finished his coffee. "I don't know what to do with information like this. I don't know where to start. You do, right?"

"I start digging, Father. Our morgue, coroner's report, police reports—we start putting things together, like a puzzle. That's what we do."

"I'll phone you before I leave town."

"Okay. Very good. No, here, let me get the coffee."

Glen was right. Dragomir must be getting sicker. He was not, to Jack's eye, in good shape.

They'd come into the old man's bedroom, all oak paneling and heavy beams overhead. The air was pungent with incense; maybe the smoke kept him alive. Or helped. He was in bed, propped up with pillows. Three of his people were standing there beside him, by the bed. And he was holding on to his cat, the fat yellow cat he liked so much. Must have the soul of his grandmother in it or something, he was so attached to that cat.

But the eyes were burning as bright as ever, like the last two coals in a smoldering fire that won't go out.

Propped up, eyes burning, Dragomir nodded.

Glen pushed Jack forward.

Jack approached the bed, trying to figure the old man out. Was it real this time, or an act? Was it live or was it Memorex?

One of the Three Stooges beside the bed held out a hand to keep Jack from getting too close. Jack looked him in the eyes. It was Neil. He could trust Neil. If the shit was really going to hit the fan, now, Jack felt that he could count on Neil to help him out.

But Neil wasn't giving anything away, not from what Jack could see. Not a hint, not a glimmer. Cold eyes.

Dragomir said, "I'm sending you to. One of the houses. In Madeira."

Jack watched him.

"I'm not sure yet what. I'm going to do with you."

"Mr. Dragomir—I can get her. What happened was—"

Dragomir closed his eyes and grinned and turned his face away. "Don't insult my. Intelligence. Anymore. Don't say anything. You're going to stay. At the house."

"Yes, sir."

The eyes opened. "Glen, you pick. Two or three people."

Jack was nervous.

"That is all. Jack."

"Look, I can still help. I'm not—"

"That is all!"

"—a liability! I'm not!"

Burning coals. Bright.

Jack needed to know something but he couldn't tell what was going on, if this were a trick or not. Dragomir kept fingernail clippings, pieces of hair, dried skin from old blisters, old socks, anything, he kept all of that stuff on everyone, something personal from everyone, just to keep people in line. Fuck up once, he might let you get away with it. Fuck up twice, you were dead. He'd pull out the piece of dead skin or the old sock or something and start stoking the demon fires and you'd wake up in the middle of the night some night, shrieking like a terrified little girl, screaming for mommy because the bottom half of your body was gone, stripped clean, just the leg bones there, or you'd wake up and be alive just long enough to see something dark and sharp jumping at your face, splat, squish, munch, or you'd see your heart being torn out and dangled in front of you, ooga booga, the blood squirting up and blinding you, splashing in your face as you realized—

Welcome to hell.

Was this a game? Was Dragomir going to try that, was he going to pull a stunt like that with Jack?

Or was Jack really minor now, was he some puke that had fucked up and was being put on the back burner until they got Nora back?

"Jack," Glen said, and Jack turned around.

Glen looked past him and nodded to Neil, who slapped Jack roughly in the middle of the back.

Jack turned on him. "Come on, Neil! Is that hard enough?"

"Neil," Glen told him, "and Susan and Morris. They'll keep an eye on you."

Neil shoved him in the back again, maybe not so hard, and Jack moved, followed Glen out of the bedroom.

And now, turned around, he could see in a corner of the room a kind of shrine that Dragomir had built: a table, lots of candles, all that smoky incense, and shelves filled with photographs of Nora, dozens of pictures of her, from Nora as a baby to very recent pictures. Jack recognized one of them; he'd taken it himself. It was Nora and Glen and a few of the others, just a few weeks ago, standing around outside making faces, ooga booga.

Dragomir was using these to track her down, to reach her from miles away, reach into her mind, her body, to get to her.

They didn't need him. Maybe they hadn't needed him at all. Maybe Dragomir had only hauled Jack along to the Adirondacks to test him, to see what he was made of. It was all a test.

They're going to fuck you over, Jack.

He *felt* it. Simply because of the David Trevisan stunt. And it wasn't even his fault; it was those other turds.

Outside, in the hallway, as Glen closed the bedroom door behind them, Jack asked him, "What is this?"

"Business, Jack. Just business, okay? Business as usual."

"He'd better not try to fuck with me."

"Let's get your stuff and get you moved, okay?"

"I'm telling you right now, he'd better not—"

Neil threw an arm around Jack's shoulders and moved him forward. "Let's not make a scene, Jack, okay? We're all friends here. We all want what's best for Mr. Dragomir, right?"

"Yeah, right. . . ."

"Right. Now, let's get you moved."

"I thought we were friends, Neil."

"We *were*, Jack. We *were*. Friends."

"Motherfucker."

"Now, now. Don't get personal. . . ."

14

Initially neither one of them said much. David wanted to help Nora, he wanted to understand her correctly, but he was wary about how to go about it, unsure. She was scared spitless, that was for certain; but on the other hand she seemed to look at all of this as if it were some new kind of thrill, as if it were a getaway weekend or something. One last roller coaster ride before her parents insisted that everyone pile into the car to go home.

She'd probably never had very many roller coaster rides. This was the only one so far, probably. And if it was her idea of fun, grim and scary and paranoid but fun, then what other kind of thrill would Nora know about?

God, David thought. To her, this is entertainment. Her father's got her so screwed up, for her, this is the cruise, this is the trip to Aruba.

He wanted to know about her father. Get some facts on Stefan-with-an-*f* Dragomir. But Nora wouldn't open up. David got the impression that she didn't seem ready, for some reason, to talk a great deal about her father.

On the other hand, maybe she was so frightened of him that even when he wasn't around, she felt as if he were. As if he were always listening, always watching, even when he wasn't actually there.

Nora was intrigued by David, though. So this was the man her father had been looking for. So this was the man Jack was supposed to trap or whatever it was her father and Jack were going to do with him. So this is the man who killed Theodore Fry.

She wanted to know where he had come from, what had

made him into what he was, how he felt about that. What was Emma like? How did you feel about her? David, are you married? Do you have a girlfriend or something? What was this about your sister?

Emma, David told her, was a wonderful woman, but his feeling was that she wasn't the same once Fry had gotten hold of her. It was as if Fry had really screwed her up, and in a way Emma almost seemed to like it, at least for a while, even if it was weird, because it was thrilling or something, or because she'd thought there'd be more to it.

But there wasn't.

And that was what had happened to his sister, too.

"And that's what happened to me, too, isn't it?" Nora asked him.

"I guess so. Maybe you're too good-hearted. Maybe you're too trusting."

"Poor, trusting women."

"Poor, trusting human beings."

"Do you think," Nora asked him, "that we're all just a bunch of victims, I mean potential victims, sitting around waiting for something to do it to us?"

"Where'd you come up with that?"

"It's just a thought. It's just an idea."

"It's... passive."

"It was just an idea...."

They drove on for a little while longer and Nora asked David, Was he married, or did he have a girlfriend or anything?

So he told her about Cheryl, but he didn't go into too much detail, he played around the edges of it.

"See?" Nora said to him. "You want me to just tell you all about my father, but when I ask you about your girlfriend, all of a sudden you turn into Mr. Shy. See?"

"Yeah, you're right. You're right," he admitted. "It's personal, it's private. It hurts."

"It does hurt. It really does." She told him then, "You know, I don't have very much in this world, right? So even if what I have hurts me, it's still mine, isn't it?"

"Dear Christ, Nora, is that how you feel?"

"We do the best we can with what we've got, don't we?"

"God, I don't know what to tell you. I don't know what to say to that."

"David, you don't have to say anything."

They were quiet for a while. After a few minutes David told Nora that whenever she wanted to take a break they could do that. Get some coffee or something. Buy her some clothes someplace.

"Whenever. I'm okay so far."

"You let me know."

"Okay."

David, looking in the rearview mirror, said, "We're being followed."

Nora turned sideways in her seat and looked out the back window.

"The tan car," he said.

"I see it."

"What is it, a Mazda or something?"

"Yes. One of my father's. I'm trying to see who it is, but they're too far away."

They were on I–71, half an hour outside of Cincinnati. David speeded up and started weaving in and out of traffic, but there weren't that many cars on the road. It was asking a lot to lose the Mazda in that kind of light traffic.

"What're you going to do?" Nora asked him.

He was thinking about that. "Look in the glove compartment."

She popped it open. "What'm I doing this for?"

"Tablet of paper. Notebook. It's in there. And a pen."

"What is this? You've got more stuff crammed in here than I've got in my purse!"

"It's a glove compartment! You're supposed to put all kinds of stuff in there! And that is a very rude, sexist comment."

"Yeah, well, it may be sexist, but it also happens to be true."

"Feminist."

"Masculinist."

"This guy," David said, watching in the rearview mirror,

THE EYES OF NIGHT

"is staying right on my ass. Come on. Come on, smart guy."

"All right. David. I've got your paper and a pen, here. What do you—ooh!"

"What's the matter?"

She'd grabbed her stomach and she was white, all the color drained from her, and she was leaning on the dash, holding on for dear life.

"Nora?"

"I'm okay, I'm okay, I'll be okay."

"You are not okay!"

"It's—Youch!"

"Are you in pain? Are you having—"

"I'm not—having the baby. . . . No. It's—"

"What is it?"

"Look at me. I'm sweating. I'm shaking like a leaf."

"This is your fucking father."

"Yeah." She shook her head and looked around, looked at the side of the road as if expecting to see him there. "This is—my father."

"What are you feeling? Nora? What is this?"

"It's gone, it's over now. . . . But I'm weak, David. I'm very, very weak."

"Pain? Nausea?"

"Yes. Pain, nausea. Incredible dizziness. I thought I was going to fall out the door or something. And now I'm super weak."

"All right, sit back. Can you get comfortable?"

"Now I can." She leaned back and David reached over and adjusted the headrest on her seat.

"All right? Better?"

"Much. What about this paper and pen?"

"It'll sit for a minute." He watched in the mirror. "Asshole is still on top of us."

"Who does he look like? Can you see? Can you describe him? Her? Is it a woman?"

"No. . . . Too far back, and I can't see in there. It's just a silhouette. It *is* a guy, though."

"Of course it is . . . masculinist."

"Feminist."

"What's he doing?"

"Staying right there, about three cars behind me."

Nora scrunched forward. "What do you want me to do with this paper?"

"Look, how are you?"

"Hey, amazing. Ask around. Now tell me what to do."

"Draw a box. Make it like a crossword puzzle, only don't blacken in any of the squares."

"How many squares?"

"Four by four. Sixteen."

"Why, David Trevisan—we're inventing gunpowder!"

"You betcha." To the Mazda in the rearview mirror, he said, "And you're the unfriendly son of a bitch who's going to find out what it feels like."

"What now?"

He dictated the letters to her; Nora wrote one in each blank. When she was done, they had a magic square.

"Fold it up. Give it to me."

She did, and put the paper and pen back in the glove compartment.

The Mazda was still there, three car lengths behind.

"What kind of game *is* this?" David asked.

Nora turned around again, trying to see who it was.

"Here," he told her. "Restaurant. Want a cup of coffee?"

"No, I don't think that right now is precisely the best time for a cup of coffee, no, I don't."

"Well, we're going to do it anyhow,'cause we're going to practice being spiders, and bozo here gets to be the fly."

Swerving, David pulled into the right-hand lane and, not using his turn signal, zoomed up the exit ramp, made a sharp right turn onto 380, and quickly pulled into the parking lot of the Memory Lane Restaurant, next door to a Marathon gas station.

It was a small box of a building, white concrete block on a windy hill overlooking the highway. The parking lot was a narrow strip of blacktop.

The Mazda followed and parked around the corner, out of sight. Whoever was in the driver's seat didn't get out, just sat there watching them until David and Nora had gone inside.

15

There were only a couple of other people in the restaurant—a young man sipping coffee at the counter and an elderly woman eating a piece of pie in a booth. David led Nora to the first free table by the door and pulled out a chair for her. Keeping an eye on the front door as Nora sat down, he told her, "Cream, no sugar."

"Where're you going?"

"Why to cause trouble, of course."

He headed for the back of the restaurant and went right through the doors leading to the kitchen. A tall blonde woman and a petite red-haired one were standing by the ovens, talking.

"Man about two-foot-four come through here?"

"What? Who are you?"

"Out this door?"

It opened onto the back of the parking lot. David saw an old Plymouth Fury and a pickup truck back there, a blue trash dumpster, Styrofoam cups and other wind-tossed litter. He ran to the end of the building, stopped, and looked around the corner.

He saw the parked Mazda and no sign of Dragomir's flunkie behind the wheel.

Coming around the corner, walking fast, David at the same time folded and refolded the magic square, wadding it into a little ball. He couldn't be seen from the restaurant; no windows looked out on this side of the parking lot, which was handy for him and which proved scientifically how stupid the driver of the Mazda was.

When he reached the Mazda, David put the magic square

THE EYES OF NIGHT

into his pants pocket and took his car keys out of his coat.

His car keys, and his trusty, all-purpose pocket knife.

He was on the passenger side. Just in case the guy at the counter decided to show up or another witness pulled in for a coffee to go, David dropped his keys on the pavement. Oops. Butterfingers.

Kneeling down to retrieve them, he shoved his pocket knife into the Mazda's right front tire. It started losing air immediately.

And when he stood up, David pushed the wadded magic square into the crease between the metal of the passenger side door and its window, forcing it down there snugly with the edge of the knife, getting it out of sight.

"Kiss this, buddy...."

Then he folded up the knife and shoved it back into his pocket and came around to the front of the restaurant. He walked in boldly and headed right for Nora.

Mazda was a guy, all right. Medium-sized, David's size, sandy haired, wearing sunglasses.

Coming up behind him, looking Nora right in the eyes, David yelled, "What the hell do you think you're doing with my wife?"

The red-haired young woman at the cash register, the guy at the counter, the old woman in the booth—all of them stared. The blonde woman appeared from the back, watching the three of them suspiciously.

"I thought I told you to leave us *alone* from now on!" David growled, reaching for Nora's hand, helping her out of her chair. "But you're going to be a real jerk about this, aren't you? Come on, dear. We're—No, no, not you! You stay right there! Come on, dear."

"Do you know what you're—"

"*Now,* dear!"

Mazda started to get up, but David pushed him on the shoulder and he fell back into his chair.

"You just give us a few minutes, all right, Tom? So that we can have a little talk about this, a little privacy, if you don't mind, thanks so much."

Pulling Nora behind him, David gave the red-haired

woman a disgusted look as they headed for the front door.

"Like we're supposed to be his best friends or something and he pulls this. It hurts me, it bothers me, it really does. He's paying for the coffee, too."

Outside, he hustled Nora into the Toyota and slammed her door shut and nearly jumped over the hood to get in on his side and slide behind the wheel.

Breathless, she asked him, "What'd you do?"

His tires squealed as David backed up, then made a sharp turn onto 380.

"Gave him a flat tire. Who is he?"

"Name's Randy."

They could both see him coming out of the restaurant.

"One of your father's?"

"One of the *mean* ones."

David speeded down the ramp onto I-71.

"Well, I hope he remembered to bring along a spare, because he'll need it."

"You really gave him a flat tire?"

"Yup."

Nora said, "You should've killed him."

"Yeah, well, I didn't kill him, okay?"

"You're capable of it."

"If it comes down to it, I'll kill him, all right?"

She said, "He'll certainly kill you if you give him the opportunity. They take a blood oath, David."

"That's fine."

"They're all contaminated. They know what they've gotten into. They don't care. They've turned themselves into zombies or something." She told him, "Their lives aren't important to them anymore, so I don't know why they should be to you."

"I guess I'm just funny about things like that."

"Well, you shouldn't be," Nora said. "Not with them. Not with my father. They don't care anymore. They don't."

An hour later, thirty miles south of Columbus, David spotted the Mazda behind them again.

"That took him a while."

"Randy?" Nora said.

"Uh-huh."

"Oh, shit."

"Get ready for Act Two."

"Act Two?"

"If it comes down to it, I'm capable of it, right?"

"Oh, God, David."

He pulled off at the next exit. Route 38. There was a fireworks place, actually a renovated gas station, and right across from it a county road. Blue Road. Dirt and gravel. David drove down it as fast as he could.

Farmland, wide fields on both sides of them, cattle grazing, sparse woods under gray skies, the occasional wood or brick farmhouse, and the occasional side road, little more than tractor paths, really, cutting straight back into the fields.

Chill winter morning in Ohio. David's Toyota kicked up a light cloud of dust. There was no other traffic, no other cars. He speeded past the fields, around sharp bends in the road. As he came over a hill, David saw Randy taking a corner, far behind him.

He dipped into a shallow in the road and, as he started up the other side, he saw the Mazda in his rearview mirror, topping the hill.

"He really thinks he's a fucking gladiator or something, doesn't he?"

Nora looked at David but didn't say anything.

The road made another bend. David took it as fast as he could. The road curved again, and once more, zigzagging. He lost sight of the Mazda.

Immediately on his right there was a tractor path, leading into a cold brown field flanked on one side by sparse woods, tall, black, spindly trees, no leaves. David hit the brakes, twisted the steering wheel, and downshifted.

"Jesus!" Nora yelled, slapping a hand onto the dashboard.

"Hang on!"

"I guess so!"

He followed the path nearly to the end of the field, then came around in a half circle and parked in the middle of the field, so that he could see the Mazda coming when it showed up. But as soon as the car settled still, David threw it into park and unfastened his seat belt and got out.

Nora yelled to him, "Hey!"

David ran as fast as he could, back to the path. He couldn't see Randy yet and he didn't hear the Mazda. He took out his pocket knife and used it to draw a circle around himself, cutting into the dirt of the path. He invoked his spirits and prepared himself, purified himself, without the benefit of any cleansing water—or even Father Kendrick's whiskey.

Props.

It all happens in your head anyway, right?

He heard the Mazda.

David stood solidly in the middle of his defensive circle and crossed his arms at the wrists, raised them in front of him.

"In nomine Agla Sabaoth Elohim..."

The Mazda was moving fast. David could see Randy, the sunglasses behind the windshield, the sandy hair.

Legs braced, feet shoulder-width apart, head down—

"*Aeior!*"

The Mazda grinned at him, the front of it, the headlights and bumper.

Randy was smiling at him, too, from behind the sunglasses.

They take a blood oath, David. They're all contaminated. They've turned themselves into zombies or something.

David said, "Well, kiss this, you fucking zombie. *Aeior!*"

The magic square, jammed between the glass of the window and the inside of the door, answered him, caught on fire, and the Mazda began to shake. A black streak, a line, a burn mark, shot up along the inside of the window.

Randy's smile vanished.

David stared over his crossed arms at the shivering Mazda.

In the field, Nora screamed.

Randy had no control over the car. His hands were frozen on the steering wheel, but he couldn't do anything with it, the steering wheel wouldn't move. The Mazda pulled one way, then the other, as if a powerful wind were rocking it, buffeting it back and forth between two walls. And it was happening in mere seconds, within mere heartbeats.

David felt no wind.

Nora felt no wind.

Randy screamed. At the last moment he let go of the steering wheel and crossed his own arms at the wrists, an attempt at some kind of defense, and as he screamed he shook his head back and forth.

His sunglasses flew off.

And his Mazda never hit David. As it came at him, the car tilted to one side, bouncing back from the line David had drawn in the gravel, his circle. It skidded and leaped off the path, bouncing into the woods, and rolled over twice, with loud crunching and snapping sounds, then came to rest between two trees.

For the space of a heartbeat, all was silence.

Then David and Nora heard Randy screaming, crying—trapped, his sobbing voice, a thin howl.

The Mazda exploded.

David watched it explode.

An enormous tower of black smoke lifted into the air, carrying with it reaching arms of flames, orange and purple and black, stretching and curling flames that began to move up the trees and jump to other trees, flames that waved and danced, moved—

Moved, and for one moment—

"Dear God..."

—for one moment created a face, a demonic face, a Bezemoth or an Ordiel or a Valefor or Kus, some leering medieval thing. Demon...

They take a blood oath. They're all contaminated.

In agony when he got back to his car, breathless, eager to get out of there before sirens sounded, before somebody saw them and came running, David found Nora shivering in the front seat, holding herself, her arms held tightly against her, and she was looking straight ahead, not at the fire, eyes wide, terrified.

She was utterly terrified.

David didn't say anything. He put the Toyota into drive and steered it, bouncing and scraping, back onto Blue Road.

Behind them, pulsing and smoking, all red and purple and black and orange, was what was left of Randy and the Mazda and what was left of his soul.

"He's just started," Nora said.

"What?"

"He's just started. He won't stop." She turned around in her seat and looked out the back window.

Black smoke, flames, gray sky.

"Dear God, we don't have a chance."

16

"How are you feeling, Mr. Dragomir?"

"What time is it? Glen."

"A little after noon, sir."

"No word yet from. What did you say? Whom did you send?"

"Randy, Mr. Dragomir. No, we haven't heard anything yet."

"Send someone else."

"If you wish, Mr. Dragomir."

"Send someone else now. He killed Fry. He may have killed. Randy, too."

"Yes, sir. Can I get you anything else?"

"Just. Leave me alone."

"Yes, sir."

"She's still alive. Glen."

"Yes, sir."

"If anyone hurts her, I'll. She's not to be. Hurt."

"Understood, sir. I'll send someone better than Randy, this time."

Around eleven in the morning, on the other side of Columbus, David stopped to put gas in his car, fill it up at a Sunoco station, and he and Nora decided that it was safe enough for them to have something to eat. They went into a Wendy's for lunch and sat at a table by a window and spoke quietly as they ate.

For the hundredth time she asked him, Did he see anyone else at all, a hint of anyone chasing them, now that Randy was—gone?

For the hundredth time, No, he hadn't seen anyone, Randy was the only one. But didn't Nora think that her father would send someone else?

"He will, absolutely. Either that, or he'll just—hurt me somehow, keep trying to hurt me." She asked David, "What do you intend to do? Just run away, just keep trying to run away?"

"That wouldn't be very practical, would it?"

"Are you going to try to fight back?"

"What else can I do?"

"You're not really going to try to *fight back*, are you?"

"What else am I supposed to do?"

"God, get serious. Do you know how strong he is?"

"Well, remember Mr. Fry. I'm the guy who—"

"Yes, I know, I know, but—"

"Nora, you came to Father Kendrick for help, so he's trying to help. I walk into this, *I'm* trying to help."

"I know, but—"

"And we can do it. We can. We can help."

"You," she told him, "you and Father Kendrick, you can walk away from this anytime you want to. Me—I can't. Me, he owns."

"He doesn't 'own' you, Nora."

"David, I'm his fucking daughter. All right? He *owns* me. Okay? You think that way, you'll see what I mean."

"You fully expect him to get at you again, don't you? I mean, the nausea, the headaches."

"Anytime he wants to. I expect him to show up any second."

"Push him away, Nora."

"Yeah, right."

"Push him away!"

"He can *do* whatever he *wants* to, David."

"No one," he told her, "can *do* whatever he *wants* to."

"Stefan Dragomir can."

In his room in the rectory, Father Kendrick stared at the half-packed suitcase sitting open on his bed.

Finish packing or not?

He'd done what he'd told David and Nora he was going to do, told the police about Jack Starkis, alerted the newspapers, a reporter. His own life was in danger, probably, so he should follow through, phone Monsignor Pantik or go over there and talk to him, get the ticket, and fly out to Phoenix.

But he didn't *feel* as if that were the thing to do.

He didn't *feel* frightened for his life, paranoid, a target, the next victim.

His little inner voice, his sense of self, whatever it was, told him to calm down. It wasn't logical, it wasn't common sense, but—

But Kendrick had long ago taught himself to listen to his little voice, to calm down when his little voice told him to, or to speak to the person seated next to him, to read the magazine article that had caught his attention, to wait five more minutes before hurrying out the door.

And whenever he listened to his little voice, calmed down, read the article, spoke up, waited—things worked out harmoniously, things worked out as if there were a master plan or a blueprint somewhere for working things out.

Finish packing or not?

His little voice told him that something was happening, something with Wayne Beck, something about the videotape or the list of famous people Dragomir knew. Something—

He went to his desk and picked up the phone, to call Monsignor Pantik and tell him no, he didn't think he'd need the ticket to Phoenix.

But then Kendrick put the phone down. If you're not going to bother with it, why bother telling Monsignor in the first place?

He went back to the bed, looked at the half-open suitcase.

What about Jack Starkis? The phone call, the threat? The elemental or whatever it was, the storm this morning? What about those things?

On top of his shirts was the talisman David had given him.

"You don't have to like it. You don't have to understand it. Just—please—keep it in your pocket. Please, Father."

Not exactly the Passion of Our Lord, that talisman.

Yet Kendrick had learned not to discount his little voice.

Finish packing or not?

"I recognize some of these people.... Dear God, that's Iva Daugherty..."

With her husband's death a few years ago, Iva Daugherty had realized her life's ambition and become a wealthy woman. Truly wealthy. Wealthy squared, wealthy to the third or fourth power. And a wealthy woman with power, lots of power. Owner of human souls, hirer and firer, mover and shaker. Dance on their bones. See them crawl. Piss on their graves.

With her husband's death, Iva Daugherty had come into the control of half a dozen businesses—a radio station, a television station, a weekly suburban newspaper and printing company, a real estate investment firm that was sitting on thousands of acres of commercial property. Odds and ends. Pocket change. Mad money. If she could have liquidated it right now, she could have filled a couple of warehouses with it. And twice that, three times that, in clout, prestige, influence.

To know Iva Daugherty was to be set up for the rest of your life, tax free.

To piss her off was to live a life of shame, degradation, poverty. You'd be better off having your throat slit by a crazed junkie, better that than try to face the society of your growth-portfolio-and-deferred-annuities peers once you were on Iva Daugherty's shit list.

She had a few acquaintances who mattered, a few enemies who didn't, many would-be friends.

Iva Daugherty, trim, attractive, admitting privately to fifty-two but no more, was lunching this afternoon with some of these acquaintances, friends, enjoying a fine meal at Orchids downtown, and on the way out, coming across the plaza, pulling her gloves on and smiling at something

Burt had said, she was approached by newspaper and television reporters.

Newspaper and television reporters, right there, a woman with a microphone and a young man right behind her with a minicam on his shoulder, and two other people, another man and a woman in winter coats, carrying notebooks and pens, hurrying toward her.

"What on earth is this?"

"Mrs. *Daugherty*! Give us some of the facts, please, about your relationship with Stefan Dragomir!"

"What?"

"Please! Mrs. Daugherty! We've heard about some of those parties that—"

"What is this?"

"—substance to any of this? What about rumors that Dragomir was influenced in the Martech takeover—"

"Get out of here!"

"Mrs. Daugherty, we've heard that Stefan Dragomir's daughter may have been involved in the murder of—"

"Get out of my way!"

"Tell us about Stefan Dragomir, Mrs. Daugherty!"

"Tell us about the parties, Mrs. Daugherty!"

"We have *witnesses,* Mrs. Daugherty!"

Wayne Beck had done his job. Spent a few hours that morning in the newspaper morgue, put some pieces together, made a few phone calls, called in a few markers, reminded some folks of a few old favors.

"Get out there and talk to these people," he said. "These rich people. Iva Daugherty, track her down. Bill O'Connell. Ted Troy at Proppco—he's ass deep in this. No, see, there's a whole group of them and they have these trashy parties, and they're starting to get real nasty with the competition, they've got a real powerful clique. Ask 'em questions. Stop just short of slander, okay? But get 'em real worked up. Make 'em sweat. Make them think we know a hell of a lot more than we do, because they'll crack, believe me. One of 'em's gonna start crying. *I* think some of them know about this nun being murdered, okay? So just lift up the rock and let's see what's crawling around underneath there.

And tell what's-his at the TV station that I'm copyrighting this in *my* name, so he can keep his nose out of it!"

As soon as she was safely home in her big old house, Iva Daugherty was on the phone, demanding to speak with Stefan Dragomir, tears running down her face, ruining her makeup.

"You tell him I want to speak to him *right now!* I *know* he's sick! I want him to be a lot sicker! He told us this would never, never, *ever* happen! You tell him to call me back!"

And immediately after that she was on the phone to one of her attorneys, a man who was Dragomir's attorney, too, who knew all of them quite well, the revelers and party goers, the doers and movers, and Iva told him to start doing whatever it was that he needed to do, because reporters, *reporters*, were starting to *ask questions,* they had asked *her* questions, and how the *hell* did that ever happen?

They were in the living room. Jack was sitting by the fireplace. Susan was in a chair in front of the bay window, reading a book.

"Permission to go to the bathroom, sir."

"Come off it, Jack."

"Permission to just get the fuck out of here and start a new life. Sir."

Susan said, "Jack . . ."

"You think I'm kidding?"

"No."

"I'm sitting around here waiting for the guillotine to fall, Soo-zannn!"

"There's no guillotine."

"Know what? I think I'm just going to get up and walk out of here."

"Fine. Do it."

"The Big D thinks he can hold me prisoner in his own home—I'm an American citizen. Is he?"

"Yes." She closed the book, reached for her cigarettes and lit one, got up and walked over to the TV and picked

THE EYES OF NIGHT

up the remote, turned it on and clicked through some channels. "What time is it, Jack?"

"Time to be moving on, partner, and start living the rest of my life sans Mr. Big S the D."

Channel twelve. "Just let me watch the news, okay?"

"Thee noose."

Susan sat in the couch and leaned toward the end table for an ashtray, and Jack watched the back of her head, wondering if he should try to kill her or if he should make a break for it, run away, if Neil would really trust him enough—

"Hey, Jack!" Susan sat up straight.

On the news they were talking about Iva Daugherty and Stefan Dragomir and their—

"Jack! *Look*!"

He stood up and walked over to the couch. "Fuck the . . . what . . . ?"

"—no further information at this time. Mrs. Daugherty and several others, including a spokesperson for Dragomir's Rose Corporation, refused to comment on the allegations."

"He's been hit!" Jack yelled, punching the couch excitedly. "He's been hit, he's wounded, he's bleeding all over the fucking rug!"

"Calm down, calm down, we don't know what—"

"He is *not* going to fucking ruin *my* life," Jack yelled at her, "when he can't even fucking—"

"Calm down, Jack!"

Neil came in. "The hell's going on in here?"

"You hear the news?" Susan said to him.

"No, I didn't hear the—"

"Shit's hit the fan," Jack told him.

Susan said, "Something's happened. There were all kinds of rumors on the TV. They mentioned Mr. Dragomir, they mentioned Mrs. Daugherty, they hinted that there were parties of some kind, maybe some kind of—"

"This is bullshit. They can't prove any of this. This is slander, this is—"

"They must know something, Neil!"

Morrie came in.

The telephone rang.

Jack yelled, "Don't answer it! Listen to me!"

The phone in the living room was on one of the end tables. Susan automatically reached for it, but Morrie went toward it, too.

"He probably thinks I'm responsible!" Jack yelled.

"Well?" Morrie asked him. "You're telling me he's wrong?"

"Get me out of here," Jack told them, all of them, looking each one of them right in the eyes. "Get me out of here. All of us, we get the hell out of here, we tell him to go to hell, all right?"

"Oh, yeah, right. We just walk away," Morrie said sarcastically.

"He has stuff on us, Jack!"

"But I have stuff on him, Neil!"

"Like what?"

Morrie said, "I'm answering the phone now!"

"Like what, Jack?"

"I am answering the goddamn phone now, everyone!"

"Like this!" Jack said, reaching into his shirt pocket and pulling out a small plastic baggie that contained a few strands of hair.

"Jesus!" Susan said. "His?"

"Yes, ma'm."

Neil said, "Where'd you get that?"

Morrie picked up the phone. "Yes? No, this is Morrie." He glanced at Jack, started to sweat, looked at Neil.

Slowly, Neil nodded to him.

17

"This is where you grew up?" Nora asked David.

"Yeah."

They were on I-80, coming into Noland. It was a little after six and it had taken them that long to get here because they'd stopped in Akron to buy Nora some clothes and all the other things she needed, and to grab some supper at a restaurant that David particularly liked in Highland Square.

"They do what here?" she asked. "Make steel or something?"

"Used to. Used to. Closed down all the mills back in the seventies."

"They just closed them down? What happened?"

"Fat cats bled all the little guys dry. Then they pulled up stakes and went somewhere else. Started making steel somewhere else."

"Did they really?"

"Yup."

"Kind of like what happens all over the place, huh? People taking advantage of everybody else."

"I guess that's how it's supposed to work."

"That's what my father did, isn't it? He's one of the fat cats."

"Yes, he is."

"So what're you? What does that make you? You're Robin Hood, right?"

"It makes me the person who got in over his head before he found out what was really going on, is what it makes me. Look before you leap, I always say."

"You always take your own advice?"

"Hell, no."
"Ouch."
"That's ri—ight."

They reached his house, northeast of the city, by six-thirty. David was surprised to see a pickup truck with a cap on the back sitting on the lawn in the front.

"What do you think?" he asked Nora. "Is that another present from your father, or am I getting paranoid?"

"God, David, I don't know."

But he didn't really feel anything, sense anything, and as he stepped out of his car the front door of the house opened and Cheryl, holding her coat closed in front of her as if she'd just pulled it on, came onto the porch. She was wearing her glasses. She awkwardly pushed them up on her nose, adjusting them.

"David?"

He said, walking up to her, "Yeah, I know, I didn't think I'd be back this early, either."

"You have a black eye."

"I had an accident."

"Um, David, Frank's here."

"Frank?"

"Frank. Gauss. From the office."

"Ah." He thought, Give me a fucking break, you really work fast, don't you, once your mind's made up?

"Who's that?"

He turned around; Nora was getting out of the car. "Her name's Nora Dragomir."

"She's *pregnant*."

"Yeah, well, I work fast."

"David, what is going on?"

"She's a friend of Father Kendrick's and she needs a place to stay."

"So you offered."

"Yeah."

"While I'm still here?"

"Jesus Christ! Correct me if I'm wrong, but this is my

goddamn house, isn't it, last time I looked? I mean, I paid for it, right?"

"Keep your voice down!"

"My fucking money, right?"

"Your parents' fucking money!"

"Well, fucking excuse me! I didn't know the fucking silver spoon was showing!"

Nora was halfway to them but she stopped now and said nervously, "This is not a good moment, is it?"

"It's fine," David told her. "It's fine. We get a little sentimental once in a while, that's all. It's fine. Come on." He held out a hand.

From inside the house, Frank Gauss yelled, "Cher-yl! *Cheryl!* You want these clothes like in boxes or can I put 'em in these grocery bags or what?"

Cheryl said, "Excuse me," and turned around and went inside.

David said, "There is no fucking excuse," and, when Nora got to the porch, told her, "I apologize."

"For what?"

"For being born, for starters."

"Oh, now, come on."

"We've got a spare room upstairs. I'm going to put you there."

"Fine."

"Cheryl's moving out, I guess. I don't know." He walked her inside and closed the front door.

Nora asked him, "We're just doing this until we hear from Father Kendrick, right?"

"Right."

"Do you think we're really going to be safe here, David?"

"I'm going to make sure we are. Trade secrets. You watch and see."

He led her through the living room and a sitting room and up the stairs to the second floor. The door to his and Cheryl's bedroom was open and he saw Cheryl in there and heard her talking to this Frank Gauss, who was out of sight behind the door. David felt a twinge in his stomach, a sick little tug. Good old Frank, right there in *his* fucking bedroom. He walked Nora to the end of the landing and showed her the spare room. It had a bed and a table, a closet, an antique dresser he'd found at an auction.

"What do you think?"

"Oh, it's fine."

"Lie down," he told her. "Take it easy. You didn't get much sleep last night."

"You didn't get any."

"I'm going to get your things out of the car and bring them up here."

"Thank-you. Thanks. David—"

He was at the door, on his way out. "Yeah?"

"I just—" Nora shrugged and smiled a little. "I guess I just feel a little weird about this, is all."

"Well, me, too. It is weird."

"It is, isn't it?"

"Life is weird," he told her, and tapped his hand on the doorjamb a couple of times and went out.

Downstairs in the living room Frank Gauss, in a brown leather jacket, was stacking boxes by the front door. Cheryl was carrying shopping bags in from the kitchen. Frank turned around when David walked in.

He was taller than David, and balding, and doing his best to cover it up, comb his hair the right way. Putting on weight. Another one of these sad suckers living their whole lives on the outside. No interior life at all. One of these guys whose best years were in high school, of all places, being a jock in high school, playing football or something. They always wound up becoming real estate agents or insurance salesmen or used car salesmen. It never failed. Once in a while coaches, where at least they could do some good. And Frank Gauss, here, had gone into real estate and had the look that told you life would never again be as good for him as it had been when he was seventeen.

Asshole.

"You're Frank?"

"Uh-huh."

"I'm David."

"Yeah, I know that."

Well, he can talk. But can he talk and perform gross motor skills at the same time?

David said, "Cheryl?"

She gave him this impatient look—*I would just pleeeeze like to get this over with now, soon, now, could we make that happen?*—and said to Frank, "Look, could you put some of those boxes in the truck, please?"

"Are you sure?"

"Frank!"

"Hey, all right? I just asked!"

He put on a show, piling boxes in his arms, then struggled to get the front door open, almost spilling the boxes until Cheryl—"Why are you doing this, Frank?"—came over and opened the door to let him out, then closed it.

"You sure can pick 'em," David told her.

"Look who's talking."

"Yeah, well . . . Fine . . ." He went to the window and looked out, just to make sure that he was indeed loading the truck.

Cheryl told him, "We'll be out of here in a couple of hours if that's all right with you."

"That might not be fast enough."

"Look, I'm sorry, I didn't plan this, I didn't want—"

"That's not what I mean." He went toward her, but stopped, waited. "This is . . . dangerous. Nora and I are in trouble."

"Oh, fuck."

"You know the funny thing I do every once in a while?"

"Oh, Jesus."

"Tends to get me in trouble? Well, it's going to be exciting around here in a little bit. Only I'm not sure how fast. But pretty soon. And I—"

"David, I really only have a few more things."

"We're talking about your life, Cheryl!"

"I understand that! As soon as I can—"

"I killed a guy on the way up here!"

She stared at him.

"Okay?" he said to her.

"You mean—like Fry, you killed him?"

"Yes."

"Oh, shit, oh, God."

"Nora's father is—" Now he went to her and put his hands on her shoulders, moved away a strand of hair that had fallen on her cheek, brushed it away gently, a memory, and said to her, "It's getting hairy. It's strange. It's very strange. I want you to leave now, as soon as possible, instantaneously. Faster than that. Please." He told Cheryl, "I don't want you to die."

"Oh, David."

"Frank I don't care about," he said. "You I do."

"Oh, God. Don't die."

"I'm not going to die."

"Please?"

The door opened and Frank came in, huffing for breath. "Truck's loaded."

Cheryl moved away from David.

"What is this?" Frank asked.

David was watching Cheryl.

Frank said again, "Hey! What *is* this?"

David snapped his head around and glared at him. "What *is* this? What *is* this?"

"Yeah!"

"What this *is*, is my fucking house! And you're standing in it! What this *is*, is my friend, this is my girlfriend or my ex-girlfriend or something, can you see that? And you're an asshole. That's what this—"

"Hey!"

"—*is*, you motherfucking—"

"*Hey*!" Frank came forward, lifting his fists. "You *got* a fucking black eye already, man! How'd you like a bloody *nose*, too, huh?"

"Jesus!" David swore.

"Courtesy of your old pal Frank, huh?"

"Don't!" Cheryl yelled, gripping David's shoulders from behind, holding his arms to restrain him or keep him there. "David, don't! You'll kill him!"

"He'll what?"

THE EYES OF NIGHT

"David, please. We'll finish loading right now and we'll get out of here right now!"

Slowly he turned around and looked at her. His hands were shaking. Cheryl, watching his eyes, frightened of him, reached for his hands and held them to help him calm down.

"David, your hands are warm."

"Get your coat," he told her. "Finish—with the truck. I'm going to see how Nora's doing. Okay?"

"Okay."

"Okay..."

Frank, confused, grunted, "The hell is it with you two, anyway?"

18

"**G**oddamit!" he swore, when he saw Nora.

She was on her back and shivering, staring wide-eyed at the ceiling, sweating. As David jumped into the room, she looked at him and let her head fall weakly to one side on the pillow.

David kneeled beside the bed and grabbed one of her hands and held it in both of his.

"Fight it!"

"I'm ... trying...."

"Fight him!" He stood up and put his hands on her neck, the sides of her neck and her shoulders, and pushed her head so that it was upright on the pillow. "Look at me, Nora."

She did, but closed her eyes as tears began to drip down her red cheeks.

"Pain?"

"No ... pain. Just—"

"All right, don't talk. I'm going to help you. Okay, now? I'm holding on to you. He's trying to weaken you and I want you to be strong, okay? So you just relax. You stay relaxed. You just let your mind go wherever it's going to go. Okay now?"

She opened her eyes and closed them again, as if signaling him, too weak to nod, then held her eyes open, and David stared into them.

Stared past her eyes and saw into her mind, felt her fever, her imagination, felt what it was that Dragomir was doing to her soul.

What Dragomir was doing to her, what Stefan Dragomir

was feeding her, pumping into her soul and bloodstream and into her mind, her imagination, to chain her and keep her down.

Flames, leaping and jumping, and demonic faces and images, wraiths and ghosts, skeletons stretched like rubber, bodiless heads and headless bodies floating through the flames, stars behind them, grotesque images, cartoons, not frightening, just familiar enough to throw her off.

And then the disjointed images, the spiritual knives and whips and chains to take her off guard, to play with her in heavy doses. Pictures of herself as a pretty baby girl, mental images of photographs of her, then the photographs ripped in two and brains and blood and pus dripping down the photographs, the pretty face contorting into a scream. Images of babies, sweet pretty innocent little babies, no doubt like Nora's own baby, the baby growing inside her right now, and then the sweet babies exploding like overripe berries, babies exploding from their skins like bananas squeezed too hard by a powerful hand. Images of Nora moving on top of the head of a horned demon, its head the size of a rock, its twin horns reaching up, curving, sharp as bone spikes, horns as tall as she was and as thick as her own body, and Nora spreading her legs, moving to sit on one of those spikes as if she were getting comfortable, positioning herself in the saddle of a horse, settling down, her white thighs sliding down both sides of this great horned spike, and then beginning to rock back and forth, laughing, loving it, and the head as big as a rock moving with her, helping her love it, no better feeling in the world or in the universe, good and raw, and Nora laughing like a harpy, loving it, laughing harder and rocking harder and faster and harder and faster as her body begins to split, as her insides begin to ooze out, squeeze down the sides of the horn, slick and shiny, fresh and exciting, spill out and run down over the brows and eyes of the demon's head as big as a rock, red gore, stringy, all connected in one long fibrous confusion of what used to be inside her, while the demon grunts and smiles and its big eyes roll back and look up at her.

Dragomir's voice, too, in there, down inside Nora's soul,

the words falling right into place like spiders scampering, hurrying to join a parade:

"*Do this and I'll kill you and the baby, you and the baby, you and the baby, I can always make more babies, but I love you because you're my daughter, why do you hate me? aren't we strong together, powerful and strong? why wouldn't I love you? I'm your father! think of what we're doing together and don't listen to anyone else who makes you feel weak or makes you hate me or convinces you that I want to hurt you, because I don't, I don't, I really don't want to kill you or the baby, I love you both and I want us to be together, together, together...*"

It was like a broken record playing constantly in the background, hostility disguised as concern, sadism as freedom, hate propped up as useful and good, nausea renamed love.

The demon was there, too, Dragomir's demon, the hate or the cancer or the lust or whatever it was that was fueling him and eating him up at the same time, keeping him alive and killing him at the same time. It was large and yellow, it looked almost like a child's toy, a great greasy yellow ball with black spots, long curling black horns, big black eyes, no legs or feet or hands to it, just this hideous floating yellow greasy thing, breathing black smoke in and out, acid smoke, black charnel smoke, with fragments of things floating in it, specks of dust, rotted pieces of old souls or something—

The thing that was killing him, the thing he was trying to escape by hiding inside Nora, by forcing his life into her, inside her, using her and eating her up, wasting her, a human sacrifice for him, so that his good clean white bright soul could go on and on....

"Nora?"

David was still inside her soul, looking deeply down into her eyes, and holding on to her, feeling her neck, her shoulders, feeling the hideous yellow greasy thing, and what he did now—

"Stay there, Nora."

—was to push it back with his own blue light, give her

strength with his own willpower, his shining curtain of light, pure and bright and blue and clean, strong as a wind, his curtain, pushing back Dragomir, her father, pushing him back, him and his—

He heard the hiss. Dragomir's voice, hissing, grunting, growling as it was resisted—

"*I love you because you're my daughter, why do you hate me? aren't we strong together, powerful and strong? why wouldn't I love you? I'm your father! think of what we're doing together....*"

"Nora?"

"It's—"

"Don't talk. You're fine, now."

"I want—"

"Shhhh. Shhhhh..."

More tears came down her cheeks, dripping and dripping, soaking into the cloth of the pillowcase, dark damp spots. She lifted a hand and gripped David's arm and held on, held on, her fingers wrapped around him for all she was worth.

"It's okay, now. It's okay."

"Dear ... God ... save me.... I don't ... want this...."

"You're going to be fine."

She sighed heavily, a strong breath. "Oh, God—"

David stood back, watched her, and Nora closed her eyes, breathed, breathed, and shuddered. Her color came back, the bright red of her cheeks, the coercion, the concentration, came away, went away, and she opened her eyes again.

"Okay, now," she told David.

"Are you?"

"It's like ... it tightens up, real tight—I can't breathe, he's right there.... He's ... powerful, and you think it's going to go on forever. Sounds ... sexual, doesn't it? You think ... he's that strong. But he's not."

"He lets go and you're okay again."

"For a while." She groaned. "For who knows how long."

"Well, stay there. I'll get you some coffee. Some tea. You want a cup of tea?"

"You know what I really want to do?"

"What's that?"

"Go outside for a walk. Get some fresh air. Feel . . . like fresh air."

They went out by the back door so that they wouldn't bother Cheryl and Frank, went down the back porch steps, and walked into the woods, cold black frozen trees, that surrounded David's house, for some fresh air.

19

Nora told David, "The thing that was weird, but it was kind of thrilling—this morning—when we were driving out of Cincinnati? I've never felt that way before. I wanted to get away, run away, just escape, and it felt like we were running up a hill or something, running through the rain. It just felt good. I'd been waiting so long for that feeling."

They were sitting on an old log. Or Nora was, anyway, because David got up now, nervous, jittery, and with his breath steaming he turned his back to her so that he could think, stare into the dark woods, feel the night around them.

"What is it, David?"

"I'm waiting for another one of those creeps to show up, any second now."

"Randy?"

"Yeah."

"You'll know if they show up. We'll know. Believe me."

He looked over his shoulder at her and smiled. "Good point." He came over and sat down beside her on the log. "You're right."

"I know."

"Oh, so you know."

"I've been right all along, only nobody listens to me."

"Right about what?"

"About my father. What he's trying to do. About dying and people being killed. It's real grim, I know that, but this is what he's going to do, he's doing it, and nobody's going to stop him."

"You know, I always liked that about you. That real fatalistic side."

"Look, I'm sorry, but that's the way it is."

"But, see, we can do stuff. You're healthy. You're baby's healthy, I guess. We ought to get you to a clinic or a doctor, though, I suppose. Have it checked out. Whatever they do to make sure babies come out all right."

"My father had a nurse there all the time. Had me taken to the doctor once a week. The baby's healthy—for a monster, I guess."

"Look—Nora—all we're doing here is keeping you far enough away from him so that we can fuck him up, trip him up. And it can be done. There are ways. The same shit he and Jack use. So just think about that, okay?"

"Yeah, well... Stop these trees from growing. That'd be easier. Make the earth stop spinning, you know?"

"That's him talking, not you."

She shrugged. "Just let me enjoy this for a few minutes, okay? Something to look back on in my old age."

"Jesus, Nora!" David stood up again. "Don't do this to yourself!" He looked away and said, "Damn it, anyway," and scratched his lower lip. Nervous habit. "Tell me about him."

"Tell you what about him?"

"Where he came from. Where he was born. Tell me about him."

"What, so you can figure out his weak spots, find the chink in his armor? Is that it?"

"Just tell me about him."

Nora said, "He comes from some village, I don't know exactly where. He was born into a cult. I don't know if it has a name or anything."

"A cult? You mean, like a church, like a religion?"

"Yeah. They claim they go back thousands of years. Look, here's all I know, and I got this from Glen and a little bit from Jack and one or two other people. My father never told me anything."

"Okay."

"They're in this cult, it's thousands of years old. They

worship demons, they take this vow of evil or something. Here's the point. I don't even know who my mother was, because as soon as I was born, they killed her."

"Who killed her?"

"They did. These cult people, my father and these cult people."

"Here? In America?"

"No. Well, yes, here. My father was born in Europe and when he was born they did the same thing. They pass it down from generation to generation. They kill the woman, the mother, the same way they killed your friend, Sister Mary."

"God."

"You see why I'm pretty sure I'm not going to live to a ripe old age? There's a kind of pattern here, wouldn't you agree?"

"Yeah. There's a pattern."

"So I don't know what to do. I can't just sit around and wait for this shit to come down. Give birth to my baby and then have my father kill me. Nail me . . . to a wall. . . ."

"What's the name of this cult? Do they have a name?"

"No."

"What do they call themselves?"

"I don't know. My father never told me anything, David!"

He started pacing back and forth. "Anything else? I mean, what else can you tell me? I just want to know anything you can think of, because it could help."

"Shit, I don't know. He's dying, you know that."

"He has cancer—what?—like, cancer of the pancreas or the liver or what?"

"Leukemia. Glen told me that, that he has leukemia. It doesn't matter what it is, though, because he thinks it happened because he fucked up some ritual."

"What now? What?" David walked back and sat beside her.

Nora said, "You know. He's being punished for doing some ritual all wrong."

"Which ritual?"

"Jesus, David! You are asking the wrong person!"

"Does it have to do with that yellow thing I saw? The demon we both saw?"

"I guess. I don't know! I don't want to know'"

"All right, all right. He screwed up, or somebody screwed him up. He interfered with something, or he was interfered with."

"Is that how these things work?"

"Kind of. It's more like baking a cake than anything else. Follow the recipe. Only you have to use the proper safeguards. And you can't walk out in the middle of it."

"Well, then, he's either the fuck*er* or the fuck*ee*, because I know he had lots of those rich people helping him, but especially Mrs. Daugherty."

"She was on the tape. We saw her on the tape."

"Yes."

"Kind of white hair."

"Uh-huh."

"Right, right."

"Her son died in a plane crash, then her husband died of a heart attack, and then my father got sick. She's got a lot of money that goes way back, and somehow it all ties together. That's the impression I got, anyhow."

"Why was your father trying to find Fry? Do you know?"

"Huh-uh. He'd already raped me. I was already pregnant, and he was already real sick. So I don't know where Fry fits into it. But my father's attitude sure changed after the nun was murdered, Sister Mary, because Jack really messed that up."

"Yeah. That and the fact that your father probably found out what he wanted to know, or what he was afraid he'd find out—that Fry was dead, that he'd been murdered."

"You."

"Yup."

"You know how you said, you told Father Kendrick about how this Fry man killed himself when he did this demon?"

"You really weren't asleep the whole time, were you?"

Nora smiled and then she said, "That's not what my father wants to do."

"I know that. He wants to come back completely aware, completely capable."

"Just pick up where he left off, doing his magic."

"Or whatever it is he's doing. Why is he here? Is he just building this business empire?"

"He has lots of people working for him. You know how he gets people? Where they come from? He's got these shelters all over the place, for street people, for families that are out of work. People like that? He helps them out, and you've always got these people that are always pissed off about things, mad at the world. He trains them, he has his people train them."

"In magic?"

"In something. There's dope, too, definitely. Coke. Crack. Lots of pills. They'll do anything for him. Shit, David, they didn't have anything. He gave them something. Why wouldn't they?"

"It's good politics, yeah."

"It's human nature, is what it is."

David said to her, "Aren't you getting a little cold?"

"I didn't think about it until now."

"Mmm, sorry."

"Maybe a little."

"Nora—I want you to understand this. I feel like I have this responsibility to help you. Can you see that?"

"Kind of. I guess so."

"If I can," David said, "to try to protect you and your baby."

"I suppose."

"And to stop your father."

"You want to get even with him because of Sister Mary."

"Absolutely. I'd be lying if I told you no."

"It does that to people, doesn't it? Getting these—powers, this feeling, whatever it is."

"It's self-awareness. And one of the things that I became aware of is that I have a mean streak in me. Very profound insight. So I'm going to fuck your father over."

"But you don't know how strong he is."

"Look at me," David said to her. "Look into these eyes.

Hear this voice. I'm going to nail him. I'm going to nail *him* to a wall, literally or otherwise."

Nora said in a low voice, "All I know is that I'm pregnant, my father raped me, with all these demons and shit, and I've gone about as far as I can go with it."

"Damn it, don't give up on me now."

"You really want to help me, don't you?"

"Come on, Nora."

"I want you to do something, then, if you want to."

"What?"

"When we go back to the house, get a pair of scissors or a knife or something and cut off some of my hair."

"I've got my pocket knife."

"Use it to help me, if you think it would."

"It would." He took out his knife. "I'll do it now, huh?"

She shrugged. "Okay."

"Tell me if I hurt you." He held out a length of her hair, gripped it so that it wouldn't tug and hurt her as he cut. When he was done, David had about three inches of glossy black hair. He put his knife away, wrapped the hair in a Kleenex, and shoved it into his left-hand pocket, so that it wouldn't get knocked around when he took his car keys in and out of the other pocket.

"Thank-you," Nora said to him.

"No problem."

He looked at her. She seemed distant, then. Amazing how she'd glow sometimes, escape all of this for a few minutes, and then just as quickly drift away again, or be pulled away.

"You know what I think?" Nora said, tilting her face to look at him. "You're going to hate this because this is real fatalistic and you think that's bad or something."

"Self-defeating. Not bad. Self-defeating."

"But I'm going to be honest with you, because of whoever this is in here." She put her hands on her stomach. "You want weird, I've got weird, right in here, boy. You want to know what I think? Here's what I think. I think everything's falling apart. I mean, historically, however you want to say it. I think that once upon a time everything was

THE EYES OF NIGHT

okay, or least anything that was good had a chance. Good people, good ideas, whatever that was. But not anymore. Too many people like my father have done too many things. We had our chance but we blew it, too much shit came down. And now everything's falling apart. It's taken a very long time. It's taken thousands of years. Because things like this can't happen in just a day or a year or a century. It takes a very long time for everything to fall apart. But finally it reaches a point where it's falling apart faster and faster, so even if you wanted to stop it, even if you wanted to try to do something about it, it's too late, it's moving too fast for you. And that's where we are now. It's taken thousands and thousands of years for people to really fuck things up, but they've worked very hard at it, and now they've done it. And even if people like you and Father Kendrick wanted to change it now, you couldn't, you can't. Too much's happened too fast. It's over. Story's over.''

David looked at her, although Nora wouldn't meet his eyes.

"Wrong," he told her.

She sniffed this patronizing little laugh, this grin, as if she were way beyond him. The rest of the class had gotten it, but the punchline had gone over his head.

"I don't think it's really evil," Nora said. She was looking into the dark forest. "I think we just call it that. I think there's some great purpose to the whole universe, some meaning, and in the long run we don't matter. I think we have this spark of a human soul all alone in the darkness and it keeps resisting, it keeps fighting, and sometimes it seems to win, but really, in the long run, it can't. It can't win. Because it's too cold. It's too dark for that little spark to last very long. Thousands of years, you know, but eventually—''

David felt a breeze brush his cheek, the wind rising.

"Everybody's outside in the cold," Nora said.

He saw heat lightning flash in the sky, mystically light up the clouds far away.

"Everybody's outside in the cold. They want to come inside and get warm, but it's so cold that it doesn't matter anymore. They'll just watch the fire for a while. They'll just watch and not move, because it's so cold.''

The wind grew stronger. Above Nora and David tree branches groaned and clacked, knocking into one another, bent by the wind.

"Because I'm cold," Nora said.

David stood up.

"What now?"

"I think we're in trouble."

"Oh, no—"

He left her where she was, sitting on the log, told Nora to stay there, just sit there, as he broke into a run, heading for the house.

20

Sounds of thunder.

In the living room, Frank had both the front door open and the storm door, even though it was cold, so that he wouldn't have to fight with them when he carried this big boxful of Cheryl's dishes out to the truck.

Thunder boomed and he automatically looked up because thunder was strange.

The doors closed. Instantly, quickly, just like that, the front door first, slamming shut with a flat dull sound, then the storm door on top of it, hollow and scraping. Leaving Frank standing there like an idiot, holding on to this box of dishes.

In the kitchen, Cheryl heard the doors close and she heard the wind. She looked out the window above the sink and dimly, by the light from the back porch, saw David running from the woods, legs pumping, coat flying behind him.

"Oh, dear God . . . Frank!"

"What?"

"Fraaaank! Come here, come here, go into the cellar!"

"For what? What's the matter with—"

"Please, please, just do it, please!" She threw down the towels she was folding and ran across the kitchen as more thunder broke above the house.

She heard David's feet pounding on the back porch, then the rattling of the doorknob, then his fists hammering on the wood. She looked back, saw him through the curtains of the door window, and ran toward him. The lights began to flicker on and off.

"David?"

"Cheryl! Open the door!"

She grabbed the knob in both hands, turned it back and forth, yanked on it. "David, it won't open!"

"Oh, shit!"

"It won't—"

"Cheryl, get downstairs!"

"David—"

"Get downstairs!" he yelled at her from the other side of the window. "Get down there now! Now! Take Frank with you!"

"Can you get *in*?"

"Move! Now!"

The wind was up, pounding against the side of the house, rolling into it, rattling the windows, and more thunder, thunder very close, tearing through the air with the sound of ripping cloth. The whole house felt strange inside, like a vacuum, as if all of the air in it were being sucked out.

Cheryl ran across the kitchen floor again. The door leading to the basement was closed. She grabbed the knob and pulled on it. It resisted, but not as strongly as the back door had, and she got it open.

"Frank!"

"Jesus, Cheryl, it's only a goddamn storm, all right? What's the panic?"

"Get down here, now! Come with me, now, please!"

"Will you calm down?" he yelled to her.

"Jesus, *Jesus*!" she moaned. She hit the light switch just inside the door, but the electricity had gone out. Cheryl ran down the stairs in the dark, gasping, her shoes clattering, and jumped the last three steps so that when she hit the floor the jolt sent her glasses flying. She heard them clatter on the concrete floor, but she couldn't see them.

"Shit, damn it, shit!"

But she was down here, anyway, and maybe she'd be safe. The basement. His workroom. David's place, David's workroom.

You know the funny thing I do every once in a while?

He'd tried to convince her, he'd asked her to perform a ceremony with him sometime, a modest ceremony.

Don't you understand? I want a normal life, a normal relationship with a normal man.

There was a laundry room down here, and a storage room, but the main room of the basement was a good ten feet across and fourteen, sixteen feet long, and it was here that David had his magic circle. He'd painted it on the floor with white paint and in the middle of it he'd built a brick table, his altar, and he'd covered it with a tablecloth, a black cloth.

It took Cheryl back to the night in the middle of the field, Fry and the demon, whatever he had done to her to give her headaches and bad eyes and blackout spells, but despite that, despite that, she wanted to live now, she had to prove something to herself and to David and she needed to *live*—

She ran into the middle of the painted circle, she could see it well enough without her glasses, and from the stuff on top of the brick altar she took what she thought would work, she wasn't sure—

If anything ever happens, you do this, you understand, Cheryl? and it'll help.

—but she thought she remembered some of what he'd told her during the past few weeks, so she took a candle and she lit it with shaking fingers, lost one match when it blew out, lit another one—

"Jesus, please, Jesus, Jesus . . ."

—and got a flame going, got the candle lit. She held it out in front of her and yelled, "Ator!" Was that what David had told her to yell? Christ, she couldn't remember! Did it matter? She turned in another direction—right or left? she wasn't sure, just do it, just do it—and yelled, "Enor!" but she wasn't sure and she was terrified, she was—

Cheryl threw down the candle and screamed at the top of her lungs, "What the hell am I supposed to do?" and began crying, and shrieked for Frank to get down here—

She heard him.

Heard his body.

She stared at the ceiling, wishing she had X-ray vision, so that she could see him, because all she could do was hear him, hear Frank being thrown against the floor, against the walls—

"Frank!"

Against the walls, being slapped against them—

"Fraaaank!"

His footsteps.

Come on, come on, he's a big guy, he's a big fucker, he fucking played football, just get him down here—

The sounds of breaking glass.

—just let him get to the cellar door—

Footsteps, loud hollow crashing sounds, his knees on the floor, but the sounds came from the kitchen, not from the living room, so he was going to be okay, he was going to—

—just get him down here, just get him down—

The door at the top of the stairs rattled as Frank kicked it, pushed and pulled on the doorknob—

"*Open the fucking door, Frank, just kick it in, God, please!*"

She heard it open, but it sounded as if the whole door had cracked in half, the whole door.

And then Frank—screaming—as he tripped down the stairs, fell down the stairs, tumbled, and Cheryl saw him—

"*Fraaaank!*"

He was rolling over, his body curled up, his feet and his arched back and his head, rolling over. Then he straightened out, she could see his face now, all white, he was a big man, for God's sake, but he was crying and there was blood on his face, he was stretched out on his belly at the bottom of the stairs and it was as if something were holding on to his feet, something Cheryl couldn't see, hidden at the top of the stairs, but she could see Frank's face, she could see the top half of his body, even though he was blurred because she didn't have her glasses on but she could see his eyes, his eyes, the blood on his face, and his arm as he reached for her, his hand waving as it reached for her—

"Frank! Frank! Frank!"

"Help—meee—"

She screamed and screamed and screamed, stopped breathing almost completely, stopped living and simply became that scream, a pitched note, one long voice, as Frank, blurred, indistinct, wavering and shifting back and forth as if he were underwater, as Frank, staring at her, reaching for her, begging her, begging her—

"Help—meee—*pleeeeease*—"

—as Frank's flesh boiled up like oil in a pan, quickly, like lard or grease in a pan, just boiled up and exploded and dripped off his face and dripped off his arm, but then came back again, stretched back like glue in reverse, plastic and rubbery, and Frank, blurred and white and bleeding, staring at Cheryl, his arm pushed out, fingers wagging helplessly—

Frank exploded.

Head, brains, heart, lungs, intestines, all in slow motion, splashed against the cement blocks of the basement walls and against the ceiling tile—

"Fraaank!"

—but didn't really, because Cheryl blinked, she wiped tears from her eyes, and sweat, and there was Frank again, his body or his soul or whatever was being dragged through it again, some new torture, because he was still there, belly down on the bottom of the stairs, eyes wide, arm out, fingers wagging—

"Help—meee—*pleeeeease*—"

—and some things, they looked like the ghosts of lizards, they looked like demons, some of them, and like hideous little children, some of the rest of them, and some of them looked like snakes, huge long wet snakes, wrapped around Frank, squeezed him tight, and tighter, so tight that, as he screamed, his eyeballs shot out and blood flew out in a long trail from his mouth—

"Fraaank!"

He was dying. He was dead. He was in hell. Whatever it was that was inside the house, that had shut out the world and smashed the doors closed and the windows—

It had Frank.

But he came back, all of him again, stretched out on the bottom of the stairs, and as he stared at Cheryl, fingers wagging, he groaned and vomited worms and his own insides, his own guts; they spilled down the front of him, down his chin and neck—

And again. Over and over again. Tortures, horrors, blood and vomit and flames, everything horrible that can happen to the flesh and to the body, over and over again, hell on earth, images of hell on earth, pranks, jokes being played on her with the soul of Frank Gauss being used as the—

Until she fainted.

Until Cheryl, inside the circle, seeing Frank trapped in a ball of gray fire, seeing the skin burning from him, peeling from him like the layers of an onion—

Sobbing—

"Fraaank!"

—before she collapsed.

Still with thunder booming outside, where David was, the storm still there, and hell inside here, and the wind rolling in hard airless waves against the walls of the house.

21

Sounds of thunder.

David ran onto the back porch, rattled the doorknob, pounded on the door with his fists.

He heard Cheryl inside, running toward him. "David?" The lights began to flicker on and off.

"Cheryl! Open the door!"

He heard her struggling with the doorknob. "David, it won't open!"

"Oh, shit!"

"It won't—!"

"Cheryl, get downstairs!"

"David—"

"Get downstairs! Get down there now! Now! Take Frank with you!"

"Can you get *in*?"

"Move! Now!"

The wind was up, pounding against the side of the house, rolling into it, rattling the windows, and more thunder, thunder very close, tearing through the air with the sound of ripping cloth. David jumped off the back porch and looked toward the woods.

He saw Nora standing at the edge of the trees, staring at him. He waved at her and bellowed, "Stay there!"

"Over here!"

"What?"

"*Over! Here!*" She was pointing frantically off to her right.

"All right! Now get the hell back!" And then he swore— "*Je*-sus!"—when a bolt of lightning, not really lightning but a wave of green fire, etheric heat, flashed through the air like sunlight bouncing off a mirror. Nora vanished for a moment and David knew that she was dead, she'd been hit.

He started running toward her, but as the air cleared, as the hissing sound died away and as his eyesight came back, the burning brightness like the glare of a flashbulb melting away, David saw that she was still there, although why she wasn't in shock or hadn't aborted her baby right then out of sheer panic, he didn't know.

He waved at her again—

"Get back!"

—but Nora was already in a hurry, running into the woods to hide.

And around the corner of the house, from the direction Nora had shown him, came a pair of black boots, camo pants, a heavy winter parka—

"Oh, fuck!"

The black woman from Cincinnati, from Jack's house.

She didn't say anything to David. She smiled and waved to him, then crossed her arms in front of her parka before raising them in his direction.

David backed up, backed away, but that was stupid because there wasn't enough time to think about anything, create a master plan or anything. So he dropped to his knees and crossed his arms at the wrists and screamed—

"Aeior!"

—and threw his own hands out and pulled it up, strength, energy, his light, his concentrated power, pulled it up from inside himself.

It was pure willpower, and they held on to one another, David and this black woman with one side of her head shaved, for a long minute, the air hot between them, charged and brilliant, a seething sound between them, crackling, before the black woman, grunting, broke it off and jumped away.

David pushed it.

Pushed it to get her before Nora got hurt, before she put herself inside some kind of defensive circle. Make her use

THE EYES OF NIGHT

her imagination, her own strength of mind, nothing else, psyche her out, and do it now.

David yelled, "Fuck you!"

The black woman laughed out loud, a great whooping laugh, and reared back and sent a wall against him, a wave, all heat and strange light and power, mental light and power.

As it came at him, blurry like the superheated air above a campfire, David screamed something startling and ridiculous, a loud animal sound from some old kung fu movie, and slid to one side, so that he felt her lightning as it swept past him, missing him, grumbling in the air like the groan of a bullwhip in slow motion.

And instead of meeting her head on again, David hunched down and pressed his hands onto the wet earth.

Show it to me before it happens, he thought, calling it up from deep inside, seeing it in his brain like a movie.

She was defenseless. She might have blocked an air current, because she would have expected that, another wall slicing through the air, but this took her by surprise. The wet brown grass between her and David lit up as if he'd lit a trail of gunpowder. Before the black woman could step out of the way, touch the earth with her own hands, scream an oath, do anything—

It hit her like a heart attack, the hot line of energy shooting across the ground, and it took her away in a blue curtain of cold light, that strange fire that always combusts when the spiritual world touches the physical. She jumped up and down, or was pulled and shaken up and down, her cheeks wobbled, her breasts bounced around underneath her parka, and then she fell over, hot streaks branding her neck and face, white burn marks in her hair. Mist floated over her body, some of the plastic of her parka had melted and stuck to her skin, and there was the sick smell of burnt flesh.

David said, "God damn it...."

You spend all your time sitting around meditating, storing up all this shit, and what do you do with it? Why, you kill people, you psyche them out, you set them on fire like you're hot-wiring a car, don't you, Mr. Wizard? Profound, sorcerous, elemental bullshit....

There was a last bit of thunder in the air, now that the two of them had finished with their dumb damned game, and loud noises, too, suddenly, from the house.

The front door and the storm door swung open again, the pressure that had closed them suddenly released.

The back door opened, abruptly swinging into the kitchen, as if David's pounding on it or Cheryl's pulling on it had finally had some artificially delayed effect. Lagging behind in time, the back door opened with such force that the window in it broke, the glass exploding in a tinkling shower all over the back porch and into the kitchen.

"David!"

The lights were back on, the electricity. The wind began to die down. David looked up at the sky. Heavy clouds, gray clouds. Snow started to fall.

"David!" It was Nora, coming out of the woods.

He walked toward her, steering clear of the dead woman. "Stay back. Are you all right?"

She nodded.

"Any idea who this is?"

"Oh, God, who knows? There were so many, David. I didn't know any of their names."

"Well, I met her at Jack's house last night. This was one of them."

Nora asked him, "What about Cheryl? And Frank?"

He took her hand and walked her toward the back porch and said, "She attacked the house. So I don't know."

"Dear God, they're not dead, are they?"

They went into the kitchen. Furniture had been overturned, pots and pans that had hung on the walls were scattered everywhere, the refrigerator door was open and food, milk, orange juice splashed all over the place.

David closed the door behind him and called Cheryl's name.

No answer.

He crossed the floor and peeked into the living room and it was the same story. The room looked as if it had been caught in a tornado—shelves torn off the walls, furniture overturned, walls cracked.

Nora called to him from the kitchen. "David?"

He found her standing at the top of the stairs leading into the basement, all the color drained from her face. She stepped back, gave him room.

David saw him immediately, Frank sprawled on his belly at the bottom of the stairs, his head twisted around, neck broken. Pretty obvious that he'd run down here in the dark and tripped on the stairs and fallen and broken his neck.

Pretty obvious to anyone other than David.

Nora was all eyes, staring at David in fear, the fingers of one hand fluttering near her mouth. She whispered, "Cheryl?"

The basement light was off; David turned it on and went down the stairs, jumped over Frank's body, and landed on the concrete with a heavy sound.

He saw Cheryl lying on her side, curled up within the protective white circle.

Nora called to him, "Tell me! Tell me she's okay!"

"She looks all right to me." But there wasn't much emotion in his voice. Exhaustion. He was exhausted. "You can come down."

Nora took the steps carefully and when she reached Frank's corpse, she leaned on David and he helped her to the floor. Then they walked over to Cheryl and Nora watched, nervous, tears in her eyes, as David kneeled down and felt Cheryl's neck, felt one of her wrists, reached under her neck and lifted up her head.

"Cheryl?"

She moaned.

"Cheryl, come on. Wake up."

Nora whined, "Oh, God, oh, God . . ."

"Come on, Cheryl, let's go."

Her eyes opened suddenly, white and frightened, and she hissed a gasp and threw out a wild arm. David caught it and tried to steady her—

"Frank! Frank!"

—and held her tightly, pulled her to him.

"Frank!"

"It's David, Cheryl!"

"Oh, God, where is he? He was—"

But she could see it in his eyes.

Cheryl's face twisted and the tears came and she began to gasp and sob, heavy airless shuddering breaths. "Oh, God, you should have seen him, you should have seen what they did to him!"

"I know, I know."

"You should have seen what they did to him!"

"I know, Cheryl!"

"It was—!" And she began screaming, screaming to keep her sanity, to remind herself that she was still alive, screaming, sobbing, kicking, and David held on to her as best he could so that she wouldn't hurt herself.

"Why did you do this to me?" Cheryl shrieked. *"Why did you do this to me?"*

He just held her and didn't say anything. Fighting her was like fighting part of himself, and he hated it, he hated it, so he simply held on as best he could.

"It's what you are."

"They're all contaminated."

"It isn't what you do. It's what you are."

While Nora watched them and listened to Cheryl scream, listened to her scream the same words she'd asked herself over and over, again and again since the rape, since her own father had raped her.

"Why did you do this to me? Why, dear God, why, why, why?"

22

They'd moved, the four of them, into a motel room on the far west side, at Jack's insistence. He'd convinced them that they'd all profit if they would let him take charge of the situation. Dragomir, he told them, had been playing games with him for some time now; not even Dragomir so much as Glen.

"I don't know where he thinks it's going to get him, what it's going to prove," Jack lamented. "But he gets to whisper in the Big D's ear, and I don't, so I always come out smelling like a big pile of shit on a hot summer day."

Neil was already feeling anxious about things, the atmosphere that was hanging over everything, whatever secrets Dragomir and Glen might be concocting. So he coolly and professionally decided to side with Jack. Susan was swayed after a half hour's discussion. And Morrie came along when he flipped a quarter that came up heads. Neil, though, always healthily suspicious of Jack, wanted to know where the hair had come from.

"From the big guy's very own flesh and blood. Isn't that grand? From Nora, guys. She's had a bee up that gorgeous butt of hers for some time now, I daresay. The sweet child shot this past me weeks ago. *Weeks* ago."

"Then you could've done something weeks ago," Neil said. "Why didn't you?"

"Friends," Jack smiled, "the secret of success in this life is—what? Anyone? *Timing!* The secret of success is *timing!* Am I right? And aren't all of you glad that your parents had their timing down? We all are, we're all real glad about that."

"I'll be real glad," Neil said, "when Dragomir's history. And until then, I'm going to be real nervous."

"Then you need some of Dr. Jack's magic tonic."

"Which is?"

"Which is—a mere seven digits away. Listen up."

He got on the phone and, persistent, charming as only he could be, he stayed on the phone, dialed and kept at it, until finally, at quarter to midnight, he got through to Iva Daugherty.

The cretin on the other end of the line at first gave him the trademarked song and dance; but Jack, annoyed, said to him:

"You tell her who I am. You do that. Now. Jack Starkis. Can you say that? No . . . No, *you* listen! *You* listen! This is—Stefan. *Stef*an. Understandez-vous, my genius friend? Well, you tell her. That's right. No, she *knows* who I am. That's right. That's right. Yes, she does. Gee, I'll bet you have a diploma and everything. Is your mom like real super proud of you?"

"This is Iva Daugherty."

"This is Jack Starkis."

"You have thirty seconds, Mr. Starkis."

"You want him dead, he's dead."

"So *you* say."

"I can do it."

"I doubt that."

"I can do it."

"And what will it cost me?"

"Frankly, my overhead's not that high. I'm more interested in safe passage out of here than I am in making a mint."

"Go on."

"It'll help us both. Put it that way."

"Your reputation precedes you, Mr. Starkis."

"Not so formal, please. We've met."

"I already *have* an asshole, Mr. Starkis. Why would I want another one in my life?"

"Mrs. Daugherty! Such language!"

"Mr. Starkis—such affected naïveté."

"It could be on the news tomorrow night, Mrs. D. He bites the big one in his sleep. You and your friends get to tidy up and lay it all in his stone-cold lap. Nuns, parties, nosy reporters—one flush and all your troubles are down the drain."

"And you're going to manage all of this?"

"I command an entire rebel outpost, Mrs. Daugherty. But it's lonely out here. My friends'd all like to graduate summa cum laude and they'd like some start-up capital after that, if you get my drift."

"Where can I reach you, Mr. Starkis, if I decide to, oh, support higher education?"

"I'm going to give you the number of a pizza parlor."

"You're not staying at a pizza parlor?"

"It's near here."

"I see."

"Well, Mrs. Daugherty? The clock is running."

"Indeed it is, Mr. Starkis."

"And the winner is—"

"The winner is . . . Well. *I'd* better win, Mr. Starkis—if you get *my* drift.

"Loud and clear."

"To whom should I plan on making out that check?"

"I'll get back to you on that."

"Do so. I'll be watching the news tomorrow night."

"Then I'll have to make some news for you to watch, won't I?"

He buried her in the woods, this anonymous woman who'd sold her soul to Stefan Dragomir, who'd mastered the profound arts and then turned around and been destroyed by those same proud arts, magnificent abilities that she'd used to cheat herself.

Concentrating, he warmed the earth to soften the cold ground, and worked as quickly as he could. David did not, however, give her much of a funeral oratory. He couldn't quite bring himself to be that noble, or hypocritical. She had, after all, intended to murder him, and murder is not particularly profound or magnificent.

He found her car. She'd parked it off the road and hiked through the woods, walked all the way to his house to try taking him and Nora by surprise.

Try?

She'd succeeded.

And she'd murdered, too, though not the way it had been planned. Give her some credit, David thought.

And over it all, the car that he drove deeper into the woods and left there, the buried body, the charred ground that marked the spot where David had murdered *her*—

Over it all fell the snow, soft and silent, clean and cool, coming down as neatly and perfectly as if he'd ordered it.

The dirty work was done by eight-thirty. Nora had insisted on helping him and so she'd fixed up everything indoors, straightened up the living room and the kitchen, all of it. Cheryl, completely overcome by what had happened, they'd put into bed, and David made sure, with one of his magic massages, that she stayed in bed, asleep, wholly out of it.

That left Frank's body, and they called the paramedics to take care of that, and notified the police, too. Hell of a stupid accident. The poor luckless s.o.b. David and Nora fixed up the basement so that it looked like anybody else's basement, piled with boxes and other garbage. Then they carried Frank's body upstairs and laid him on David's couch.

To the paramedics and the police David explained how Frank, a friend of his girlfriend's, had been helping them move her stuff into his truck. There'd been a storm, the lights had gone out, and Frank had fallen down the basement stairs.

He showed them the basement, and Nora introduced herself as Cheryl, David's girlfriend.

You know, one of the police officers told him, a million people die each year in stupid accidents like this, and it's a damned shame.

It sure is, David agreed. It sure is a damned shame.

Afterward, he fixed himself a Scotch and asked Nora if she wanted something to drink, too.

"I'll have some coffee, actually."

"I'll make it."

"I'd like to go upstairs and sit with Cheryl. Is that all right?"

"Sure."

"I'd just like to sit with her."

"I'll bring the coffee up, then."

"Fine."

And while he was waiting for the coffee to brew, he went out onto the back porch and sipped his Scotch, and looked at the pine tree he'd cut down three days before, for Christmas.

Christmas, less than two weeks away. Brother.

And, he thought, then, with Nora here, with Cheryl way off in slumberland, with—how many now?—with three people dead, not counting Sister Mary, and with Dragomir and his goons out there acting like this was some kind of gangster movie from the thirties—

He thought, David realized that Jack was right.

"Don't you understand what you are? *... Nobody knows we exist! And we're the people who run the show! Don't you know how things get done in this world? ... Life is pain, David. ... Life is fear. And terror. ... We're brothers now, you and me. ... Get rid of this middle-class morality act. You're one of us."*

Wasn't he?

Wasn't Jack right?

He looked at the Christmas tree again and thought of Father Kendrick. *"True sight, true seeing. Everything is in focus, everything fits together and makes sense."*

If it all fits together and makes sense, then why did he feel like shit right now, feel like a murderer, feel so responsible?

We're all just sparks, he told himself. We're all just pieces of God, pieces of the All, playacting, pretending, pretending unto eternity.

True. True.

And yet—

That didn't, right now, for him, seem to explain everything, seem to explain Sister Mary, and how he felt about Cheryl, and Nora, and how Cheryl felt about him.

How terrified she was of him.

"David, your hands are warm."

Maybe Jack was right, after all. Maybe it was just middle-class morality and bullshit.

The coffee was done, he went into the kitchen and made Nora a cup and took it up to her, made small talk for a minute and smiled and pretended that holding down the fort was going to work out just fine, everything was fine.

Then he went downstairs to the basement, got rid of the boxes and junk they'd used to fool the police, and took from the big old dresser he kept down there about a dozen talismans on chains, necklaces.

He wore one himself, of course, and he gave one to Nora, and put one around Cheryl's throat. The rest of them he hung up around the house, nailing them to doors, over windows.

Would they help?

Maybe he should use garlic, instead. Or crucifixes. Or silver bullets. Silver bullets might do it.

Would they help?

Well, sure. Couldn't hurt. But so what if they'd help and so what if they couldn't hurt?

After all, Jack was right.

"What did you see?"

"What do you think I saw? . . . I saw life. I saw reality."

"Go to hell, Jack."

"I've been to hell."

Jack was right.

This was the big roller coaster ride, the cruise, the trip to Aruba. For Nora, no doubt for Jack, and for David, too.

For him, too.

Father Kendrick, God love him, just wouldn't have understood.

23

A little after one in the morning, Jack pulled to a stop within sight of a great black hulk of a building, a mining or processing plant of some kind, off one of the long gravel roads down in Newtown. He wasn't driving the Ferrari, since no doubt the police were still looking for that one, but an old Ford Pinto wagon, of all things. Nothing like hiding in plain sight.

"Everybody ready?" he asked.

"Let's just get it over with," Morrie grumbled. "It's cold and I'm tired. Let's just get it over with, okay?"

"Oh-kay. Let's just, shall we?"

The four of them crawled out and Jack opened the back of the wagon and took out what they'd need, a knife and a sword, incense and a bowl, all wrapped together in an old woolen blanket. Then the other three followed him in a file, past the dump trucks and earth movers that stood around like cold, unmoving dinosaurs, into the woods and weeds that surrounded the plant. They made their way through tall grass to a flat area guarded by tall trees.

"We absolutely have to do this here, I suppose," Susan complained to Jack.

"I saw this a couple of weeks ago, driving around. It called out to me. It looks like modern death. Rust, metal, grime. Poetic, I thought, for the big kahuna's demise."

Neil looked at him and said, "Let's get to it, huh?"

"Why, sure." Jack dropped the blanket onto the ground and unrolled it, sword and knife and bowl clattering noisily. He picked up the sword and freed it from its metal sheath.

"Anybody need to use the john before we get started?" he grinned.

Susan gave him a weary look.

"No? Onward, then."

He turned with the sword and faced Morrie, who was holding his hands cupped in front of his face, blowing on them to keep them warm. His breath came out in clouds in the cold night air. Jack moved forward with the sword, point up, and shoved it into Morrie's belly, low through the abdomen, then pulled it back out.

"Jesus!" Neil said.

Morrie's expression was one of total surprise.

Susan said, "Jack?"

Morrie smiled. He smiled at Jack. It was a joke; it hadn't happened; he'd wake up in a second, here, right?

Jack shook the sword and black drops of blood flew from it. Morrie was still staring at him, still smiling, but now a dark line of blood appeared between his lips and seeped down his chin from one corner of his mouth. Jack walked over to him and said in an irritated voice, "Damn it, Morrie," and gripped him by one shoulder and shoved him backward.

Morrie groaned. His mouth opened and he coughed and now a thick runnel of blood came out of his mouth and washed over his chin and down his neck.

"Jack!" Susan yelled at him.

Neil moved, or started to move, his feet noisy in the grass as Morrie fell, and Jack looked up at him quickly, alert as an animal.

"What are you doing?" Neil said to him.

"Saving our asses. Is that all right with you? What do you need, Magic Theory 101 here, or what? I'm killing the big guy and I'm going to save our asses while I do it."

"You didn't tell us this, Jack!"

"I shouldn't have to tell you this, Neil!" He shot a cruel look at Susan. "You too? What? Come on!"

On the ground, Morrie groaned and kicked his feet a little, wiped his hands back and forth in the cold grass.

"While we still have something to work with here, huh?"

Jack said, and nodded at the dying Morrie. "Whaddya say, gang? You want to do it while dipshit here can still help us out?"

They didn't say anything, didn't move, just watched him.

"Assholes," Jack grunted, shoving the sword into the ground, keeping it close by, away from Neil and Susan.

Susan said in a low voice, "He trusted you—"

"*What?*"

"He *trusted* you, Jack!"

"Well, life's tough when you're stupid."

"He was *part* of this, he *trusted* you!"

"So now he gets to be a real big, very *important* part of this. He gets to carry his own weight. He gets to be the star of the show, and that's because I don't want to hog the whole thing myself. It's just the kind of guy I am. And where's the applause? No, please, no heavy-duty thanks. I'm just doing my job, okay? So *do not fuck it up*, okay? *Okay?*"

He took the knife that had been rolled up in the blanket, unsheathed it, and straddled Morrie.

"Hang in there, youngster. You're bound for glory, now."

He slit the front of Morrie's jacket and pulled it open, then tore open his shirt and undershirt so that the white, damp skin was bared to the night.

"Hocus pocus, razzmatazz," Jack said, and cut a design in Morrie's skin.

The blood drooled up between the puckered nipples. What Jack had cut looked like a tattoo that had pushed to the surface from inside Morrie's body and bled from the pressure of it. Thin lines of blood began to stream down both sides of him, staining the inside of Morrie's shirt.

Jack deftly threw the knife aside; it spun in the air and landed squarely, point first, in the ground.

"Well, call me Daniel Boone."

Then, from one of the pockets of his winter coat, he pulled out a lunch bag, a paper sack that he'd filled with table salt.

"Smile for the camera, now, partner."

He sprinkled fistfuls of salt above the dying Morrie, and as the salt landed on his cut chest and pierced belly, Morrie sobbed and whined. The pain, the pain.

"Jesus, Jack, you're a fucking *sadist*!" Neil yelled at him.

Jack shot him a look and growled, "Jesus, Jack, maybe you're the only one here who knows what the fuck he's doing! Huh? Huh? Maybe? Huh?"

"Morrie," Susan said. "We didn't know about this. That's the truth."

Morrie sobbed and rolled his head back and forth, and with slick red-stained hands tried to wipe the salt from his chest. But it hurt, it hurt, and he was dying, he was in terrible pain, he really couldn't move his legs anymore and he was becoming dizzy, he was trying to breathe and finding it very difficult to breathe.

Jack threw the last of the salt on him, crinkled up the paper bag, and tossed it into the grass.

"Morrie, Morrie, Morrie. Here I am, looking out for your immortal Christian soul, and what thanks do I get? Complaints. No gratitude, only complaints. Jesus. You kids today, I just don't know."

From his shirt pocket he retrieved the plastic baggie with Dragomir's body hair in it, and placed this on top of the mark he'd cut on Morrie's chest.

"Now, don't touch that," Jack warned him, "or you'll fuck up the program, all right? Can you hear me down there? Hey! Hello? Hello? Earth to Morrie. Come in, Morrie! Bzzupp, come in, please."

Morrie was shivering, he whined, groaned, mewled, tried to scream, tried to do something, anything—

Jack stepped back and picked up the sword and with it quickly drew a circle all the way around the bleeding Morrie, muttering in Latin as he did it. And when he was done he looked at Neil and Susan, who had stood there, watching everything so far, stunned and frightened, uncertain what precisely they should do, now that they were accessories to a murder committed by a madman.

"A little closer," Jack told them.

"For *what*?" Neil yelled.

"For your own fucking good, smarty pants!" Jack picked up the bowl and some incense from the blanket and handed them to Susan. "Or do you want to be on the outside looking in? Want to stand out there in the cold all night long? Or would you prefer to come in here where it's nice and warm, hmm?"

Susan carefully stepped closer, and since Jack didn't make any threatening moves with the sword, Neil came ahead, too. Jack moved around them both, outlining a circle to contain all three of them, then stuck the sword into the ground again.

"Don't touch it," he told Neil. "You're still only freshmen, both of you. You've got to bring your grade points up and get to be seniors first. You just haven't applied yourselves yet, that's the problem with you two."

Neil said, "You're sick."

"And you're a dear to say so. Now—class—what's going to happen when we light this bowl of incense and start speaking in tongues?"

"What are you calling, Jack?"

"That most demonest of demons, the evil and terrible Joe-Bob, Sheik of the South! Only we've got be very formal about it and call him Arzethiel. Ar-*zeth*-ee-el! Rolls off the tongue."

"And you're giving it Morrie, you're sacrificing Morrie."

"Crude way of putting it. So judgmental! But, yes, in the vernacular, I suppose *we* are sacrificing Morrie to cover our own asses."

Susan made a sound.

"Oh, God," Jack said, "I love it when you make that little *uh* sound. Right here. Oh, Jack—*uh*."

"You'd better be right," Neil told him.

"I'm so right, I'm an honorary Republican. Our demonic friend gets the prime rib dinner, here, the better to waddle around on the ground, and—Right? Class? Demonology 101? And the little hairs are for sniffing out Mr. D, right? True or false."

"What?" Neil said.

"True. Or. *False*?"

"What is this, Jack?"

"There'll be a quiz later. Fuck it. Forget it. Now turn around. We show Joe-Bob our backsides. Maybe we'll moon him. You *really* don't want to see this, do you? Burn your eyeballs out or your retinas? Shit. We should've brought sunglasses, I forgot. My fault."

He lit the bowl of incense and began his prayer, the invocation.

Susan, her back to him, glanced at Neil and reached for his hand. He got hold of hers and gripped it, held it strongly.

"... veni, o Arzethiel, in nomine Das, et Othiel, et in nomine Inaxas..."

Behind them, Morrie whimpered.

Instinctively, Susan moved to turn around, to look—

Neil tugged hard on her hand. Don't. Don't. Don't you dare. Let it see us, it can see us, but do not under any circumstances, do not look it in the eyes, do not turn around.

"... veni, o Arzethiel..."

Or you'll be blinded.

"... et Inaxas..."

Or worse.

Morrie *moaned*.

Thunder boomed in the sky, energy coming in, waves of it curling down in a whirlpool, and the cold winter air warmed, Susan and Neil both felt the warmth on their backs, warmth seeping through their coats.

And light.

She held up her free hand, her right hand, looked at the back of it. It was shining, reflecting the brilliant green light that was building behind them, rising up from the ground or forming out of the air—

"... o Arzethiel..."

Morrie, *crying*, sobbing, these great garish heaving sounds—

"... in nomine Das et in nomine Inaxas..."

More heat, and the green light more brilliant.

Neil squeezed her hand harder, harder—

The *fear* of that grip—
Morrie *screamed*.
Loudly.
Wherever he found the strength, wherever he found the voice to shriek—
"... o Arzethiel..."
Shriek, sob, whine, kick, moan, pule—
And the green wind, the green light, shining brilliantly almost all the way through Susan's hand like some kind of nuclear brilliance—
Screaming, Morrie screaming.
If animals could scream when human beings cooked them and ate them, if plants could scream when human beings chopped them down, cut them up—
Jack chanting—
Oh. Dear. God, she thought. Kill me now, I'm sorry, I am sorry, I have sinned, I am wrong, I never—never thought—never meant—never *did* this—
Screaming and sobbing and crying as he was eaten—
—never *dreamed* of this—
Eaten by the demon.
—never *dreamed*—
The chomping sounds behind them, the gnawing sounds, teeth on bone, scraping, ripping the meat free, as Morrie *screamed*—

24

Before it made any noise, Stefan Dragomir heard it. Before it left its burning trail of smoke in the air, Dragomir smelled it. Before it tried to grip him and take him, try to drag his soul away, he felt it.

Outside, first of all. Outside, as it grew out of the air, as it pulled molecules into itself and sucked light into itself, as the wind swirled around it and as thunder grumbled overhead—Dragomir could sense it, feel it outside his house.

Then, at the door, pounding at the door, washing against it in rolling charges, until the locked doors gave way.

The lights in the house flickered on and off; radios and televisions, blenders and garbage disposals exploded with noises, with chanting and singing and whirring and clanking.

From his bed, then, he heard alarms ringing and voices, and dozens of footsteps running up and down stairs, up and down hallways.

And he heard the first of the screams.

The echo, the heavy *pounding* of the thing's feet as it came up the stairs, and the smell of it, like burning cork, burning cloth as it moved up the stairs, heavy as a giant—

Screams, men screaming—and someone's scream cut short as he was hurled downstairs, over the banister, the scream cut short by the abrupt snapping of his neck or his spine.

The wind, then, as the lights flickered and as the sick burning odor, burning cloth, carpeting, burning human flesh moved up the hallway and up the stairs toward him—

More screams—

And the heat coming at him—

Dragomir sat up in his bed, finding the strength in reserves he'd built within himself from the beginning of his sickness—sat up and called his cat to him, the great yellow cat—

—hissing, knowing what would happen to it—

—and held on to his cat, gripped it as strongly as he could, and watched the door of his bedroom, watched—

Burning coals—

The door blew in violently, first with lines of fire streaking down the length of it, then the wood splintering and the charred pieces of wood flying across the room—

"*Mr. Dragomir!*"—from the hallway.

"Stay there! Glen. I can. See to this. Myself."

"Are you sure, Mr. Dragomir? Let us—!"

"Glen! Stay! There!"

It was close, now, shuffling across the carpeted floor of his bedroom, almost invisible, only its footsteps visible, burning their marks into the carpeting, and some of the light of it, brilliant, cryptic, glowing and howling with its burning sound—

Dragomir smiled at it.

"Who," he whispered. "Sent. This?"

It had no mouth; it could not speak. It had no eyes; it could not see. It had only burning energy, and burning feet, and was only partially there, being carried on the strength of whoever had sent it, and that strength, while great, was not enough, not great enough—

"This is Jack. Starkis."

It howled, as only it could howl.

Arzethiel, demon, formed only partially from blood and hair and human flesh, burning it up, using up that fuel of blood and hair and human flesh as it attempted to slay, as it built a road on earth to seek and find and slay, to burn and rend—

Dragomir laughed at it and gripped his cat strongly.

"Show me!" he hissed. "Show me! This! Fool!"

It could not come closer, for Dragomir's bed was guarded

by a circle built into the floor, a great wooden circle, bare of carpeting.

Arzethiel, the burning light, the smoking puddle of fumes and energy and human blood, the eyeless, sparking thing that Jack had brought imperfectly onto the earth, reached out with a line of light in an attempt to touch Dragomir, kill him with awful hellish light—

Dragomir threw his cat at it.

The cat shrieked as it arced through the air, its hair lifted, claws out, eyes wide—

It struck the invisible wall that marked Dragomir's circle, reached that curtain in the air and died in a sudden flash, vaporized, stolen away in a breath of light, stretched and shimmering like a sheet of light pulled rubbery and thin—

And through it Dragomir saw into the sparking, smoking, surging energy of the trapped Arzethiel, saw and recognized, for only a moment—

He laughed arrogantly.

For he saw them there, out in Newtown, saw Jack and Susan and Neil with their backs to him, inside their circle.

Saw them—

"Begone!" Dragomir howled at Arzethiel. "I! Command this! I! In nomine! Inaxas et! Abraxas! Veni! Arzethiel! Ad locus! Vestrum!"

It hissed, it glowed, it tried to do more, but it was fading, sparking, making odd sounds, and was not strong enough, not fed enough to be on this earth for more than a few hate-filled, anguished minutes—

"*Begone!* And wait for! Their souls to! Meet you! In! Hell!"

And he laughed, as the thing vanished, Arzethiel, the sending.

Laughed.

And laughed.

As Morrie laughed.

Morrie, dying in the field of grass surrounded by tall black trees at night.

Morrie, blood pouring from his mouth, his body half eaten.

Morrie, howling louder than a stormy wind, howling to Jack and Neil and Susan as the green light died, as Arzethiel died away—

Laughing, and howling—

"You! Failed!"

They moved as quickly as they could, left Morrie to die there, and Jack drove insanely fast to the motel room so that they could get whatever it was they needed—clothes, suitcases, whatever—and then leave the city immediately.

"Stupid! Stupid! *Stupid!*" Neil kept saying, pounding the side of his fist on the dashboard of the Pinto. *"Stupid!"*

"Will you please shut the fuck up!"

"It's your fault, Jack! You did this! We're dead! We're fucking dead!"

"He will know that it was us, Jack!" Susan said from the backseat.

"He can kill us!" Neil hissed. "He's got our fucking *boogers*, Jack! He can kill us whenever he wants to!"

He pulled into the motel parking lot too fast and hit the brakes abruptly and kept the car running, held on to tightly the steering wheel.

"They'll send those fuckers after us, too," Neil whined. "Fucking idiots, they'll come after us—"

"So I'm supposed to do—what?" Jack asked him, in a voice that was tense and quiet, almost a whisper.

"Come with us," Susan said. "Give up."

He barked a laugh and lowered his head and shook it back and forth. "No, no, no, I don't think so, no, no."

"We don't have a choice here!"

"Out," he ordered them. "Get out. Now."

"Do it, Jack!"

"I'm driving away from here as fast as I can," he told them. "He's not going to kill us. I know how to protect myself, and he can't do anything about it. I am not—"

"Jack, come—"

"And I am not," he suddenly howled at the top of his voice, losing it, slamming his hands up and down on the steering wheel, bouncing them up and down and shrieking

insanely, *"I am not going to go to him and beg him for mercy! I am not! I am not! I am not!"*

Neil moved quickly, frightened of him, opening his door and jumping out and calling in to Susan, "Come on. Let's go."

"I am not!"

Susan moaned, "Oh, God, dear God," as she opened her door, put one leg out, looked up at Neil, and reached for his hand.

Jack threw the Pinto into reverse and gunned it. Susan screamed. Neil yelled at him. Half inside and half outside the car, Susan was caught by the rear door as it tried to slam shut, then was knocked outside when Jack threw the car into drive. She slipped under the wheels, face down, and was run over by the rear tires.

Neil ran after him. Jack saw him and stopped, reached over to close the front passenger door, then threw the Pinto into reverse and backed up again.

Taken by surprise, Neil tried to jump up but was knocked down, run over, and dragged for several feet across the parking lot until Jack, for the final time, shifted into drive again and escaped.

It was three o'clock in the morning. He drove up Erie Avenue, talking to himself, cursing and swearing, pounding the steering wheel, while the rear door that Susan had never closed flapped back and forth, click, click, click, as the dome light flickered off and on, off and on, off and on. . . .

When the police arrived, and the medics, Susan was dead; but Neil was still breathing and still conscious.

Call Dragomir, he begged the paramedics. Call Stefan Dragomir, call this number.

It was Glen who met him at the hospital, who spoke to Neil in those few minutes before he was prepped for surgery. Neil told him about Jack's plan, the plan he'd concocted with Mrs. Daugherty, and how Jack had tricked them all, tricked them, and Neil begged Glen in a taut whisper, so low that Glen had to lean close so that no one else, the nurses or orderlies, would overhear, "If I die . . . please . . .

Glen, please... let me die... don't hurt me... don't hurt—my soul... *please*...."

"I'll do what I can. I'll talk to Mr. D."

"Please..." Neil moaned, tears running down his face, gasping as he watched Glen walk away. "Please, please, don't hurt me, let me die, *please*...."

The papers that morning were cautious. There were allegations, there were opinions, but only a small handful of facts, and none of those facts connected Stefan Dragomir to anything particularly felonious.

There was speculation that he threw some wild parties. There was an investigation pending into personnel who operated two of his community outreach shelters; some of these individuals were allegedly involved in the trafficking of controlled substances. But attempts to get further information from prominent members of the community who were known to have close business ties with Dragomir had led nowhere.

And there was absolutely no mention of the illegal bribery of several politicians, the substantital donations to certain campaign war chests, the unethical marriage brokering of buyout capital with poorly managed business firms, or the brutal murder of Sister Mary Francisco a week and half earlier.

It was apparent that Stefan Dragomir was not involved in such things; or, if he was, it was apparent that proving such would be quite difficult.

Difficult and, no doubt, dangerous.

"Are you feeling better?" Glen asked him.

Dragomir, in bed, appeared pale and weak but did not seem incapacitated. He had circled a number of names in those front-page articles and he was copying them now on the top sheet of a legal tablet.

"Much. Better." He tore off the page. "Handle these. All except. Iva. Her we are. Visiting. Ourselves. The phone."

Glen brought it to the bed.

"We will see her. This morning. And then we take. A

trip. What day is. Today?" He looked at the papers for the date.

Glen told him, "Saturday."

"Did you find. The information. I asked for?"

"About the priest, Mr. Dragomir, or about David Trevisan?"

"I assume. You have found. Both. But. David Trevisan."

"Yes. He lives in Noland. Apparently a new address. It seems somewhat isolated. A five-hour drive at the most."

"No word from. Lona. Was that. Her?"

"Yes. No word, sir."

"I think. This young man. Is. Quite adept. Jack will. Go there."

"I assume so, Mr. Dragomir."

"Tell everyone. To get ready. Bring. The pictures."

"Yes, sir."

He picked up the phone and dialed Iva Daugherty's number.

25

Early Mass was over at seven-thirty; by quarter to eight, Father Kendrick was returning to his room at the rectory. Walking in, swinging his door wide open, he stopped cold and growled, actually, from low in his throat, growled in shock when he saw Jack Starkis standing there, posed by the broken window on the other side of the desk.

The window over which David had taped the cardboard desk blotter.

"Did I do this?"

"What the hell are you doing here?"

"Nice way to phrase it. Close the door."

"No."

"Please."

"What are you doing here?"

"*Pretty* please." Jack crossed the room, meeting Father's stern glare, and reached around him to push the door closed. "Now..."

"Answer my question, Jack. I'm not afraid of you."

"Too bad. You should be. Padre, what are *you* still doing here? Don't you realize that you're in trouble? The Big D is without a doubt going to send some of his ace storm troopers after you. Do a better job than I did." He regarded the window with regret. "I really fucked up, didn't I?"

"Actually, I thought it quite impressive."

"Yeah, I'll bet, to the inexperienced eye. Damn. No, maybe I'm not being fair to myself. I *am* good, aren't I?"

"I'm asking you once more, Jack. What are you doing here?"

"Buying some life insurance, Father."

"If that means you want me to help you, then I might as well tell you right now, I refuse."

"I'll kill you."

"I'm not afraid of you."

"I know some nasty ways to do nice people in."

Kendrick reached inside his pants pocket and pulled out the talisman David had given him.

When Jack saw it, he let out a cruel laugh. "That won't help you!"

"Not by itself, no."

"What, David give you like the beginner's course in low ceremonial magic or something?"

"Jack, I'm going to turn around, go out the door—"

"Father—"

"—and make one phone call."

"Don't do it."

"That one phone call will end all your troubles. Mine, too."

"Father, I've got troubles you never dreamed of."

Kendrick sneered at him and put the talisman back in his pocket.

"And you're going to help me, or—"

Father turned around and opened the door.

"Don't do it, Padre!"

He moved into the small front room, headed for the outer door.

"We're after the same thing, Father Kendrick! I can help David and I can help Nora, too!"

He waited a moment before slowly turning around. He stayed where he was, though, and said, "Make it good, now."

"Jesus Christ! I tried to *kill* him last night! And he knows it was me!"

"Stefan Dragomir?"

"Yes." Jack raised his right hand. "Father, I'm an asshole and a liar and a thief and a pimp, but this is the whole truth and nothing but, so help me."

"You keep saying that. Me helping you. You helping me."

"Look—Dragomir would like to just erase all of us, okay? And it's not exactly an impossible request, given the man's scores on certain aptitude tests. Are you following me?"

"Oh, yes."

"I want to get to David. I want to get to him and Nora."

"Why? So you can continue to hurt them?"

"Look, *I'm* the one who's hurting now! Okay? I've got about half an hour to live if I stay in this fucking town! That's about it, that is it!"

"There's still something missing here."

Jack told him, "David killed a magician named Theodore Fry."

"I know that."

"If I know how he did it, I could probably kill Dragomir."

"Ah. A noble ambition."

"Stop jerking my chain, Padre. You don't want to die any more than I do. I'm asking you to help me."

"By doing what?"

"Tell me where he went."

"He went home, Jack."

"Home? He went—You mean, Noland? He's back in Noland?"

"Yes."

"That's the first fucking place they'll look!"

"Is it really?"

"Why the hell did he go there?"

"Because it's his home, Jack. He feels safe there. He feels that he can protect Nora there. Does that make sense to you?"

"God, I don't know. I guess. Only he better not stay there."

"He'll stay there until I tell him not to."

"The hell does that mean?"

"It means that the three of us, Jack, aren't as stupid as you seem to be. We're doing everything we can to stay away from you and Stefan Dragomir, to keep Nora safe.

That *is* a noble ambition. Because you tried to kill us, let's not forget that part."

"Yeah, well, I was a lot younger then."

"How time flies."

Jack coughed and looked at his watch. "Then I'm driving to Noland."

"Good. It'll save me bus fare."

"Don't start with me, okay?"

"Fine. Leave. As soon as you're out of here, I phone him and tell him and Nora to go to Pittsburgh or Atlanta or Phoenix or someplace else."

"Don't."

"I'll do it."

"Father, don't bullshit a bullshitter."

Kendrick raised his right hand. "I swear. I'll do it, so help me."

Jack looked at him and grinned in amazement. "Jesus," he said. "I'm outgunned. I am out-fucking-gunned. By a priest!"

"Yes," Kendrick told him. "We have quite a reputation for that sort of thing."

"I'm not going. To kill. You," Stefan Dragomir told Iva Daugherty, as he stood before her in her ornate blue room, leaning on his cane. "Because you can. Help me when. I come. Back."

"Stefan, he lied to me. He tried to trick me. He threatened me!"

"Yes. I know this."

"He said he'd kill me, Stefan!"

"That would be. Enough. Yes. I can. Imagine."

"He did! I wouldn't lie to you, I wouldn't *do* this to you!"

"Iva." He took one step toward her; the cane thudded on the floor with the sound of a final heartbeat.

She was sitting on the edge of a divan and two of his people flanked her, one on each side. Glen was there, too, guarding the door. She was trapped, even though she was in her own home.

THE EYES OF NIGHT

Iva Daugherty stared up at him, at Dragomir the sorcerer, her face white, lips trembling, her whole body trembling.

Trapped.

"Iva. You would. You would. Do this. To me. After all we've. Done. For each other. Don't. Start this. Nonsense. Now. Please."

"All right. You're right. I'm sorry."

"That's. Better."

"I'm sorry." She couldn't look into his eyes anymore; she glanced away. Still, she felt his shadow lingering on her, felt his breath, smelled him there, leaning over her, and when she looked back, anxious, fearful, the eyes were still there, burning coals, and Iva Daugherty almost broke down, then, she was so frightened, her heart was beating so fast, she was *terrified* of this man who'd made everything happen for her, given her everything.

"Iva."

"Yes, Stefan."

"I will be. Back. Tomorrow, or. Next day."

"All right."

"When I come. Back. You will help. Me, then."

"Yes, certainly."

"Joel"—he nodded to one of the giants standing at one end of the divan—"will stay here. With you. Your. Bodyguard."

"Fine"—although the implication worried her.

"Other business is. Being attended. To. You. However. Are to help. Me."

Oh, God, that chilled her. Other business? She thought, don't kill me when this is over, don't, don't, please, oh, why had she even *spoken* to that incredible asshole, Jack Starkis, that *psychopathic maniac*?

"Iva."

"Yes, Stefan, yes?"

He stepped back and held out his right hand.

She looked at him, looked at the others there, the two beside the divan and Glen Dennison. Slowly, then, uncomfortably, she moved and kneeled on the floor, awkwardly straightening her dress over her knees, smoothing her belly, arranging her belt.

Dragomir watched.

Iva Daugherty moved forward, wiggling in her dress, crawling across the floor on her knees.

One of the flunkies, not Joel but the other one, sniffed, repressing his laughter.

Iva Daugherty's face reddened.

Glen looked away.

Just as she reached Dragomir's outstretched hand, he took another step backward, pulling away from her.

Iva whispered to him, "Oh, please . . ." and tears started at the edges of her eyes.

But she continued to crawl, reaching out now with both of her hands, reaching for him, and the tears fell over her cheeks, tears of humiliation and fear.

"Please . . ." Iva whispered to him again, when she reached his hand.

Dragomir let her take it.

He let her press it to her face, he let her kiss his hand, kiss each of the fingers of it, he let her suck on some of those fingers and wipe his hand all over her face, wetting it with her tears, smearing it with her powder and rouge and lipstick.

"Please," she said to him, mouthing the word as carefully as she could, tears beading her eyelashes. "*Please*, Stefan . . ."

Please, God, don't kill me, don't do to me whatever you're going to do to Jack Starkis or even to your daughter, don't, please, *please* . . .

Looking down at her, Stefan Dragomir read her mind, and smiled.

26

Exhausted, David slept in until ten-thirty. He'd curled up on the couch, figuring that it might be best to let Cheryl have the bed to herself, and he woke up now, jarred by sounds she was making and by the smell of coffee.

"Oh, shit, David," she said.

Yawning, rubbing his eyes, he swung his feet to the floor and readjusted his underwear. He'd used an afghan for a blanket and now he pulled it around him because the living room was cold.

"What're you doing?" he asked Cheryl.

"Putting the last of the stuff in the truck." She was dressed for it, in heavy corduroy pants and her down jacket and gloves. She pulled open the front door and picked up what looked like the only box left and lugged it outside.

Standing up, David pulled the afghan over his shoulders like a cape and started toward the front door to close it, but Cheryl shut it from the other side before he could get there.

Shaking his head, yawning again, he headed for the kitchen and coffee.

He'd just gotten the first few sips down when she came in, pulling off her gloves and unzipping her jacket.

"It's going to snow," Cheryl said.

"Mmm." He looked at her. "How are you?"

"What?" She draped her jacket over the back of a chair.

"How are you?"

"How am I? Is that what you said?"

Dear Christ, he thought. "That's what I said."

She went to the counter and poured herself some coffee

and brought it to the table and sat down. "What did you do to me last night?"

"You needed to sleep. I made sure that you got some rest."

"And what happened to Frank?"

"Frank's dead. Remember that?"

"Yes," she said snidely, "I remember that. What happened to him?"

"We called an ambulance, Cheryl. We called the police and we filled out a report. They'll tell his family or something. Then they'll bury him."

"Jesus!" she said, looking away, cupping her chin in the palm of one hand. Tears started.

"It was an accident, Cheryl."

"It was *not* an accident! It was—you, it was *you*!"

"My mistake. It was me. I take it Nora's still sleeping."

"I take it."

He pushed his chair back; it squeaked on the tile. He picked up his coffee cup and nearly threw it into the sink, furious with her. "She sat up all night with you," he told Cheryl. "She held your hand—"

"Fine."

"—all night long because she knows—"

"Fine, David, fine!"

"—because she fucking knows what the hell this is about, and you don't!"

"I don't? I *don't?*"she screamed.

"Where is she?"

"Is that what you said?"

"Fuck you," David told her, and went out of the kitchen and up the stairs to the spare room.

"Don't you *ever* say that to me!" Cheryl screamed at him as he walked away. "Don't you dare say that to me, ever again, *ever again*, do you understand me?"

He came down the landing and said, "Fuck you," one more time, traded in his afghan for the bathrobe hanging in his bedroom closet, then went to the spare room and opened the door and looked in.

"Oh, shit."

Nora was lying flat on her back, sweating and shaking. David flicked on the light and hurried to her, picked up one hand and held it. There was a pulse. He felt her neck; there was a pulse. But she was drenched with sweat and she was staring up at him.

"Nora? Nora!"

"Can't," she whispered between clenched teeth, "move."

"Oh, *damn it!*"

"Kill me. Please..."

"Jesus!" David swore, curling both of his hands into fists and looking for something to hit in his frustration. "Jesus, Jesus fucking *Christ!*"

Footsteps on the stairs, coming down the landing.

Cheryl. She took one look and gasped, "Oh, my God!"

"Come in here."

She did, staring at Nora, then looking at David. "Call a doctor."

"She doesn't need a doctor."

"Call a doctor!"

"She doesn't need a doctor!"

"Then *I'll* call!" And she turned and left the room.

"Cheryl!"

Nora hissed, she wheezed from the bed.

David swore and ran down the landing, followed Cheryl down the stairs, into the kitchen.

She jumped for the phone, took down the receiver, started to dial. From behind, David grabbed her wrist, gripping her so strongly that she almost dropped the receiver.

"You're hurting me!"

"Stop it!"

"You are hurting me, David!"

"Stop dialing!"

"Let me—fucker!—go right now, goddamn it!"

He did, he let her go. Cheryl dropped the receiver and it banged into the wall and hung there at the end of the cord, twisting back and forth above the floor, while she glared at him.

"You are sick! You are *sick!* You hurt me! My wrist

hurts! My wrist *burns!* You want to explain that?"

"She doesn't need a doctor!"

"She doesn't need you, either, Mr. I-Fuck-Up-People's-Lives!"

He walked away, heading for the stairs.

"She doesn't need that and neither do I and neither does anybody, David!"

He went up the stairs, listening to her behind him, sobbing and yelling.

"Neither does *anybody!*" Cheryl screamed at him. "Neither! Does! *Any! Body!*"

They didn't take I-75 or I-71 because Jack was afraid they'd be followed, that the interstates would be too obvious. Instead, he took Mill out of the city, but as he did, he wondered if he were supposed to think they'd be too obvious, the interstates, and so maybe Dragomir's people would expect him to take the back roads anyway? But then, if they expected him to think that way, then he should probably take the interstates after all. Only, if he did that, then—

Fuck it.

From Mill he kept making ragged turns, right and left and right again, zigzags that gradually led him north and east, toward I-71, because he'd have to get on the interstates eventually, he'd have no choice. But he'd sacrifice the time now, though, figuring that staying alive a little longer was worth it, figuring that his own peace of mind was worth it.

Yeah, right, peace of mind. He sure had a mind full of peace right now, oh, absolutely.

"You're the one who made the phone call, aren't you?" Kendrick said to him.

"What phone call is that?"

" 'You be careful and keep away or you're next.' Words to that effect."

Jack flashed him a big grin.

"I thought so. I knew it. I told the police."

"Why, thanks."

"Christ," Kendrick said. Then, sarcastically, "You can drive faster than this, can't you?"

"You know what, Padre? You can help by keeping an eye out, how's that?"

"An eye out for what?"

"Anyone or anything."

"That's a pretty substantial order."

"He's going to have people everywhere. Think about it. They're going to be ready to jump on us and take care of business any second, at any time."

"Jack, he is not going to have people on every road out of Cincinnati!"

"He's not?"

"Damn it, we can't be suspicious of everyone!"

"We can't? Why not?"

"Dear Lord!"

"Jesus!" Jack said then, nearly jumping out of his seat, glancing quickly in his rearview mirror and in the side mirror.

"What? What is it?"

"Didn't you *see* him?"

"See *who*?"

"It was one of them, it was—I forget his name—it was one of his motherfucking—"

"Jack, let me drive."

"No-oho, boy!"

"Pull over and let me drive!"

"Father, you just sit, you just leave the driving to—"

"You're sick, Jack! You're sick in the head!"

"Hey, I'm so sane, you don't know how sane I am, I'm sane enough to—I'm *scared*, that's how *sane* I am, that's how *sick* I am, Padre Father—"

"Jack—!"

"—Father Hail Mary Fuck You Full of Graceful—"

"Jack, look out!"

The car jolted, it jumped, and Jack braked, grabbed the wheel, stayed on the road, straightened it out—

"Shit! *Jesus!*"

"Stop the—"

"Who was that?"

"Jack, you hit him!"

"Did I? Did I hit him?"

He'd been standing right there on the side of the road, thumbing a ride, kid with a backpack—

"Stop the car! Dear God, dear Christ, stop the car, go back!"

Now someone was honking his horn at him, a car that had just gone past him in the other lane.

"He saw you, Jack!" Kendrick yelled and turned around. "Oh, *Jesus*, I can't see him, you hit him, you knocked him off the road!"

"He was one of them!"

"He was not one of them!"

"He was! They're sneaky! They're so fucking crafty, you think they aren't, but they are, they are!"

"That car is turning around. He's following us. Jack, he'll get your license number!"

"He better not."

"He's... Oh, God, God. He stopped, he's... Slow down! He found him, he found the body!"

But Jack drove, kept driving, faster, moving faster down the road, looking for signs that would take him to I-71.

Trembling, Kendrick leaned back, closed his eyes, swallowed, tried to swallow. His throat was dry, his lips were dry, he could barely speak now, he couldn't think.

"Dear God," he said. "Dear... God..."

"Him, too," Jack said. "And anybody else who fucking thinks they're going to get me and stop me...."

"Is she going to be all right?" Cheryl asked him.

"Yeah. For the time being."

She said, "I'm... Then I'm going to leave now."

"Yeah." He walked her into the living room.

"If anyone calls here, you tell them where I am."

"I will."

She had on her down jacket, her gloves, her boots. She looked out the front window. "Still snowing. We're going to get a couple of inches."

"Oh, yeah."

"All right, David, look—"

"Your car's over at your mother's, right?"

"Yeah. Sure. We left it there when we . . . Damn it."

"Oh, hell."

"*Damn* it!" Cheryl swore. "Dear Christ, this is insane! This isn't real. None of it. This is all—"

"Cheryl—"

"—like it's some kind of *game* or something? No, no . . . Don't—don't you touch me, don't—do anything, David, don't talk to me, you listen to me! Don't talk to my mother, don't—"

"Cheryl!"

"Just *stay away* from me! All right? Just *stay away!*"

She ran away from him. Slammed the front door hard. He heard the truck start up and it sounded stupid and obsolete and mechanical, the gears shifting as she drove away.

He watched the snow falling outside the window.

He was aware of how warm it was in the house and he went across the living room to turn down the thermostat a little. Then he walked upstairs to look in on Nora, wondering if he should watch television or read or listen to the radio or . . .

What he should do.

27

"*Other business is,*" Dragomir had wheezed to Iva Daugherty, "*Being attended. To.*"

He returned home, then, to wait throughout the morning for that other business to be transacted.

Phone calls were made to the many people not mentioned in the newspaper articles, people who were told that airline tickets were waiting for them and that they had better be on flights leaving the city this afternoon. They were to hurry and answer no questions; Mr. Dragomir's attorneys and public relations people would answer any further inquiries that might be directed toward him or his business associates.

And other phone calls came in regularly, all morning long, to be intercepted by Glen and other members of his inner circle and reported to Stefan Dragomir as soberly as if they had been stock market quotations or fluctuations in the prime rate.

Neil Banyon had died on the operating table; the surgeons with their skill and their machines could not save him, though they had done their best. They complimented him afterward, saying that Neil was a fighter. But the human body is only so resilient, the will only so strong.

Wayne Beck, who'd written the lead article for the *Post*, had been found dead in an alley behind a parking deck downtown. He'd fallen about four stories; there wasn't much left of his facial features, or most of his head, for that matter.

Ted Troy, who'd founded Proppco eight years ago and who was known to be a sometime business associate of Mr. Dragomir's, was killed early Saturday morning in a horrible fire at the paint manufacturing plant he owned. Thirteen of his employees died with him, when one of the buildings went up in a tremendous explosion. An investigation was pending.

Violent murder claimed the life of E. William O'Connell, another associate of Mr. Dragomir's and the owner of a large chain of car rental agencies. Apparently Mr. O'Connell had become involved in a difference of opinion with the driver and passengers of another car on the I–275 bypass, and one of the passengers had discharged a twelve-gauge shotgun into Mr. O'Connell's Lincoln Town Car. Conflicting eyewitness reports were of little help to investigators.

Norman and Celia Vernon, real estate magnates and acquaintances of Iva Daugherty's, suffered an unfortunate accident that Saturday morning, as well, when an electrical appliance fell into their heated indoor pool while the two of them were enjoying a relaxing swim.

And a little before noon, Stefan Dragomir received a message from the driver of one of his cars equipped with a cellular telephone. A Ford Pinto station wagon, resembling the one stolen from Mr. Dragomir a few days ago, had been seen about an hour and a half earlier, heading north toward Columbus on I–71.

Mr. Dragomir thanked the alert driver, hung up, and reminded Glen to issue the man a bonus next week in his paycheck.

"We leave for. Noland. Immediately," he said.

"Do you want Jack's file?" Glen asked him.

"Oh, yes."

"Why not just kill him now?" one of the others asked.

Dragomir smiled at him. "And miss the. Look in his. Eyes? No. No. What we. Appreciate. In life," he said, "Comes down to. Only a few. Moments. In life. The. Occasional. Rewarding. Moments. Don't you. Agree?"

"I guess I'd better."

"Everything. Else," Dragomir said. "Is. Pretense or. Prepar. Ation. Waiting. The antici. Pation. Of certain. Moments. Correct?"

And his smile grew deeper still.

* * *

David answered the phone around two in the afternoon. It was Father Kendrick.

"How is she, David?"

"Not good. She's very weak. She's sick. He's worn her down. She's paralyzed or something. I'm doing what I can, but he's got a lock on her."

"We can't let him hurt her. You've got to tell me what we can do to stop him."

"Father, where are you? Did you go to Phoenix, or—"

"No, we're very close to you, as a matter of fact."

"What?"

"We're near Noland."

"What're you doing here?"

"Long story. Can I tell you when we get there? Give me directions."

"Where are you now?"

"It looks like—it's an important interchange of some kind. Route forty-six and some other highway."

"Eleven."

"That's it. Route forty-six and Interstate 11."

"And you're right on top of six-eighty, too. All right, I'm going to steer you here, but write this down. You have some paper there, something to write with? Okay." Kendrick answered with grunts and uh-huhs and got it all, and finally David asked him, "Who's 'we,' Father?"

"Hm?"

"Who's the 'we,' as in, 'Can I tell you when we get there?'"

"Jack Starkis and me."

"Jack Starkis!"

"Yes."

"What the hell is *he* doing here?"

"It's gotten rather complicated, David."

"Jesus Christ, it was *already* complicated! This takes it—"

"I know, I know, but . . . Please. Calm . . . Listen to me, calm down." And Kendrick told him what had happened, about Jack's attempt to kill Dragomir.

"Father, do you know what this does?"

"David, I really don't have much choice at this point."

"You do realize, don't you, that since he tried to kill Stefan Dragomir, Stefan Dragomir is going to follow him here and kill Jack?"

"That's my general impression, yes."

"And he'll have Nora, too, at that point."

"Unless we can stop him, yes."

"Please tell me this is a joke."

"It's not a joke."

"Please tell me this is a dream."

"It's not a dream."

"Father Kendrick, I've never been this serious before in my life."

"David, we can't say that we didn't know this would happen."

"Yeah, I know that, but . . . I know, I know."

"David?"

"Why do I just know I'm not going to be here for the Traci Lords film festival next week."

"The what?"

"Oh, God. Never mind. Look . . . Shit."

"David, we agreed to help Nora."

"Yes! Nora! But bringing Jack into this is—"

"Could we discuss this over a cup of coffee?"

"Yes, Father, yes. We could."

"Well, we'll be there in about—what would you say?—fifteen minutes, twenty minutes?"

"Twenty minutes, yeah."

"It's snowing out here. Very light."

"Well, it's snowing here, too, Father."

"Twenty minutes, then."

"Yes, but . . . Yeah. Yeah. Father, look. Get here as fast as you can. Are you driving, or is Jack?"

"Jack is, if you can call it driving."

"Tell him to get you here in one piece, but get here as soon as you can. All right?"

"Yes."

"Because I've got some work to do if we're going to get ready for the big showdown."

"That's what this is leading to, isn't it?"

"Yes, sir, it is."

"I, uh, still have that talisman you gave me, that piece of jewelry."

"Then you hold on to it for dear life because, Father, you could get caught in the crossfire here."

"I just don't want want Nora getting hurt. That's my main concern."

"Well then, you're a brave man."

"I owe Mary something, David. Let's put it that way."

"Get here," David told him. "As fast as you can. Because as soon as you're here, we're putting up roadblocks."

"Roadblocks."

"We're going to give them a show, Father Kendrick. We're going to give them a show."

"I was wrong, David. You're not like him at all."

"No, you were right. I'm a lot more like him that I was willing to admit. And maybe I need to be, Father. Maybe that's exactly what I need to be."

When he hung up, he went upstairs and sat beside Nora, held one of her hands and looked down at her, the pale skin, she was so damp and ill, she was so far away.

"Nora? Can you hear me?"

And he thought of his sister.

"They found her in a field, did they tell you that?"

"Yes."

"It's kind of a state of shock. We don't know what triggered it. And frankly, we can't reach her."

"Nora? Can you hear me?"

"We can't reach her."

No movement, no sound. The eyelids didn't flutter, she didn't recognize him at all.

"They're on their way," David told her. "Nora, I know you can hear me. You're in there somewhere, damn it, and so's your father. Can you hear me, Ste*fan* with an *f*? We're going to *f you*, Ste*fan* with an *f*. We're ready. We're ready."

He gripped her hand tightly and tried to make his threat

sound meaningful, but it was all bluster; he was unnerved, he wasn't sure that he believed it himself.

"I expect him to show up any second. He can do whatever he wants to, David."

It was too much. It was too much, all of it.

"It's real grim, I know that, but this is what he's going to do, he's doing it, and nobody's going to stop him."

"Damn it," he said to her. "We did it once. We invented gunpowder once, goddamn it, and we can do it again."

He put a hand on her belly, leaned over, and rested his cheek there for a moment, his ear, so that he could feel the baby inside her, the life inside her.

He supposed that he heard it. He didn't know what babies sounded like. He didn't know what it was supposed to sound like in there.

"I owe Mary something, David. Let's put it that way."

Well, he thought, maybe I owe Mary something, too, and Nora and Cheryl.

Maybe I owe Cheryl something, too.

He stood up, letting go of Nora's hand.

"It is time," he announced to her, "to invent gunpowder."

And may God, he thought, have mercy on your soul. . . .

28

He went downstairs and, within his circle, he lit candles and incense and took off his shirt and ritually washed himself with water from a brass bowl.

Salt water.

Salt, to keep away demons, to protect his soul if, indeed, he were to be killed.

Then he crossed his arms over his chest and prayed.

"In nomine Agla Sabaoth Elohim. Elion. Amathia. On. Non declinet cor meum in verba malitiae. Defende me in proelio contra spiritus malignos qui ad perditionem animarem pervagantur. Veni, spiritus magnus, neco mea inimici. In nomine Agla Sabaoth Elohim."

He thanked his guardian spirits and blew out the candles, covered the bowl of burning incense to extinguish it, pulled his shirt back on, and went upstairs.

"Nora? Now listen to me. You can hear me now. I'm going to do a ritual. I'm going to protect you and the baby and I'm going to make you feel strong. You're going to feel powerful. All right? You're going to have to help me as much as you can. I'm going to get inside again and I'm going to help with your father. We're really going to fight him. I know he's coming here, and we don't want him to hurt you or the baby, so we're going to make ourselves very strong, now. Okay? You're going to live and your baby's going to live. I want you to understand where this is coming from, because you're going to feel it when I start the ceremony. You're going to feel it."

He pulled the bed out from the corner of the spare room,

THE EYES OF NIGHT 177

moving it as carefully as he could, trying not to disturb Nora, although she probably couldn't feel it at all. There wasn't a great deal of room to maneuver but David did the best he could, giving himself enough space to get behind the headboard and along the one side so that he could draw a white chalk circle around Nora and himself. More of a square, really, not a circle, but enough to do the job.

Then he sat down beside her, in a chair beside the bed, and held one of her hands in both of his. He closed his eyes and felt her pulse and listened to her breathing, felt Nora's breathing, and let his own breathing move with hers, coincide with hers, rise and fall with hers. He gripped her hand tightly; there was the merest response from her, a very light flinching of her fingers, a small spasm of movement.

Very small, very slight, but she might have been shrieking to him because that's what it meant, that movement, a cry for help. She might as well have jumped up and screamed at him to help her.

Breathing as she breathed, breathing as she breathed, trying to get Nora to relax, holding her hand, and nodding to her and sending her energy and strength, breathing as she breathed, seeing as she saw—

The baby, a happy healthy smiling baby, a warm and sweet and lovely vision, and one no doubt sent by her father, another lie of her father's, because as David smiled with Nora and rocked back and forth with her, enjoying the baby and appreciating it, it changed and became demonic. The baby stopped smiling; its face tightened and stretched and the baby began to cry loudly, cry as it changed colors, from white, from pink to green and purple and red. Its head changed, from a baby's head to an oversized demonic head, the face chiseled and grisly, the mouth full of teeth, the eyes mere pinpoints of light deep in skull-like eye sockets.

David said out loud, "It's all right. He's playing games. He's trying to keep you weak and afraid, Nora, that's all, that's all this is."

He took a deep breath and called up imagery of his own, his blue light, a curtain of it, an electric shimmer thin as a butterfly's wing, as delicate and as strong.

With the blue shield around him, David moved forward into Nora's mind, into her soul, whispering to her to stay strong.

His blue shield was attacked. Violent colors, brilliant and sharp as spears, sharp as knives, assailed him from all angles. He was swimming in long rows of colors, a maelstrom of colors that buffeted him and tried to break through his blue shield, tried to pierce him and shred him.

The colors changed into their true shapes, then into demons, a swarm of demons, flying at him and laughing, a wild assortment of them, some of them like animals, others like serpents, some furred and others as shiny as oily water, all with bold and exaggerated eyes and mouths and teeth, all of them nightmares from somewhere deep inside Nora, all of them the monsters and animals and reptiles and insects and shadows and dreams she feared and had always feared, the sharp teeth and horns and claws without names, the flames and eyes and nets and traps and edges that had terrified her since childhood.

Then, the yellow thing.

The small scampering and swimming and flapping demons, flying toward David, toward the blue light that protected his spirit and Nora's, the moving army of demons parted, as if they were pilot fish directing a shark, and the shark appeared.

That great greasy yellow ball, Dragomir's demon, his demon or his illness, his sick soul warped through centuries of evil, born and reborn, his soul dragged shrieking from the bloody wombs of women sacrificed time after time throughout history—his demon, the great yellow ball with black spots on it, long black curling horns, great black eyes like a shark's dead eyes, no legs or feet or hands, floating, and breathing its black smoke in and out, suspirating its acid smoke, black charnel smoke with its blackened bits of old dead souls floating in the mist of it.

David pushed his blue wall of light against it.

He told the yellow thing, the demon, he told Stefan Dragomir: I have protected her and her child from you.

The great yellow thing laughed, discharging more black

smoke from its maw. The great yellow thing made sounds, the sounds of a newborn human baby, mewling and whimpering. It took on the appearance of a newborn baby, Nora's baby, white and pink, a lovely vision, healthy and correct, a smiling baby, smiling, smiling, and the smile enlarged, the smile grew and increased until the nose vanished behind it, and the eyes, and finally the last of the head, until the head was no more and was completely a mouth, a mouth filled with sharp teeth atop a pink baby's body.

Nora, on the bed, moaned and began to cry.

David held on tightly to her hand.

The baby's body began to rip, rip like the lining of a suit or an old coat. Tentacles erupted from the ripping baby's body, writhing dripping tentacles all alive, more demons from Nora's unhappy soul, pulled from the depths of her spirit...

The tentacles reached for David, tried to smash through his blue wall of light.

David told them: Go away, get back to hell, I'm stronger than you are, *we* are stronger than you are!

But the vision began to go black, the more he resisted, go black and red, as if his brain behind his eyes were filling up with blood and blinding him to the—

Black. Erupting. Suddenly. And splinters of red, sharp splinters trying to wound him and wound Nora—

She whimpered, she moaned....

David pulled back. He moved away as quickly as he could to safety, pulling his strong blue curtain of light, spiritual light, with him, pulling back—

He opened his eyes, and gasped.

He released Nora's hand from his and his fingers opened with a moist sticky sound, perspiration.

"God..."

He couldn't fight him, couldn't fight Stefan Dragomir, not this way, not like this, it was too dangerous, it would endanger Nora and her child both...

She sobbed.

David looked down into her eyes. Nora's eyes were open

and she was staring up at him, and the tears were moving down the sides of her face—

"Kill . . . me . . . David . . . please . . ."

He took her hand and moved it to her belly and placed his own hands on her swollen belly and pressed there—

"Live!"

—pressed down with his hot hands, hot hands.

"Live . . ."

But Nora moaned and whimpered beneath him on the bed, looking at him and whispering, "Please, no, please—just kill me—just kill me now . . . give me the strength to . . . kill myself . . . please. . . ."

29

When David answered his front door, he was holding a decorated longsword in his left hand, its blade inscribed with magical symbols, the wooden handle wrapped in colored ribbons.

Father Kendrick's response was a politely restrained, "Well, no suit of armor?"

"Still snowing, I see." David stepped back to let him and Jack in.

Both of them stamped their feet on the welcome mat, knocking ice from the bottom of their shoes.

Jack said, "Good afternoon, David."

"Well, let me be the judge of that, okay, Jack?"

"Oh, sure."

He closed the front door and rested the sword against it while Kendrick and Jack took their coats off and looked around.

Jack said, "How's that nose of yours?"

"Still hurts. How's your hand?"

"Still hurts."

"Uh-huh."

Father complimented David on the decor. "This is a wonderful home you have here."

"Thank you."

"Small and cozy. Rustic," he said. "Lots of wood and stone. I like that. I like the fireplace. It's big. I like the furniture. And lots of bookcases."

"You can put your coats in here," David suggested, opening the closet in the corner by the front door. He took

Father's and hung it in there and took Jack's when he handed it to him. "Coffee's in the kitchen."

"And Nora?" Kendrick asked him.

"Upstairs. I'll show you."

Jack was surveying some of the odds and ends on David's bookshelves. "Nice work," he commented, handling some of the talismans and amulets.

"Emma Daedalus."

"And nice work!" he said again, picking up a framed photo of Cheryl. "This's the lady who makes it happen, huh?"

"Was. Was the lady."

"Very nice. Very pretty. Excellent bod. Outstanding tits, I must say."

"Jack."

He put the photo down and glanced at David.

"Coffee?"

"Oh, yeah, right, sure."

He led them into the kitchen, took down two mugs from the rack on the wall and retrieved his own from the counter, then poured for all three. He took milk out of the refrigerator and put it on the table.

Then he asked them, "How long do we have before Dragomir and his hit squad show up?"

"Hard to say," Kendrick frowned, looking at Jack. "Two hours? Three?"

"We'd better plan on two hours," Jack said.

David looked at the clock above the stove. "So we're saying they'll be here by five o'clock."

"That's right."

"Unless I can slow them down or stop them."

Jack looked at him. "And how're you going to do that, if I may ask?"

"You may ask, Jack, but I'd really prefer that you sit this one out, if you don't mind."

"Hey, no problem. I'll leave it to a pro. This is your neck of the woods, anyway. I'm just a visitor here."

David purposely set his cup on the table with an audible sound. "It's this way, Jack. I don't like you. And I don't trust you. If you're going to help, help. If you're here to cause trouble—wait your turn. Got it?"

"Got it, Dave."

"Good."

"Nora," Kendrick said.

David led him back through the living room, through the sitting room, and up the stairs to the spare room at the end of the landing.

They went in quietly and David, whispering, told Kendrick what he'd tried to do an hour earlier. "She came around a little bit, Father, but he's still got her. It's like he has her in his fist. And he's squeezing. Her and the baby both. She's so weak, she can't even move. And if I try to move her, put her in a cold tub or something, he sends the pain right through her, really zaps her with it. She can't eat or drink anything, and she's sweating like crazy."

"Dehydration?"

"No sign of it yet, but it won't be much longer."

"He'll kill her if he keeps this up."

"I think he intends to be in control of the situation before that happens. Get his hands on her, get her home, force her into labor—get the baby born."

"Can you stop him?"

"I don't know. I think so. The idea's to put a lot of pressure on him and his goons, distract them if nothing else, just keep piling it on so that he's weakened, too. If we can do that, we might be able to hurt him."

"Kill him, you mean."

"I don't know yet, Father. If we can just *stop* him, we could get Nora to a hospital here and take it from there. I thought about doing that tonight if you hadn't called. But we're here, so we'll make the best of it."

"We may still have time to do that, a hospital."

"And we may not have the time, either. We're quite a ways out here and that means we can contain the damage, I guess you'd call it. But if we take this thing into a city hospital, lots of other people are going to get hurt."

"You're right."

"No matter how it comes down, Father, people are going to die."

"I know that."

"Yeah. Yeah . . . Let me get going now."

"David, tell me what *I* can do."

"At this point, not much. Stay with Nora."

"There must be something!"

"Not a lot, sir."

"Damn it, I can pray to Almighty God!"

"Father, this isn't between Stefan Dragomir and God. It's between Stefan Dragomir and us." He moved past him then, to leave the room, but paused by the door. "Go ahead, though, if you want to," David told him. "I suppose we can use all the ammunition we can get."

He left, and Kendrick stayed in the room. And as David went down the landing, he thought he heard Father behind him, whispering to Nora.

To Nora—or putting in the request for extra ammunition.

Downstairs, he took his coat and hat and his scarf and gloves out of the closet. He saw Jack in the kitchen, sipping coffee and looking out the window at the falling snow. David walked into the kitchen.

"How's it hanging, Jack?"

"David—I want to help."

"I knew this was coming."

"I mean it."

"I'm sure you do."

"Damn it, you could use my fucking assistance here, you know!"

"You're right. I could. Only the problem is that you're extremely fucked up. You're sick in the head, Jack. You're poison. I'd rather go upstairs right now and kill her than count on any help from you."

"Don't do that."

"I mean it."

"I'm sure you do. I understand that."

"I'll put her out of her misery right now and go out in a blaze of glory because, Jack, you're not trustworthy."

"I know that, I know."

"Look at me."

"What, David?"

"This is another one of you goddamn stunts, isn't it? You don't really want to help. You just want to make sure your grass doesn't get mowed when all this shit comes down. Am I right?"

"Look, damn it! You're not the only person backed into the corner here, you know! I'm here, too, you know! If I fuck you over, then I'm fucked, too! And I'm not that fucking crazy!"

"Some experts disagree."

"We're the only two people who even understand what the hell's happening here! Huh?"

David said nothing.

"Am I right, or what?"

"Oh, yeah. You're right."

"See? See what I mean?"

David tightened his scarf around his neck and buttoned his coat and said, "Let me do this, and we'll talk."

"Okay."

"We'll *talk*."

"David, we're brothers."

"We are not brothers."

"We're the same kind of people."

"You're scared shitless, aren't you, Jack? I mean, you're incapacitated."

"He made a fool out of me!"

"I'd've never guessed."

"He did. He really made a fool out of me."

"Jack, be honest—Mother Nature beat him to it."

When Father Kendrick came downstairs a few minutes later, he found Jack still in the kitchen and joined him, stood beside him and looked out the window.

The daylight was nearly gone, the snow was still gently falling, and Kendrick saw David, quite some distance away, making a circuit around the house, dragging the longsword beside him, pushing it into the ground, cutting a deep groove in the earth.

"What's he doing?"

"Building a wall, Padre. Building a wall."

"A wall?" Kendrick noticed that where the falling snow struck the sword, the metal blade, the snow melted instantly, vaporized as steam.

"The metal's hot, understand?"

"I see...."

David finished the circle and they both watched him as he lifted the sword and, pointing it to the sky, gestured with it in a formal prayer or benediction. Then he turned around and started walking toward the back porch, but stopped to begin tracing another circle about ten feet inside the one he'd just outlined.

"Well, I'll be damned," Jack whispered in admiration.

"What's he doing now?"

"He's building another wall, is what he's doing. He's creating a real obstacle course for these fuckers, is what he's doing."

"This is what he did in my room at the rectory, with you and the rest of them."

"Yes, it is."

"That thing of yours, that elemental—"

"Yeah."

"It couldn't get past the line David drew. It was like a wall."

"You got it."

"It pulled away, it drew back."

"If we'd forced it, Father, we would have gotten into very serious trouble. It would have backfired on us."

"Meaning?"

"One of us would have died."

"That's what David said."

"David was right."

"And that's what will happen if Stefan Dragomir and his people try to get across these lines, as well."

"Uh-huh. The only question is, how many people is he bringing with him? How many people do we have to stop?"

"What you mean," Father Kendrick said, "is that the only question is, how many people are going to die?"

30

When David came back in, he told Jack that he wanted to see him downstairs.

"Nice setup, Duh-veed."

"Go ahead, Jack."

"I'm touched. I really am, old buddy."

"Everything you need's right here. Incense, the candles—that's salt water in the bowl, there."

"Partners. The two of us. Who would ever have thought? Well, I must tell you—whatever you need, you can count on me. I mean it. Just ask. Anything."

"A new life."

"Within reason."

David sat at the bottom of the basement steps while Jack lit the incense and candles, stripped off his shirt, and began his ritual purification.

"I tried to kill him, David."

"Dragomir?"

"Yup. Last night."

"That's got to rank right down there as one of your more egregious acts of outright stupidity."

"Yeah? Look who's talking. In nomine—I didn't let the sweetie in the picture frame walk out of my life, now, did I? In nomine Agla Sabaoth Elohim. Elion."

"It's a little more complicated than that, Jack."

"Amathia. Is it really, now? On."

"How many's he bringing with him?"

"Truckloads, is my guess. Non declinet cor meum—"

"Great."

"—in verba malitiae. You know, I recall predicting this."

"Predicting what?"

"That you'd come down off your high horse some day. Join the rest of us in the trenches. Get your hands dirty. Defende me in proelio—get your feet wet."

"You're a real seer, Jack. I have another question."

"—contra spiritus malignos—Ask. All will be revealed."

"How much longer has he got to live?"

"Good question—qui ad perditionem—"

"Do you know?"

"No—animarem pervagantur. But it won't be much longer."

"No?"

"No. He is sick, he is walking death, really. Fucker's in bad shape. Veni, spiritus magnus—"

"Been hanging in there for at least seven and a half months now."

"—neco mea inimici. Yeah, well, I have a question for you, David."

"And what's that?"

"In nomine Agla Sabaoth Elohim. Did you kill Theodore Fry?"

"I don't know. You tell me. You're the seer."

"Just yes or no."

"I guess I never really did get around to answering that one, did I?"

"We know you did, all right? It's pretty obvious."

"It is, huh?"

"Listen." Jack pulled his shirt back on, put out the candles, covered the bowl of burning incense, and walked over to David, leaning back against the basement wall in front of him and crossing his arms over his chest. "Tell me how you did it. Because we can ice Steverino that way, what do you think?"

"I doubt it."

"Why not?"

"It's two entirely different things, Jack."

THE EYES OF NIGHT

"Different how?"

"You killed Sister Mary, right?"

"Will you get *off* that?"

"You killed her."

"Me, Dragomir, guy named Glen Dennison, about four other people—yeah. Guilty as charged."

"I'd like to nail you for that one, I really would."

"It's over. It's a long time ago. It's—"

"Two weeks!"

"It wasn't my bright idea! I'm an employee, remember?"

"You dick."

"Do I call you bad names? Do I? I'm a guest in your home here, and I respect that, I hold that sacrosanct."

"All right, Jack, fine. Jesus. You want to know why we can't kill Dragomir that way? Here's why. What'd you get when you killed Sister Mary? The conjuration, I mean. The calling."

"The first thing we got was real bullshit. Maybe Bezemoth, maybe not. The big D figured out that Fry was dead and that you'd probably done it, and that's what he needed to know. That's what came through."

"That was it?"

"David, this was not like an earth satellite linkup or something! It was some fucking demon hiding behind a nun!"

"God, Jack!"

"And Dragomir never told me what Fry *did*, what was going on, there. Understandez-vous, now?"

"He committed suicide."

"No fuck!"

"That's how he made his compact with Bezemoth."

"No shit! What balls! So how'd you nail him?"

"I found his book. I found his grimoire. Destroyed it, destroyed the link with his demon. Gone with the wind."

"Brilliant, I must say. True genius."

"I was nervous as hell for weeks afterward. What if the police found me or something? They have these bones in the middle of a field. Try and identify them. Figure out who it was."

"Nobody complains, cops don't care, right?"

"I guess."

"But I see what you mean. That's got nothing whatsoever to do with what Dragomir's doing. That's not how this one goes at all."

"We can nail him, Jack. I'm just not sure at this point that we have the right tools to nail him with."

"I don't know. I've been around the guy for months and he's protected, he keeps it all close to home, believe me. He does."

"I believe you."

Jack yawned and said. "Toe to toe. That's all I can think of. Keep piling it on, keep him busy, get him weak. Find his weak spot and keep hitting him there with combinations."

"That's the master plan. Jack, go upstairs. You're tired."

"No sleep last night, you believe that?"

"Fix yourself a drink. Relax. Don't fall asleep, but relax."

"While you're doing what?"

"Building another wall. Throwing some more punches— I hope."

"You know, Mr. T. . . . I won't let you down."

"I know."

"What, you know?"

"Jack, you said it yourself. Neither one of us has any choice in this. We sink together, or we swim together."

"You're right, that's it."

"Understandez-vous—*partner*?"

He sat in his circle, he purified himself and prayed, and he concentrated. Dreamed a dream that was not a dream, but reality, in the same way that Dragomir's demon, molesting Nora, and his child, festering within her, were not dreams but reality.

Upstairs, Jack sat on the couch in the living room and

listened to David's CD player, an old Stones album, and leafed through the sports section of the paper and tapped his feet and sipped from the brandy he'd poured for himself.

Father Kendrick came downstairs, saw him, and said, "That looks good."

"Those cabinets above the fridge, Padre."

"Where's David?"

"Downstairs."

"I wanted to—"

"But don't go down there, okay?"

"Why not?"

"Because he's busy." Jack smiled and nodded toward the front window.

Kendrick looked, not at first understanding. "Is it snowing harder? Harder than it was?"

Jack's grin improved and he lifted his glass of brandy in a mock salute.

"It is, isn't it?" Kendrick went to the window.

"Dumbfuck sure is showing me a thing or three."

Kendrick leaned over the table David had sitting in front of the window and watched the snow come down in fat, heavy flakes, come down quickly.

And then they both heard his footsteps on the basement stairs and the door opening, and watched him as he staggered into the living room.

"Jack," Kendrick said.

Jack got off the couch and moved around the coffee table and stood to one side.

David was exhausted. He fell onto the couch and flopped onto his back, half sitting and half lying there, and wrapped his arms around himself. His teeth were chattering. He yanked the afghan on top of himself and curled up.

Kendrick walked over to him and handed him Jack's brandy.

David sat up and sipped it greedily, gasping at first, but appreciating it.

"Thank—you! Whoo. Good stuff."

Kendrick felt his face, his forehead. "You're half frozen."

David nodded. "I know, Father. It's cold out there."

Five o'clock.
Five-thirty.
No Stefan Dragomir.
Six o'clock.
"What else can we do?" Jack asked David.
"Nothing."
"The talismans on the doors and on your windows?"
"They're fine, Jack."

David was sitting on the couch, listening to—the silence, the feel of it, the sense of it, what was coming.

Jack sat in a chair by the fireplace, sipping more of the brandy. It was getting to him a little, the brandy—and the waiting.

The ritual sword was on the coffee table.

They heard Father Kendrick coming. He walked into the middle of the living room, hands clasped behind his back.

David gave him a look that asked, Nora?

Kendrick shrugged.

"You have your talisman, Father?"

"For the hundredth time, David, yes."

"Yeah. Well, are you hungry? Jack? Anybody hungry?"

"What do you want to do?" Jack asked him. "Order a pizza?"

Kendrick said, "I'm not hungry. I don't need anything."

"Maybe they'll deliver," Jack said.

"Anybody want anything, help yourselves."

"This is crazy," Father Kendrick said. "I'm sorry, but this is . . . it's crazy. It makes me want to jump out of my skin."

"It is, it is," Jack agreed.

Father went to the living-room window and looked out.

There was nothing to see but the ice fogging the windows and the darkness outside and the wall of falling snow, thick and heavy. There was nothing to hear except the blowing wind, howling when it picked up and moved wildly through the woods behind the house.

"Bad night out there" was his comment. "Bad night."

"Thank-you," David said.

Six-thirty.

Seven o'clock.

31

"There must be a foot of snow out there," Glen complained. "Look at this shit."

"Snow," someone in the back said, "is white shit."

"Still coming down, too."

Dragomir, beside him in the front seat of the van, was smiling.

"Mr. Dragomir," Glen said to him, "are you all right?"

"This is. Him."

"Him? What? He's doing this? Trevisan?"

"Yes."

Ahead of the van, the Oldsmobile slid off the icy road and into the ditch. Glen checked his side mirror to see how the pickup truck, behind him, was doing, then hit his warning lights. They started blinking.

"Mr. Dragomir, we have to stop to get those people into the van."

"Do it."

There was no other traffic on the road; no one else was crazy enough to be out in this kind of weather tonight. They were in the middle of nowhere—north of Noland, Glen knew, out in the country somewhere but with no house lights to be seen in any direction—just fields of grass and woods around them and everything obscured by the dense white snow coming down, driving down, piling up and clogging the grass, woods, road. Glen had never been around here before; the area was totally unfamiliar to him, and it felt strange and desolate and threatening to him. It made him feel foreign, an outsider, and cursed.

He downshifted and let the van slide still in the middle

of the road. He glanced at the clock on the dashboard.

Nearly seven-thirty.

"Heads up," he called to the four in the back. "The Olds is off the road! Got to make room for four more back there!"

"All four of them? Back here?"

"They can squeeze one or two into the truck, can't they, Glen?"

"I don't want that truck stopping for anything. I want it to keep going. I don't even like us stopping here."

He opened his door and jumped outside, his boots vanishing instantly into eight inches of heavy snow that felt like cold quicksand. Glen shielded his eyes with a gloved hand and waved for the truck to keep moving.

"Come on! Come on! Don't stop, damn it! Keep going!"

It did, making its way around the van, tires spinning and whizzing on the icy road, kicking up geysers as it plowed through a snowbank and got past.

"Go, go, go!" Glen rooted, waving a fist after it as he high-stepped through the snow to reach the Olds.

All four of them were trying to get it moving, Nolene behind the wheel, trying to steer, the other three pushing on the rear bumper. Every time the wheels spun, snow and gravel and dirt flew into the air and the stench of burning rubber came up.

"Enough! Enough!" Glen yelled.

"Get behind us with the van! Give us a push!"

"Forget it! Just get into the back!"

"Are we all going to fit?"

"You'll fit. Just do it. Dragomir's orders. We're almost there."

"You sure?"

"The house is right around the next bend. We've been following the county map."

As he slogged past Glen, one of the men said, "Why don't we just melt all this shit for about half a mile, you know?"

"Save it for when you really need it."

"We need it now."

"Team work, Barry. Mr. Dragomir's orders. Save the fireworks for what's important."

"Whatever."

"Party poopers," Jack said. He finished his brandy and set it on the stone step of the fireplace and picked up the back section of the paper.

David and Father Kendrick were standing by the front window, watching the snow, the night, watching.

Father told David quietly, personally, between the two of them, "I have what I call my 'little voice.'"

"Yes?"

"If I calm down and listen to it, it usually tells me what to do. I rely on it."

"I have a little voice, too, Father."

"Do you?"

"It's like a heartbeat. Only it's a mental heartbeat. It's like a mental heartbeat."

"That's exactly what it is. And if I stay calm, if I can keep calm when I feel pressured, when I'm under stress, then I can hear the little voice."

"Yes," David said. "What's your little voice say now, Father?"

Kendrick looked at him with regret in eyes, pain, not wanting to reveal it, not wanting to admit it.

David said, "Father, he only has as much power as we give him. If we make him waste his energy, and if we don't panic, if we can think the whole thing through—we'll make it. Panic is false; the secret is not to panic. The secret is to feel the whole thing, not break it up into bits and pieces. He's been looking at the whole thing from the beginning. You and I walked into the middle of it, but we can deal with it if we can see it the way he does."

"I'll try, but I'm not sure what that means."

"If you could see through the eyes of God, you know, from the beginning of time to the end of time, you'd see it all happening at once, one big picture, everything, all of life, happening just the way it's supposed to, everything connected, working itself out. Just life. We have to try to think that way. The whole thing, and not just the bits and pieces."

"Hey, David!" Jack called behind him.

"He thinks we don't understand that. He's counting on us to deal with the bits and pieces, with his leftovers. But he's put together this net, this web of things, and now I've done the same thing."

"Da-vid!"

"But what about him?" Kendrick tilted his head toward Jack, behind them. "He could be the weak link in your chain, in your web. What if Dragomir has seen that from the beginning? What if part of his web is to cripple you by having Jack here?"

"You want to hear your horoscope?" Jack asked.

"I don't know, Father. Maybe. But we don't have any choice. You have to deal with what you've got. That's something I forgot to tell you. Deal with what you've got."

"Lis-ten! Do you *want* to *hear* your *horoscope*?"

"No, Jack."

"You're a Leo, right?"

"Yes, Jack."

"Father, you want to hear yours?"

"No, Jack."

"Scorpio, right? 'Prepare for an important new challenge in your life. You are at a—'"

They saw lights down by the road, headlights cutting through the darkness, sliding across the snowdrifts, slicing eerily through the wet lines of falling snow.

"'—crossroads that could lead to—'"

"Heads up, Jack!"

The newspaper crumpled loudly.

"Visitors."

"Whoa."

David slapped Father Kendrick on the back and said, "Nora. Just stay with her. You have the—"

"—talisman, yes, David, yes."

"Go, now. Go, go."

Then he jumped across the room and ran into the kitchen and looked out the window over the sink, just to make sure that no truck or sled or something else ingenious was coming at them from behind, through the woods.

When he came back into the living room, Jack was standing up in front of the window.

"Just take it easy, Jack."

"Yeah, right."

"Nothing's happened yet."

"Like it's not going to. Do I have time to use the john first?"

"Yeah," David grinned, a little puzzled, but, "Yeah, you do."

"Never mind. I'll try to hold it."

"Hang on," David told him. "I'm going to see how Nora's doing. Just sit tight."

And as he came up the stairs, he called out, "Me, Father! How is she?"

Kendrick didn't say anything. David hurried down the landing and came into the room. The overhead light was off but Father had the desk lamp on, and it cast long, sinister shadows along the walls.

"I don't like it," Kendrick said.

He was standing on the other side of the bed with his back to the window, because neither he nor David had ever pushed the bed back against the wall. The chalk circle David had drawn this afternoon was a powdery smear on the floor.

Nora was paler than David had yet seen her, and thinner, her skin yellowish gray and covered with a thick sheen of perspiration.

David felt the pulse at her neck and leaned over to listen for breathing, pressed his ear to her breast to hear a heartbeat.

"God, she's still alive."

"He's killing her!" Kendrick insisted. "He doesn't want her to live at all! He's killing her, David!"

"She's weak. She's so weak, she's almost dead. But, Father, he won't kill her."

From the living room, Jack yelled, "David!"

"Now what? Father"—he pointed to the window behind Kendrick.

Kendrick turned around and looked out, but from this far back and from this angle, it was hard to see much of the front yard or the road. David took a quick look, then told him, "Please, stay with her. Hold her hand—anything, just so she knows another human being is here!"

"Yes, all right, all right. . . ."

And he ran down the landing and down the stairs into the living room.

"What is it, Jack?"

"See for yourself. I don't care for this at all."

"Jesus Christ," David said, looking through the window.

Lit by their own headlights in the driving snow, he saw the van and the pickup truck, and around them a mob of people, at least a dozen of them, all bundled in heavy winter clothes, getting out, standing around, beginning to move toward the house.

"Sons of bitches!" Jack swore.

"There," David said. "Is that Dragomir?"

"Yeah. I see him. And that's Glen."

"Which one?"

"Big fucker, right there. Nolene . . . Barry . . . Audrey—this is the SWAT team, all right."

"Well, they're surrounding the house," David said, "and they'll start moving in toward us. Which is exactly what we thought they'd do."

"Look at him," Jack grumbled, his hands curling into fists. "Just look at that rotten son of a bitch."

"Please, Jack, don't lose it."

"I won't lose it."

"And kill that light. I'll get the lights in the kitchen."

Jack turned off the lamp that sat on the table in front of the window.

David yelled up the stairs to Father Kendrick, "Father! Turn off all the lights, please! All of them! We're going to keep the place dark!"

32

Dragomir lagged behind, walking very slowly, leaning on his heavy cane, while Glen took command. The others moved through the deep snow and fanned out to cover the house from all directions. The sky was dark and the house was dark, the wind blew shimmering crystals of ice through the air, and the drifting snow went on forever, a desert, rolling and gliding, while more snow hurried down, and human beings left behind them winding trails of disturbance on its skin.

"Be alert!" Glen yelled. "Stay alert!"

Anything might happen, he told himself. Who could say what Trevisan and Jack Starkis were capable of doing together? Glen thought of things jumping out suddenly from windows or from behind doors or trees, things erupting from the earth, knives or demons. Anything might happen.

"Fucker acts like he's in charge," Jack said, watching from the front window, watching as Glen yelled and pointed to the rest of them while he fought the wind and lifted his legs in and out of the deep snow.

David said, "He's getting real close, I hope to tell you."

"He is, isn't he?"

"He sure as hell—"

There was a brilliant blue flash. Jack said, "Holy shit!" and covered his eyes. David squinted but kept looking.

Caught in the outer perimeter, Glen screamed, or tried to scream. He was inside the wall, in the airless blue haze. He waved his arms uselessly and kicked his legs as he was quickly pulled up into the high, cold sky.

From far above came the rumble of heat lightning. The

wild blue glow, iridescent, tall, lit the snow and lit David's house, a circular blue curtain, like shimmering paper, like thin glowing skin, reaching into the clouds.

Glen's screams trailed away in the distant sky. More heat lightning flashed. Thunder rumbled. The thin blue wall, glowing, vibrated and began to vanish and then was gone.

Dragomir grunted, leaned back, looked up. The last of the heat lightning faded away and a drop of blood struck him on the cheek.

Another drop fell, and another, and then more of them. A rain of blood came down, dappling and staining the pure white snow, falling in a circle around the house.

Dragomir smiled.

"Excellent," Jack hissed. "Excellent, good, good."

David said nothing. He left the living room and went into the kitchen, looking out the window above the sink, then came back into the sitting room and pulled back the drapes and looked outside from there, left to go into the spare room—

Another brilliant blue flash, electric and sudden, and more heat lightning high above, and grumbling thunder, and blood, the drifting rain of blood.

"David!" Jack yelled. "They're getting real close, they're here!"

David came back into the living room and stepped behind Jack. Together they saw Dragomir pointing to the house with his cane, ordering his people to continue.

Father Kendrick came downstairs. "David! There are too many of them! Don't you see?"

"I see!"

"There are too many of them!"

"Father, there's only one of them! Just one of them! Now, please—stay with Nora."

Kendrick growled something and went back up the stairs.

"Come on, Jack!"

He picked up the sword from the coffee table.

"Right here, buddy, right here. Let's do it!"

They stood together in the center of the living room. David drew a circle around them with the point of the sword, and he and Jack both incanted their prayer of defense.

"In nomine Agla Sabaoth Elohim. Elion. Amathia. On. Spiritus magnus, Agla Elohim, veni, defende me in proelio. Spiritus magnus, Agla Elohim, neco mea inimici. In nomine Sabaoth Elohim."

David set the sword down between them, flat on the rug, and pressed his arms over his chest, and Jack did the same thing. They faced the front door, because that was where Dragomir was coming from, and they would meet him, they would meet him there, look him in the eyes and confront him there, and bring him down, send his energy back against him and send him down to death, flaming and screaming in a rage of spiritual fire, etheric fire.

Behind them, then, from the kitchen—

"David?"

The door.

Someone kicking it in, the sound of it, the splintering of wood and the abrupt, heavy crash—then the electric snapping sound of the charged talisman, and the roar of fire, the scream—

Lights all over the house blinked on, went out, flickered off and on; the microwave came on, and the dishwasher—

A window—the window in the sitting room—an explosion of breaking glass, and then the wild sound of heat and flames, of flesh erupting, and shrieking, the surge of power as the barrier was crossed, the line snapped—

The front door—

Let it be him, David thought. Let it be him.

They heard the storm door being pulled back outside, twisted loose, and then grunts and howls as someone huge threw himself against the front door and smashed it, splintering the wood of it and making the whole living room tremble with each attack—

"Aeior!"

—and a tall man stumbled in, David saw him, a tall blond man in a heavy winter coat, David saw him and his manic blue eyes just before he was swallowed up by a curtain of flames, blue fire, and was sucked back into the darkness and the blowing snow, shrieking, a black corpse shrieking

THE EYES OF NIGHT

as fire and lightning danced from him, snapped and danced on the ground, making him look like a strange glowing spider with thin legs, before he dropped to the snow and sent out a long, huge hissing sound, sizzling sound, like hot steel dropped into a bucket of ice—

"Shit, David, fuck, oh, fuck, there's too many of them—"

"Shut up, Jack!"

"There's too many of them!"

Another one, a red-haired woman, Nolene, and a man, Barry, beside her, came into the living room but didn't do anything, simply stood there, one on each side of the great hole where the door had been, flanking it, guarding it as—

Stefan Dragomir.

He lurched in, melted snow running down his bare head and down his coat like fresh rain, leaning on his cane, walking in a halt, full of pain and death, aching, in agony, full of heat—

David could feel it rolling from him in great waves of power, the heat, the psychic evil, the chaos and pain of him, the incredible strength of him.

Dragomir the sorcerer, a walking furnace.

He could see the evil yellow thing in him, see that demon in Dragomir's eyes, smell the stench of it and feel the power of it, the power David had been fighting all along, the power of this thing, this raw thing of evil—

"So you. Are the young. Man. Who killed. Theodore. Fry."

David's hands tightened, he pressed his fists against his chest, his arms were crossed, and he lowered his head—

But Dragomir looked away from him, looked at Jack, and held up his free hand, his right hand.

There in the palm of his hand was a small plastic bag with fingernail clippings in it, and a wadded-up facial tissue, an old Q-Tip, maybe some dental floss, and a small color photograph.

David looked at Jack then, too.

His arms were at his sides, hanging limply.

Tears ran down his face and his mouth hung open.

He was staring at Dragomir, staring at him and sobbing—
"Jack!"

Dragomir threw the plastic bag away, cast it to the floor, and held out his arm to Jack, held out his hand.

"Jack, *no!*"

And he collapsed, Jack fell to his knees and crawled forward, crawled on his knees—

"*Jack, no!*" David screamed and reached for him and caught the back of his shirt.

The shirt tore.

But Jack continued crawling, his eyes on Dragomir, sobbing, the tears falling as he cried and cried—

"Forgive me!"

"Oh, Jack," Dragomir breathed.

"Forgive me!"

"*Jack!*"

And he grabbed Dragomir's hand, grabbed it and held it and pressed it to his wet face, kissed the hand, kissed the fingers and licked them, sucked them into his mouth, drooled and cried—

"*Forgive me-he-ee!*"

—and collapsed there, fell on his belly at Dragomir's feet and curled up like a baby and sobbed and sobbed, his whole body shivering and pulsing, heaving as he sobbed—

"*Goddamn you!*" David shrieked, and brought up his arms.

Dragomir lifted a hand.

"*Aeior!*"

But Jack, crawling, had broken their circle.

Light filled the room, light and heat. David's brilliant blue heat, his guardian strength, his soul energy, his mind and heart and his sorcerous strength, the spirit of himself, the blue curtain that was his strong wall—

Dragomir's lightning broke it.

The green evil waves of light, snapping and arcing and bouncing from walls and ceiling and floor, reaching like snakes, like worms, across the living room, danced on David's strong blue curtain of light and exploded with fiery sparks, black and red—

David screamed.

The fiery red was there, the hellish molten fury he'd fought in Nora's soul, it was attacking him now, and it ate him, it tingled in his hands and in his arms as it pierced his blue curtain, his wall, it clawed its way up his legs, it pushed into his heart with a million needles, it grabbed at his heart and squeezed it, stretched it; it filled up his vision until Dragomir and his outstretched arm and the sobbing Jack and Nolene and Barry and the dancing green electricity in the room were all washed red, until all of them disappeared behind a thick murky wave of red that went deeper, deeper, swallowing him and pushing him down, became a deeper red, became black, black, airless thick heavy cold black, no light, no bridge there, no light—

"*No!*" Father Kendrick screamed from the stairs.

—as David was thrown backward, his arms and his hands glowing with a green fire. He was lifted into the air and one foot struck the coffee table as he was sent smashing into the bookcase behind him. He slid down, bringing half the books with him, on top of him, and he slowly curled up there at the foot of the bookshelves and died.

"*No!*" Kendrick watched David fall, slide down, and die. He looked at Dragomir, the sick demon, the dying man, the thing, the thing—

Dragomir frowned at him.

And Kendrick howled, backed away, and turned then and ran back up the stairs to Nora, ran—

Dragomir faced Nolene and Barry and indicated Jack, nodded to him there on the floor, and they understood.

They grabbed him by the arms and lifted him up and walked him out into the snow. Jack was strengthless; his legs didn't move; he couldn't walk on his feet.

They threw him into the snow.

He lay there on his back, sobbing, legs spread wide and arms flung out, eyes open, looking up as faces appeared to him, as faces looked down at him, as a dozen hands stretched toward him—

He screamed.

Screamed.

Laughed and screamed—

Six of them in a ring, surrounding him, unleashing their fury at him and their strength, burning Jack alive as he laughed and screamed.

In the living room, the plastic bag with Jack's old fingernail clippings in it and his dental floss instantly burst into flames and burned a hole in the carpet.

And when they were finished, they left in the snow a charred corpse, his black skeleton, hot and smoking, the legs spread wide and the arms flung out.

From the living room of David Trevisan's house, Dragomir listened until the screams had gone silent, watched until the stench and smoke of Jack's death were floating across the white landscape of snow, waited until the six looked up at him, their master, and nodded, bowed their heads to him, and moved away, done.

Then Stefan Dragomir went up the stairs to confront the priest.

33

Father Kendrick was standing on the other side of the bed, behind Nora, facing the doorway so that he could watch as Stefan Dragomir came down the landing. He held a pair of scissors in his right hand. He'd found the scissors in the kitchen and he'd brought them up here deliberately, this afternoon *Almighty God, forgive me, forgive me* so that he'd be prepared in case it came down to this, the inevitable.

And step by slow step, Dragomir came down the landing, his cane thudding like a primitive heartbeat. No one else was with him; he was alone.

When he reached the open doorway he stopped, threw out a hand and slapped it against the inside wall, reaching, blindly, and flicked on the light.

The two old men stared at each other.

Father Kendrick looked into the eyes, the yellow eyes, demon eyes, hell eyes, and he lowered the scissors, pressed their point into the softness of Nora's throat.

He said, "I'll do it." But his voice was raspy and his hand was moving back and forth, shaking uncontrollably with fear.

Dragomir held up his right hand and waved it in front of him, back and forth, very quickly, the fingers loose and sloppy.

Father Kendrick winced, then cried out as his right arm shot up suddenly, completely out of his control, lifting the scissors high above his head.

Burning coals—

And a wicked smile.

His arm jerked again, as if it were being pulled on a

207

string, snapping back and forth on a rubber band. He brought the point of the scissors to his own throat, pressed the point of the scissors against the softness of his own throat.

Dragomir lifted one eyebrow, arching it in an unspoken question. The evil smile faded into a weary grin, sad, strained.

Kendrick, not flinching, not taking his eyes from the demon's eyes, whispered, "Then—kill me. . . ."

Dragomir blinked slowly.

Kendrick braced himself, but instead of the sudden push of pain that he expected, the scissors grew hot in his fist, the metal burning his palm and fingers.

He yelled and opened his hand, and with an electric snapping sound the scissors dropped. They bounced lightly on the bedcovers beside Nora's arm, leaving a burn mark there, and clattered on the floor.

Dragomir leaned forward and took one, two, three steps, thud thud thud, until he was in the middle of the room. Still he faced Kendrick; he hadn't even bothered to look at Nora yet.

Father Kendrick reached into his pants pocket for the talisman David had given him. He held it out, showing it to Dragomir—

—and it, too, the talisman, like the scissors, quickly turned hot, burning him. Kendrick let go of it and the talisman leaped across the room into Dragomir's hand, where the sorcerer crushed it in his fist.

Kendrick gasped.

When he opened his fingers, it was to show Kendrick a misshapen lump of hot silver, which Dragomir threw onto the floor.

"He is. Dead. His magic. Is. Dead."

It was over. Kendrick didn't know what else to do; his fingers automatically reached for the crucifix he wore around his neck. He gripped it, pulled on it strongly so that the chain broke, and held the crucifix in both of his hands, gripped it tightly and pressed it over his heart.

Dragomir grunted.

Kendrick said to him, "This is all I have left. What shall I do? Curse you? Pray?"

The sorcerer told him, "You get. To live. Father. Kendrick. That is. Your hell. You get. To live. What do you. Think. Of that?"

Kendrick stared at him. He tried to hold them back but he could not, he could not, the tears came, the sobs, and then a brute howl of anguish, an unbelievable cry of pain, as if he had indeed stabbed himself with hot metal, as if he had indeed been slain, or cursed by his God and sent down to hell.

Dragomir rapped loudly on the floor with his cane, and footsteps answered him, running up the stairs and down the landing and into the room.

Nolene and Barry and Audrey. They entered and took hold of Nora, Nolene roughly pushing Father Kendrick out of the way so that he almost fell into the window. They wrapped Nora in the bedclothes and blankets that were there and carried her out, down the landing and down the stairs.

Dragomir followed them. He said nothing more to Father Kendrick, made no imperial salute, offered no cruel jest or witty insight. He simply followed his people downstairs and out the front door.

Kendrick stood there, off balance and listening, feeling like a ghost, like an intruder, feeling as if he had been cut in half, his soul separated from his body, feeling mechanical and incomplete, conscious but unable to move.

This couldn't be it. This couldn't be it. It had happened too quickly and it had all gone wrong. It was *only a few minutes ago* that he had talked to David. David had had a plan, and the plan should have worked, the fear and nonsense should have gone on all night, it was—

It was ridiculous, it was unfair.

He looked at the bed, the depression that had been left by Nora's body, and he wanted to die, he wanted to go back in time.

This was all wrong and he knew it now, Kendrick saw where it was all completely wrong; they'd boxed themselves in, it was ridiculous, making snow fall and nailing talismans to doors, when they should have gone to the police or used guns or simply driven all night to get Nora somewhere, anywhere else, why hadn't he spoken up earlier, why hadn't—

He heard engines start up outside, far away, down by the road, the truck and the van, the tires spinning and whirring and making high-pitched sounds in the night, then gears shifting and the truck and the van going away, the sounds of gears shifting fading away.

Dear God.

He forced himself to move, and he walked, though he couldn't feel himself walk.

Kendrick got across the room and he noticed, as if he were someone else, that he came down the landing. He headed for the stairs and he felt cold air coming into the house, a great deal of cold air. He thought that a window or the front door had been left open and that he'd better close—

There was no front door, there was no front door, there was no front door anymore. He wanted to cry some more, he came down the stairs and pushed a hand out in front of him, as if he were chasing away cobwebs or shading himself from a bright light.

"David . . . ?"

No, wait, David's dead, he's dead, he died.

"Are you dead?"

In the living room he looked at the pile of snow growing inside the front door, watched the blowing snow dance in the air and crawl across the carpet, reach with cold fingers toward David's body, curled up, huddled at the base of the bookshelves.

Kendrick looked at him and he walked toward him. His mouth fell open and he tried to cry, but there was no sound, he was in agony but he could not breathe, his breathing had stopped and he could not suck in enough air to—

He fell to his knees above David's body and found his breath and Father Kendrick howled, howled, howled, one long anguished cry, an animal howl, a cosmic howl of pain and defeat.

THE EYES OF NIGHT 211

"Where are you?" Kendrick screamed to his God. "Where are you? Why did you do this? Where are you?"

He screamed, "Answer me, answer me, answer me, answer me!"

He screamed, "There is no God!"

He screamed, "Where are you, where are you, what are you, why did they all die, why does that thing live?"

He beat his head, he pounded himself on the chest and the thighs, frantic, lost, out of control, frantic—

The cold wind bit into his back, and the snow, and Kendrick looked up, tears pouring down his face, his whole face wet, and he looked at books, at a bookcase, at the ceiling of a rustic house—

The room tilted.

Kendrick was breathless, he was gasping, breathing too hard, and the room seemed to lift before him, he felt dizzy, the cold wind surrounded him, and he heard something, a humming sound, a low whining sound, very far away.

He sobbed and blinked away tears. The room settled, but he still seemed to be falling to one side. He blinked and, in that moment, as he blinked, there was a bright flash, white and sudden like a light bulb exploding, a flash bulb going off.

The humming sound was still there, the whining, and for one crippling, sorrowful moment Kendrick imagined that he heard voices, people speaking in another room of the house, or below him, far away. The cold wind wrapped around him, thin and piercing, sinking into him like a second spirit. David's voice? And a woman's. It made him think of Sister Mary, that voice, and he was in anguish when he thought of her.

He looked behind himself, suddenly frightened, suddenly terrified. Someone here with him? Who had come back?

"God, don't let—"

The smashed door, the snow coming in, the cold air—

But he'd *heard* them....

Then Kendrick felt warm, it lasted only for an instant, but he felt very flush, almost ill, as if a sudden surge of heat were passing through him, and he smelled something, an aroma, like perfume, sweet, pungent, like incense.

He blinked.

He screamed, "Answer me, answer me, answer me, answer me!"

He screamed, "There is no God!"

He screamed, "Where are you, where are you, what are you, why did they all die, why does that thing live?"

He beat his head, he pounded himself on the chest and the thighs, frantic, lost, out of control, frantic—

The cold wind bit into his back, and the snow, and Kendrick looked up, tears pouring down his face, his whole face wet, and he looked at books, at a bookcase, at the ceiling of a rustic house—

He remembered then. He thought—

"Oh, dear *God*, what—?"

The room lifted again, Kendrick felt very dizzy, he was breathless, gasping, and someone grunted, it wasn't him—

Grunted, and grabbed his wrist.

Kendrick looked down.

Scratched at his hand, as if clawing for life.

"God, no! *No!*"

Clawing and staring at him, David was staring at him, and moaning, gasping for air, grunting and trying to speak—

His eyes were open and he caught hold of Kendrick's arm and held on, held on—

Warm.

David's skin was warm, his eyes were bright and alive, full of fear—

Alive.

"Oh . . . dear . . . God. . . ."

David Trevisan was alive.

34

*W*hen I come. Back. You will help. Me, then.

Early Sunday morning Nora, under an assumed name, was admitted into the maternity ward of one of the hospitals on whose board sat Iva Daugherty and other associates of Stefan Dragomir. She was given a private room. Two nurses were assigned to her exclusively. Personal employees of Stefan Dragomir acted as security guards on a round-the-clock rotation.

"What's with the mystery bimbette at the end of the hall?"

"Got me. Nobody knows nothing and they got the file locked up in Claudia's office or something."

"For crying out loud."

"Hey, they don't pay me enough to worry about all the weird shit goes on in this place."

"You got that right."

A memo in the mystery bimbette's file indicated that, unless developments dictated otherwise, labor should be induced within forty-eight hours of her admittance into the hospital.

The Sunday morning papers contained the initial write-ups on the rash of odd accidents and crimes that had occurred in the city on Saturday. Reporters following up on these incidents, however, soon ran into a maze of peculiar developments—"deliberate obfuscation," one of the women with the *Enquirer* called it. A couple of them were outright howlers.

The man charged with shooting E. William O'Connell

on the I–275 bypass, for example, was a seventeen-year-old semiliterate drug addict who did not have a driver's license, could not remember his current address, and who did not know how to operate the style of shotgun identified as the murder weapon. When asked how he might load shells into the shotgun, his best guess was to force the ammunition down one of the the barrels; he'd seen that done once in a movie.

Files of two other investigations had simply disappeared overnight. In one instance, a needed jacket was located but was found to contain, not the case's paperwork, but a large number of poorly photostated dirty cartoons, some of them featuring Santa and Mrs. Claus.

Also missing was an electric space heater identified as the cause of the swimming pool deaths of Mr. and Mrs. Norman Vernon. A police officer walking through the evidence room noticed that, while the space heater was gone, two D-cell batteries had been tagged as possibly contributory to the Vernons' deaths.

Attempts to reach persons who might have been able to answer important questions were stonewalled, as well. Many of them, explained receptionists or official spokespersons, had left the city for extended holiday vacations—sudden, pressing engagements in Europe or tours of the Holy Land. No doubt they would be happy to comply with the investigation when they returned early next year.

In Noland, Ohio, Father Kendrick, to restore his sanity, set about nailing lengths of plywood over the broken windows and the ruined back and front doors. As he did this, he tried to avert his eyes from the burnt bodies and the burnt pieces of bodies that lay on the ground around the house, Jack Starkis's and others'. He was concerned that passersby, cars or trucks going past the house, would see the corpses. But the few motorists who did go by that morning paid no attention to David's little house in the woods, and the snow that had started yesterday afternoon continued to fall, which helped to obscure the bodies.

Besides, as David had pointed out to him, people will

look something right in the eye, look right at something and not see it. Someone comes up the driveway and sees four corpses lying in the yard. Oh, I see you have four burnt bodies in your yard. It wouldn't happen. They'd deny it. Look right at it and not see it. Odd-looking logs you got there; damned things look like human bodies, ain't that one for the books? Where'd you find them logs, back here?

Kendrick looked in from time to time on David, whom he'd put to bed upstairs, and who slept through the morning and through the early afternoon. Kendrick wanted to sleep, too, but he could not. Once or twice he had lain down on the couch and tried to drift off, but had come awake suddenly, heart pumping, seeing people on fire, running in the snow, seeing yellow eyes staring at him in the dark.

He made himself some tea and drank it, but was not in the mood to eat anything.

He straightened up the house, the books that had fallen and the things in the kitchen that had been knocked down. There were scorch marks on the walls and burn marks on some of the carpeting; he wasn't sure what to do about those.

And occasionally Father Kendrick would stop what he was doing, sit down on the couch or in a chair, and cry. Just let himself cry like a child, get it out, release it, let it come out.

Late in the afternoon, David woke up and Father brought him a cup of tea.

"How are you feeling?"

"It only hurts when I—breathe. Like—that."

He sipped the tea and Kendrick watched him and desperately wanted to talk with him.

"Do you want anything to eat, David?"

"No. No."

"Let me know when you do."

"Yes. I will."

"Can we talk—later?"

"Yes."

"I know you need to rest."

And, later, over another cup of tea on a snowy winter

day, Kendrick told David what he had done, boarded the doors and the windows, straightened up.

"Thank-you. Thanks. We'll get some . . . lumber, buy some new doors. . . . What day is today?"

"Sunday."

"Right. Yeah. It would be Sunday, wouldn't it?"

Father told him or reminded him that Jack was dead, that Dragomir or some of his people had killed him, and that they'd taken Nora—no doubt back to Cincinnati.

David said nothing, seemed to think about it as Father told him these things. His skin, which had been very pale, seemed to be regaining some of its color.

"I think I'd like to rest now, Father."

"Certainly."

"Could you . . . just turn the light off for me, could you, please?"

"Surely."

"The light seems awfully bright."

That evening Kendrick phoned Monsignor Pantik. He'd been rehearsing the phone call all day long, not certain how much he should tell Phillip, or even how much he plausibly could tell him.

"What's happened to you? Where are you, Mike?"

"You're never going to believe this." He explained that he'd disappeared yesterday because he'd literally been kidnapped by Jack Starkis, who'd panicked because of the police investigation into Sister Mary's death. He'd wound up here, in Noland, where he'd been able to escape from Jack, and was staying with a friend of his, a young man who'd once attended the seminary.

"You're safe, then?"

"Oh, yes. Quite safe. Only we weren't certain whether or not to tell the police here, so I thought you might tell Sergeant Pomeroy. Here—Jack Starkis was driving a blue Duster, I don't have the license number, and he was going to head south, or told me that he might go south, maybe to Atlanta. Could you forward that to Sergeant Pomeroy?"

"I will do that, yes, immediately."

Kendrick explained that he'd be back in a day or two, take the bus or accept David's offer for a drive back to Cincinnati.

"That sounds fine."

"Oh, yes—Phillip? You might tell Bud, too, that Jack's no longer associated with Stefan Dragomir."

"No?"

"No. Dragomir fired him."

"Your jokes," David told Kendrick, when he overheard that one, "are getting to be as bad as mine."

He'd come downstairs in his bathrobe and, moving slowly, full of hurt and pain, managed to sit down at the kitchen table.

"Hanging around with the likes of you," Kendrick said, "I'm bound to pick up some bad habits."

"You're right about that. But you can't—ouch—you can't call me a liar. What do you say? Do I throw killer parties or not?"

Kendrick made them sandwiches from cold cuts he found in the refrigerator, and some coffee, and they ate supper. The snow had stopped, and outside the house now everything was snowdrifts, snowdrifts and blowing cold wind.

"I'll bury the bodies as soon as I feel up to it," David told Kendrick. "Believe me, nobody'll report them missing. Get rid of Jack's car, too."

"Doesn't it make you feel like a criminal?"

"I'm already a criminal."

Kendrick built a fire in the firepalce—"This takes great courage for me to do this, do you understand why?"—and asked David, "Why aren't you dead?"

"Because of you."

"Me?"

"Because of what you did."

"What on earth did I do?"

"Father, I saw it all. Jack. You and Dragomir. I knew I was dead but—still, you fight for your life, you still want to be connected. Animal instinct or something. And I was still fighting for my life. All of that energy of Dragomir's.

And you called me back. Everything was set up for a ceremony, for a ritual, and you completed the ceremony, even though you didn't know it."

"But, David, things like incense and that sword of yours—I never did those things."

"Props. Props. Get your mind right. The ceremony is nothing but focused energy. And your energy was focused. We had a lot of focused energy in this room, let's face it."

"I've been thinking about it all day long. Can't get it out of my mind, trying to make sense of it."

"People die and come back, Father. Happens on operating tables, probably happens—"

"But not like this. This was something I'm not familiar with at all."

"It was there, Father, and you just became part of it for a moment. That's what it was."

"Don't make it sound blasé."

"Believe me, I'm not being blasé."

"I must have been out of my mind."

"You were, in a way."

"It was as if time stopped, time seemed to stop. The room spun around... I heard voices. There was a bright light." He looked at David intensely, questioning him with his eyes. "I was somewhere else, wasn't I?"

"You were listening in on things most of us don't get a chance to hear. Mystics, maybe."

"Magicians."

"Yes."

"I thought I heard your voice, like it was far away. And Mary's. Maybe Mary's, too. Or did I just imagine that?"

"Trust it, Father."

"Trust it?"

"Oh, yes. Trust it. You were touching some very deep stuff."

Kendrick said then, "There is a God, isn't there?"

"You can call it God."

"What would you call it?"

"It has about a million names, I suppose. But it all comes down to just the one thing. Everything is alive. Everything

THE EYES OF NIGHT

in existence is simply alive. That's what it is."

"So that's what death is. We become aware of so much. Do we . . . We become part of so much, really become a part of it."

"Nothing dies," David told him. "Nothing ever really dies. Everything's always alive, in one way or another."

"Yes, alive. . . ." Kendrick looked into the fire and said, "I've made myself into a criminal, too, haven't I? Lied to Father Pantik. I won't be able to tell Bud Pomeroy the truth."

"Oh, some day you probably will."

"It . . . infuriates me . . . to know that Stefan Dragomir has . . . won. Is going to murder his own daughter and do whatever it is he can do to her baby. Foul—*thing*. I would never have imagined there were such things on the earth."

"He hasn't won yet, Father."

"What do you mean, he hasn't won?"

"Just what I said."

"David, what can you do now?"

"Watch and see. All will be revealed."

"But you're too weak, you're sick, you're—"

"I'm alive, Father Kendrick. I'm alive. For which I thank you. But I'm alive, and so is Stefan Dragomir, and so is Nora, I'm sure. And that makes all the difference. You know the old joke about Jesus?"

"I don't know. Which one?"

"Second Coming. 'He's back and he's pissed.' Well, that's the way I feel. I'm back and I'm pissed. I'm real pissed."

35

He got rid of Jack's car that night, hid it where he'd hidden the black woman's car, deep in the woods, in a gulley of mud and rocks and tree roots, where both of them would disintegrate over the winter and over many winters, rusting and corroding, picked apart by the elements and by nesting wild animals and helped along by human scavengers who'd take the engines and the tires and all of the metal, the seats and the nuts and bolts, every last part of those cars, not even leave a hubcap or a spare wire.

David buried the bodies, too, the four burnt corpses, husks, shells. He hollowed out a long ditch, using a pick axe and a shovel, and dumped them in there, feeling like a criminal, they really did look like old charred logs, and as he covered them over, he thought, Jack, you complete asshole, you asshole.

"Whatever you need, you can count on me. I mean it. Just ask. Anything."

"A new life."

He remembered talking to a police officer once, years ago, a friend of his father's, and the police officer had commented that the easiest thing in the world to get away with is murder. A sudden, sloppy, insane murder is impossible to trace. Don't be neat; don't be polite; don't plan it too well; just lose it, go nuts, and run the son of a bitch off the road in the middle of the night, surprise him and shoot him in the face and run away. There's so much death, so much insanity, so much incredible nonsense in the world, no one can straighten it all out, and no one really wants to be bothered with trying to straighten it out.

Afterward, on his way back to the house, limping and aching, he stopped at the spot where he and Nora had talked yesterday.

Had it been yesterday?

"Everybody's outside in the cold. They want to come inside and get warm, but it's so cold that it doesn't matter anymore. They'll just watch the fire for a while. They'll just watch and not move, because it's so cold."

". . . it's so cold . . ."

". . . so cold . . ."

They slept late on Monday, he and Father Kendrick both, waking up a little before noon. Kendrick made them lunch, the last of some chili David had in the refrigerator. Then David went to the bank and on the way home stopped at a hardware store and bought two doors and two windows. It took him and Father Kendrick the rest of the afternoon to hang the doors and windows. The doors came out okay but the windows weren't real great. Windows are a bitch, and neither of them was a practiced carpenter.

"Well, they'll keep the snow out, anyway," Kendrick said.

"More or less," David said.

They took showers, ate supper, packed. David offered to lend Father some clothes, but the only thing that really fit him was an old, oversized sweatshirt with Kent State University printed on the front of it. So they did some laundry, and the fresh clothes helped Father Kendrick feel more comfortable and relaxed.

Then they loaded David's car.

"You're sure you're up to this, David?"

"Oh, yeah."

"We can go tomorrow."

"I really want to get there and get this over with, just get the whole damned thing over with."

"All right, then."

"Just want to make one quick stop before we get going."

* * *

Cheryl's father had died some years ago, but he'd left his wife a house that was paid for, a little land, and a comfortable income from his savings and his investments. The house was on the west side, only a mile or so from I-80. David swung by there a little before seven, and Father Kendrick waited out front in the car while David walked up the driveway and knocked on the back door.

Small two-story house. White aluminum siding. Brown plants, dead for the winter, along the side by the driveway. Dead or hiding, hibernating. Green garden hose hanging on a spool, stiff, frozen. David saw the big splotch of red paint that Cheryl's brother had accidentally sprayed on the cement block foundation about three years ago, at the picnic before he and his wife had moved to Arizona. "Damn it, Cher, there's no paint left in here now!" Clack clack clack hissss. *"Shit!"*

The back light came on, instantaneous and bright. It hurt, the light hurt. David lifted a hand to cover his eyes as the back door opened and Mrs. D'Angelo stared at him.

"David."

"Is, uh, Cheryl here?"

Long look. Thoughtful pause. Do we still know you?

"She's upstairs sleeping."

"Look, then, can I talk to you for just a second? Leave this for her?" He reached inside his coat.

Long look. Thoughtful pause.

"All right. . . ."

She pushed open the storm door and David came in and followed her up three quick steps into the kitchen. The house was warm, very warm, overheated. He could smell the dust in the air from the furnace.

David put a white business envelope on the kitchen table and on top of it the keys to his house.

"That's a letter in there, from me. A letter of intent that I want to sell the house and I'd like Cheryl to do that and keep whatever commission she gets out of it. I had it notarized today at the bank. Keys're there, too."

"Can't you just call her in the morning?"

"Well, I'm on my way out of town. I'm leaving right

now. I expect to be back in a few days, but if I'm not, if it takes a little longer, then at least she'll have this, get started with it."

"I'll see that she gets it, then."

"There's another letter in there, too. Telling her, you know, one of the doors got damaged yesterday, stupid thing, accident. Telling her about that."

"Well, I'll give it to her."

"Okay, then."

"David, is there something wrong with your eyes or something?"

"No, no, it just seems, the lights seem kind of bright, that's all. It's nothing."

He wondered if she'd think he was on drugs. He wondered if she'd ask him questions about Frank Gauss dying at his house. But she didn't, so David supposed that Cheryl hadn't told her mother yet, maybe she'd never tell her, or maybe she'd tell her that Frank had moved away or had been transferred to the office in Toledo or wherever.

"I'd better get going now."

Mrs. D'Angelo walked him to the back door. David stepped outside and looked away from the light. Mrs. D'Angelo held the storm door open a little.

He told her, "Thanks again."

"You know, David, I'm kind of sorry that it didn't work out for the two of you. I didn't think it would because you're just too different, but I feel badly anyway."

"Yeah, well . . . thank-you."

"It's difficult for young people today."

"I guess so." He looked at her then, squinting against the light. "Maybe I've been going through a rough time, you know, but I didn't mean to do anything to Cheryl. I didn't mean to do that at all."

"You know, David, Cheryl's father and I always said you have to know where you want to go with your life and you have to make your plans to get there. I don't think you know what you're doing with your life. You're a very intelligent young man, but you don't seem to have much direction, although I don't know why that is. I don't know how much this religion of yours has to do with it. Cheryl hasn't told me very much about it. Maybe some of the people in it aren't good for you, though, have you considered that? Is it one of these cults they're always talking about today?"

"Well, it's not a cult. It's not actually much of a religion. It's more like philosophy."

"I just think you need to motivate yourself and find a goal and do something with your life. Think about if your parents were still here, what would they say, you know? I think you need to look at the big picture and see where you fit in it, is what I think."

"Maybe you're right."

"I'll see that Cheryl gets the envelope in there."

"Thank-you."

"You take care of yourself."

"Thanks."

"And Merry Christmas."

"Merry Christmas, Mrs. D'Angelo."

He walked back to his car and got in and started it up and pulled away from the curb.

Father Kendrick asked him, "Well?"

"Well what?"

"That's it. Just, 'well.'"

"The kitchen lights hurt my eyes. They're too bright, Father, and they hurt."

"The kitchen lights."

"Because of my accident."

"Uh-huh."

Five solid hours to get to Cincinnati.

Father Kendrick had decided that the person to talk to, once they got there, was Mrs. Iva Daugherty.

He and Jack had had a long talk on their way to Noland yesterday, Jack naming all of the important people involved with Stefan Dragomir, all of the dirt and trash they'd done together, however much he knew, and Father Kendrick had deduced that the single most decisive one of them, Dragomir's alter ego or partner in crime or whatever, must be Mrs. Daugherty.

Yesterday, while David had been downstairs or outside creating the snowstorm, Jack had handed Kendrick a slip of paper.

"The people we were, you know, talking about on the way up here?"

"Yes?"

"In case you need them. You got your names there, phone numbers... kind of a chart, who's doing what to whom."

"Okay, Jack. Thank-you...."

" 'Cause you never know, right? Who knows? I don't know."

Five hours—which got them to the city by midnight, a little after.

They drove directly to St. Luke's and from the phone in his room at the rectory Father Kendrick called Mrs. Daugherty on her private number, the one Jack had given him.

"I think I recognize your name, Father Kendrick."

"Perhaps you do."

"I thought that you were dead."

"Perhaps I was supposed to be."

She agreed to see him, late as it was, which told Kendrick and certainly David—

"She screwed up once, Father. She's got to be real scared. This could help her out a whole lot, she kills you or sits on you until this whole thing's over. Do him a big favor, probably."

"She told me to come over. Now. Tonight."

"Okay."

"What should I do?"

"Go. Only take me with you. If she's that tight with him, then she'll know where Nora is. If she's alive, where Dragomir's hiding her, where he is. We have to try. And something else."

"What?"

"I was thinking about this on the way down here. Dragomir's dying, right? What's the first thing you'd do if you knew you were dying?"

"I don't know... buy a cemetery plot or... I don't know!"

"Second thing."

"David . . . a will!"

"Where's his will, and who'd he leave everything to?"

"Dear God! Nora?"

"Nora's going to be dead."

"Dear God."

"I think we should find out who's named in his will, is what I think. Could help us out. You know where this woman lives?"

"Jack wrote it down, here."

"Then here we go."

36

David asked Father Kendrick to drive to Iva Daugherty's. "You can handle a five-speed, right?"

"Of course I can."

"Toyota's a five-speed."

"Where are you going to be while I'm driving this five-speed Toyota of yours?"

"Right beside you, thinking of a plan."

"David, I'm convinced that you really enjoy this wing-and-a-prayer approach to dangerous situations."

"I'm just doing what I can to get through the day, Father. I'm making it up as I go along. Making it up as I go along."

"Not a particularly profound philosophy, is it?"

"But a practical one."

It was twenty minutes to the Daugherty home—an estate actually—and when they were nearly there, Father said to David, "I have an uncanny feeling of déjà vu."

"Literally? Right at this moment?"

"Not literally, no. But it wasn't very long ago that I said good-bye to you, when you and Nora were on your way to Noland, and I had the chilling feeling that we weren't going to see one another again."

"Fooled you, didn't I?"

"And now we're walking into another lion's den."

"Well, I'm the proverbial bad penny, Father. I just keep showing up."

"You're the proverbial something. We're here." He pulled into a long, black-topped driveway that curved back from the road and passed through a tall, wrought-iron gate. The doors of the gate had been left open.

Iva Daugherty's home sat quite some distance away, on top of a hill, stately beneath the bright moon and nighttime clouds.

"Rich people," David said, looking at it.

"You sound jealous."

"I am. Jealous as hell."

"How are you feeling otherwise?"

"Worried and scared."

"Have you thought of a plan?"

"Certainly have. Would you slow the car down?"

"But we're not there yet."

"I'm going to jump out here, Father, before anyone sees me, and hide in those bushes up there."

"So that I get to go in alone."

"That's right."

"I don't particularly care for this plan."

"It'll be fine. No one's going to hurt you."

"Oh, really?"

"Not immediately, anyway."

"I think we'd better talk about this a little more before—"

"Here. Stop the car. I can get behind that tree."

Kendrick braked. David opened his door and stepped out and quickly looked back at him.

"Just go in and keep her busy. Keep talking. Small talk. Charm her."

"I'm a priest! I'm not some bon vivant!"

"You'll do fine. Wing and a prayer."

"And where will you be?"

"Scoping it out."

"And how long am I supposed to keep this up?"

"Give me ten, fifteen minutes."

"Fifteen minutes!"

"I'm going to break in and prowl around. See if Dragomir's there or something."

"Fifteen minutes with that monster? Pretending that I'm—I'm small talk?"

"Father, be a pro. You can do it. It's for Nora."

"Dear Christ! David—"

THE EYES OF NIGHT

"Bye." He closed the door and jumped into the darkness.

He was mildly surprised that his jaunt up the lawn, keeping as well as he could to the shadows cast by all the trees, didn't attract the attention of any watchdogs. No watchdogs?

She'd have something looking after her place, though, that was for sure.

David came to a carriage house, unlit and apparently vacant, and he stopped there for a moment, stood in the shadows and surveyed the back of the Daugherty mansion. Long stone wall there. Maybe a patio of some kind behind it, a garden of some kind.

It looked promising so he aimed for it, glancing in all directions as he did so. No watchdogs and, so far, no people around either. The scariest thing was that he seemed to be getting away with this.

He jumped the stone wall and landed in a small garden. There were paths. David glided down one of them until he reached the back of the house.

There was a wide, flat, elevated porch and off to one side of it a service entrance of some kind—steps and a back door leading to another porch, a small, enclosed porch.

He took the steps and tested the doorknob, trying not to rattle it—

The door opened.

Now he was nervous. Had he tripped an alarm somewhere, a burglar alarm?

Or was there sorcery guarding this entranceway? Was he about to walk into a web stretched from floor to ceiling or a sheet of goo that would suffocate him or would he suddenly fall into a hole or have to face leaping things shooting at him suddenly from the darkness?

Calm down, calm down . . .

So there was no burglar alarm. Maybe Iva Daugherty was one of those people who thought that installing a burglar alarm would automatically attract burglars. Or maybe she'd just never gotten around to it. Or maybe she'd just forgotten to turn it on.

Or maybe she'd never thought about protecting this place at all, certain in her patrician pride that no one would come all the way out here to hurt her. Reputation and arrogance can act as shields. Or seem to.

He closed the door softly behind him and moved forward as carefully as he could, afraid with each step that he would make a sound, boards creaking or something, and bring guard dogs down on top of him, or demons blowing up out of clouds of vapor—

But the house was completely unprotected, or apparently. David moved through room after room, kitchen, pantry, hallway, access rooms and storage rooms, stepping carefully, listening but not hearing anything—

Perhaps Mrs. Daugherty wasn't here?

Had something happened since Father Kendrick had phoned her?

In yet another small room, David moved cautiously around a coffee table of some kind and stepped into another hallway, and saw light at the end of it.

A line of light at the bottom of a closed door.

Sweating, he eased down the hall. It was carpeted, which comforted him. He heard voices on the other side of the door, and they grew louder as he approached. David recognized one of them—Father Kendrick. He assumed the other to be Mrs. Daugherty.

And he sensed something, too. Didn't hear it or see it, but felt it.

Felt it, the presence of it in the air.

We know our own kind. We're like cats in the dark.

Here was the guard dog. Here was the burglar alarm.

If this clown on the other side of the door knew his job, he'd feel David coming, too. If he were paying attention.

If he weren't—

Hell, even if he were, David had the advantage of surprise.

He reached the door. He leaned against the wall, listened, but couldn't make out the words.

Footsteps.

Too heavy for Father Kendrick, certainly too heavy for Iva Daugherty—

David rapped quickly on the door, pounding loudly several times—

"Yoohoo!"

—then grabbed the door handle and held on to it, gripped it firmly—

"In nomine Agla Sabaoth et—"

The voices, Father and Mrs. Daugherty, went quiet.

"—in nomine spiritus magnus—"

No. Mrs. Daugherty was saying, she called out, "Joe" or "Joel."

The footsteps stopped, right there.

David could feel him on the other side of the door, almost see the outline of his energy through the wood, a big son of a bitch, as tall as—

The big son of a bitch gripped the doorknob from the other side—

"*Aeior!*"

—and David let him have it.

Energy, energy, pure, raw, loud, shrieking, real, pouring through the metal door handle—

Joe, screaming, shrieking, and the abrupt, sick smell of burnt human flesh in the air.

Or Joel.

Whatever his name was.

Mrs. Daugherty cried out.

David let go of the doorknob, pressed his back against the wall, and, at an awkward angle, brought up his left leg and kicked at the door.

It swung open, banging loudly against the inside wall.

David walked into a large room, a library, with very tall ceilings, very tall drapes at the windows, an enormous number of volumes on the shelves all around, a large fireplace, two library tables, and some splendid antique lamps.

On the other side of the room, Father Kendrick and Mrs. Daugherty, staring at him.

David glanced at the corpse on the floor. It had been, yes, a big man—but a big man taken by surprise. He stepped over the blackened body, no way to get around it, and kept his eyes on Mrs. Daugherty as he did so.

"Hard to find good help these days, isn't it?"

"Who are you?"

"I'm—"

"Are you—"

"—David Trevisan."

"Oh, my God." She turned and looked at Father Kendrick.

He nodded.

"I'm here to kill Stefan Dragomir."

"But you're dead. He killed you, he *killed* you, you're *dead!*"

"I was dead. I came back."

"What?"

"For him."

37

"Mrs. Daugherty," Kendrick told David, "has been pretty forthright so far."

"You mean she's told you the truth?"

"Yes," she hissed at him. "Yes, I've told him the truth!"

"That's probably because she figured that what's-his-name over there—Joe? Joel?—"

"Joel."

"—was going to strangle you in a minute or two. They were going to mount your head as a trophy, Father."

Iva Daugherty didn't care to look at the corpse in the middle of her library floor.

David walked over to her. She was sitting on a loveseat and he crouched down in front of her, rested his elbows on his knees, and said to her, "Personally, I don't care what kind of sick fucking relationship you had with him. All I want to know right now is where he is and where Nora is."

She looked at him but refused to say anything.

"I don't have to hurt you," David told her, "but I will. I can cause you some real pain. Even do a little internal damage. Or are you into that, you and Stefan?"

"Go to hell, Mr. Trevisan."

"Everyone keeps telling me that, and I have absolutely no intention of going anywhere."

He stood up and lightly dropped a hand on Iva Daugherty's shoulder and squeezed.

"You say when."

Kendrick said, "David, don't—"

"No more fucking games, Father."

Iva Daugherty winced. She was in pain. She began to

sweat and, not meaning to, not in control of her own body, she started rocking back and forth on the couch. She was sweating.

"David, you'll kill her!"

"So be it. Her or Nora."

"David—"

"It's all the same thing, Father. I can be a nice guy, or I can be a son of a bitch. Just like our little talk, remember?"

"David!"

"It all comes from the same place."

Iva Daugherty moaned, she gasped, and, not able to stand it anymore, at last threw a hand on top of David's and cried out in pain.

So did Kendrick. *"Stop! Now!"*

David let go of her.

She fell back into the couch, whispering and groaning, tears of pain coming down her face, and she grimaced as she massaged her hurt shoulder.

"Maybe it's me," David admitted, not looking at Father Kendrick. "Maybe I should just learn to go along to get along, you know? But I really do not have a great deal of patience when it comes to the outright creeps and assholes of this world. What do you think, Mrs. Daugherty?"

She shot him a ferocious look.

"Should I try to be a little less impetuous when it comes to the creeps and assholes of this world?"

"You're out of your league, Mr. Trevisan."

"Let me explain the facts of life to you, rich lady. He thinks I'm dead."

"You said—oww—that he killed you."

"I did say that. Do I look dead to you?"

"Hardly."

"He thinks he killed me, but I'm still walking around. I'm a surprise package. What do you think of that?"

"I think that even Jack Starkis couldn't kill him."

"Look." David walked over to Joel's corpse and tapped it with his foot. "Jack's dead. I'm not. Glen Dennison is dead." He waved his hands at her. "And these little finnies did it. Now tell me where Stefan Dragomir is and I won't kill *you.*"

"You have no idea what—"

"And don't tell me how strong he is and how powerful he is, and don't tell me how many followers he has or how many politicians he owns. I couldn't care less. I don't care where he was born or how he got here. He's mortal, and he's mine. I'm killing him. Tonight."

"You'd better know what you're talking about."

"Give me something, Mrs. Daugherty."

"Dear Christ Almighty."

"Give me something!"

She said, "He's going to turn me into that, anyway, won't he?" She meant Joel on the carpet over there.

"Yup. He will."

"You really think you can do something."

"I can kill him." David looked her in the eyes, searched there. "Please, Mrs. Daugherty. Help me kill him."

Slowly, uncertainly . . . "All right."

David let out a long rush of a breath. "Thank-you."

"What do you need?"

"First things first. Here. Is Nora safe?"

"The last I heard, she was."

"And where is she?"

Iva Daugherty named the hospital and told him the room number.

Father Kendrick took a small notepad out of his shirt pocket and a pen and jotted it down.

"And where's Stefan Dragomir right now?"

"If he's still alive, and I don't know how he's stayed around for this long, as sick as he is, he's at a house he owns in Madeira." She gave him the address.

Father Kendrick wrote that down, too.

"One other thing," David said. "I want to know about his will."

"His will?"

"Who'd he leave everything to?"

"I have no idea."

"The guy's a jillionaire, he's dying, he's practicing black magic all over the goddamn—"

"I didn't make out his will, Mr. Trevisan."

"Who did?"

"Paul Honegger, probably."

"Probably?"

"Paul Honegger."

David went to her and leaned close and put his hand on her shoulder again. Mrs. Daugherty flinched, but he didn't do anything to her.

He said, "Why don't you call Paul Honegger right about now and find out for us who's in that will, would you do that?"

"I'm not even sure he's in town."

"I'll bet you could find out. And I'll bet you could track him down, too, an influential lady like yourself."

"All right, Mr. Trevisan."

"Thanks ever so much." He stood up and looked at Father Kendrick. "I have the phone number here, right? It's the one Jack gave you." He glanced at Mrs. Daugherty.

"Yes," she said.

David headed out, then, walking past Kendrick.

"Father, I'll call you in half an hour, hell or high water. No—I'll call in half an hour, high water. If I'm in hell, the phone won't ring."

"Understood."

When the front door far down at the end of the hall had swung closed, Mrs. Daugherty said, "He's quite a... strong-willed young man, isn't he?"

"Mmm," Father Kendrick agreed. "He gets it from me."

Quarter to two in the morning, in the middle of the night.

It was a small ranch house in a suburban neighborhood of wide lawns and trimmed shrubbery. David watched it as he crawled past in his car. It looked just like the other houses on this block, ordinary and plain, only this one had no Christmas decorations.

He parked along the curb about two doors up, got out,

and carefully looked the street up and down before making a move.

The night. Everything quiet, chill, very still and crisp. No traffic. No barking dogs.

David walked down the sidewalk toward the house. His footsteps echoed and carried; he moved off the sidewalk onto the lawn.

Still, silence—no traffic, no dogs—

And no hint of anything else, either. No sorcery, no—

He stopped when he got to the house, listened, waited, watched it carefully for a minute or two.

Dragomir was in there.

Stefan Dragomir was in there.

Guarded, protected, by what?

Or by nothing?

Was he going to protect himself by doing nothing whatsoever? Could he be that arrogant?

David didn't sense anything, and with Dragomir in there—

Was he in there?

Or had Iva Daugherty lied to him, set him up, or simply got him out of the house for some reason, maybe to hurt Father Kendrick, maybe for some other reason.

Jesus, Dave, take it one fucking step at a time, just take it one fucking step—

Literally.

He crossed the yard, keeping an eye on the front door, the porch, but went around the side of the house, glanced at the cold black windows, came around back.

There wasn't a porch, just a concrete slab patio, a trellis at one end and some lawn furniture still, this late, sitting out.

And nothing in the air, no sensation, no feeling, no breeze or scent or pulsation of anything unordinary or sorcerous or deadly—

David whispered to himself, "This is fucked, this is weird. This is weird."

He saw no cars in the driveway. There was a two-door

garage and David crossed the shadowed lawn to peek inside it. No cars in there either.

"This. Is. Weird. . . ."

He went back to the porch, felt the door, and pressed the palm of one hand against the cold glass of the door, expecting the glass to come alive and wrap around his hand, or to shatter and suck him inside, grab him by the arm—

He reached for the doorknob, didn't grip it but tapped it gingerly a couple of times first. Nothing. Great. He took hold of it, shook the knob, twisted it—

The back door swung open, inviting David into the small, dark, cold house.

Cold.

He walked into a kitchen. No table and chairs, just a counter with a few paper wrappers on it, some Styrofoam cups.

Nothing on the walls, no baskets or pots and pans, no clock, nothing.

No, wrong. There was a phone hanging on the wall beside the refrigerator. David went over and took down the receiver.

The phone was dead.

He opened the refrigerator. Bad odors but no light, no humming sound.

Electricity was out.

This is fucked, this is weird. This is . . . She's fucked us over, *damn* it. . . .

He wasn't sure whether to check out the upstairs first or the downstairs, but before he got to the entrance to the living room, David came to an open door, the stairs leading to the basement, so he took them, he walked downstairs.

And now he sensed something, smelled something, very raw and very real. Smoke, he smelled smoke, and he smelled blood.

Human blood.

No electricity. The basement was thoroughly dark.

With each step the stairs creaked, and David could see almost nothing, he—

He carefully put each foot out in front of him, making

THE EYES OF NIGHT

sure first with his toe that he had something to walk on, that he wasn't going to trip or fall or be attacked, as he got almost to the bottom of the stairs, got past the overhang and was able now to see—

The basement was lit, there were candles.

Not many of them but, still, what was left of some candles. Orange lights, small waving orange lights—

"Jesus *Christ*, no, *no!*"

Stefan Dragomir.

Stefan Dragomir, lit by the candles.

Stefan Dragomir, lying on his back on a table, surrounded by the candles.

Dead, lying on his back, dead, Stefan Dragomir with a knife through his heart.

38

He drove frantically to get to the first telephone he could find, a phone booth in front of an all-night convenience store, and he dialed carefully, he was excited, and stood there waiting, frightened, shivering because he was cold.

So cold.

"Father Kendrick! Are you all right, are you—"

"David? I'm fine, I'm—"

"Listen to me, it's a trick! It's a trick! They've— Is Mrs. Daugherty there?"

"Yes. David, what's happened?"

"They killed him!"

"What?"

"They've killed him, they've sacrificed him! Dragomir! They've started the ceremony, we're too late!"

"No, no!"

"Call the . . . Mrs. Daugherty, have her call, phone the damned hospital and find out what's happened! I'm coming back now, right now! Find out about Nora! Find out about the baby! Now. Now!"

"Panic is false; the secret is not to panic. The secret is to feel the whole thing, not break it up into bits and pieces. He's been looking at the whole thing from the beginning. You and I walked into the middle of it, but we can deal with it if we can see it the way he does."

"Mrs. Mortimer? Mrs. Mortimer?"

Drowsily, she opened her eyes.

"Mrs. Mortimer, would you like to see your baby?"

"Is it—" She slurred her words, fought the drowsiness, the drugs. "Is it—all right...?"

"He's fine, he's a fine little boy."

Nora flopped her head to one side, she was so weak, and tried to lift her arms out for her baby, she wanted to see it and hold it, just once, please God, just once, whatever was going to happen—

"Here he is!"

She saw him in the nurse's arms, little boy, pink little boy, all red and tiny, incredibly tiny, tiny fingers—

A second nurse came in, huge smile, and said, "Mrs. Mortimer, here's the other one!"

"The—other—"

"Here's your brand-new baby girl!"

Dear God, what was this, two babies, she'd had—

She looked, tried to look. The first nurse stepped out of the way and the second nurse leaned in, showing Nora the little girl—

"Is she—"

—the little girl that was not pink, that was not—

It opened its eyes, the little girl opened its eyes and looked at Nora suddenly like a reptile, it had intelligent eyes, it had yellow eyes—

"Kill it!"

"Mrs.—"

"Kill it, kill it!" She tried to sit up, tried to grab the baby boy, the baby boy with the black eyes, tried to get hold of it so that she could strangle it, rip it apart, tear it with her fingers and teeth—

"Stop her, nurse, call—!"

"Kill it, kill it!"

Her father's eyes.

"It's him, it's *him*, kill it, for the love of—*God! kill it, kill it!"*

Mrs. Daugherty was just getting off the phone when David, gasping for breath, came into the library.

"Twins," she told him and Father Kendrick. "Nora had twins."

"Let me guess."

"Guess what, Mr. Trevisan?"

"One of them is sick."

"The little girl was born with leukemia. The little boy is fine."

David laughed out loud. Stamped his feet on the floor and threw his arms up in the air and jumped, made fists and threw them back and forth.

"The man's a genius! The man is a fucking genius! He knew it all along, he saw it all along! God *damn* him, he's *brilliant*!"

"There's more, Mr. Trevisan."

"More?"

Oh, Jesus, he felt chill, he realized—

"Nora's dead."

Father Kendrick yelled, "No!"

"She was found . . . murdered. She was found—"

"—nailed upside down to the wall of her room," Father Kendrick said. "Butchered. Cut. Mutilated."

"Yes."

"Nora," Kendrick said. He walked to the loveseat and sat down, sank into it.

David looked Mrs. Daugherty in the eyes. They shared something then, the two of them, something neither of them had anticipated. But he made a sound and looked away, turned away from her and Father Kendrick.

He felt tears wanting to come, and he couldn't cry now, he had to stay on top of it all, he had to—

He shoved his hands into his coat pockets, furious, humiliated, feeling betrayed, and made them into fists—

He felt the Kleenex.

"When we go back to the house, get a pair of scissors or a knife or something and cut off some of my hair. . . . Use it to help me, if you think it would."

Oh, God, oh, God, he couldn't face that now, he couldn't think about that now. . . .

"David?" Father Kendrick said behind him.

"It's what you are."

He swallowed and from where he was said thickly, "The

THE EYES OF NIGHT 243

little girl—does she have yellow eyes like he did?"

"I really don't know."

"Like his demon? What about the little boy?"

"He's missing."

Kendrick looked up.

"Of course he is," David said, turning around and looking at Father. "The private security people. Dragomir's people. Killed Nora, took the little boy. And who knows where they are now?"

"On a plane to Europe," Mrs. Daugherty said. "Or soon will be."

"Those babies," David said, "were born premature, and Nora was not in good condition. That little boy is going to have to be well taken care of, wherever he is and wherever they take him."

"That little boy has Stefan Dragomir's soul in it," Iva Daugherty told him.

"And what's the little boy's name, Mrs. Daugherty?"

"I don't know. I don't know that it was given—"

"You know. If Nora didn't do it, then Dragomir's security people did, or one of those nurses that're on his payroll. Bet your ass they don't come to work tomorrow. The doctor, either, I'll bet. They all just won the lottery. What's the little boy's name, Mrs. Daugherty?"

"They really didn't say."

"What's the name in the will, then? Did you call your lawyer?"

"Honegger."

"Honegger."

"Yes."

"And?"

"Everything—*everything*—that Stefan Dragomir owns has been left to someone named Eric Mortimer."

"And there we have it, friends. I'll bet you a hundred dollars that Nora—"

"Nora Mortimer," Mrs. Daugherty said. "That was the name they used when they took her into the hospital."

David shook his head and smiled cruelly. "Man's a motherfucking *genius*! Out-thought, out-figured everyone, saw it all from miles away, played us all for fools, didn't overlook one detail—"

"He's had a lot of practice, Mr. Trevisan, believe me. Stefan Dragomir's soul is thousands of years old. It's survived a lot worse things than people like you trying to kill it."

"I'm sure. No doubt. . . ." David sighed wearily and walked over to the loveseat and sat beside Father Kendrick. "I'm sure," he said again, and yawned, couldn't fight it. "Tell me—"

"Yes?"

"Mrs. Daugherty, what was it between you two? This hot love affair? Was it that? Was it—"

"Yes, Mr. Trevisan, that's what it was."

"I wonder how long ago your husband died."

"Three years ago."

"And I wonder how long Stefan Dragomir waltzed into your life."

"Four years ago, Mr. Trevisan. I was attracted to him instantly."

"Yeah, he's a charmer. And he was attracted to your wealth. Your clout. Your connections."

"To my husband's wealth, Mr. Trevisan. Henry was one of the wealthiest men in the state."

"And he probably left you everything."

"Yes. We have a daughter in California. I rarely see her. I send her checks."

"Help him along. Why not, right? Goose old Henry so that he jumps right off the cliff. Gets you that inheritance so much faster. You and Stefan Dragomir. What were you going to do, eventually? Marry him?"

"Probably not. But we had some very pleasant and intriguing business relationships."

"And he killed your husband for you."

Mrs. Daugherty smiled.

"We're not going to say anything," David sneered. "The hell do I care, anyway? And even if other people knew, it wouldn't change anything, would it? People don't give a shit, not really. It wouldn't—" He stopped.

"David?" Kendrick asked him.

"I'll be goddamned," he said, looking at Mrs. Daugherty. "Nora told me that her father's disease, this leukemia he had, started when he fouled up a ritual."

"He confided the same thing to me."

"Care to tell us—"

In a voice as cold and brittle as iron, she told them both, "I initially agreed to help him with a ritual designed to kill Henry. But I got cold feet and tried to get out of it."

"That's what fucked him up, then."

"Yes. I . . . was responsible."

"So what'd you finally do? Push old Henry off the roof or something? Hunting accident? What?"

"Stefan completed another ceremony and he died of a heart attack."

David shook his head and laughed again and looked at Father Kendrick. "Here I am, helping Nora, helping her *baby,* trying to get her through this—and all along I'm helping him. Helping that healthy baby of his to live. Helping *him* live. Nobody said anything about twins because the only people who knew about it were his fucking killer elite, his damned Praetorian Guard."

He stood up and walked over to the one of the windows and looked out at the night. A light snow was falling, not common for Cincinnati. But it reminded David of Noland, his house in Noland.

"That explains Fry, too. If he'd have been able to get hold of Fry, he could have killed him. Big ceremony. The soul of another magician. Very powerful. Help incubate the soul of Nora's healthy baby. But I killed Fry, so he wanted to meet me. And I played right along, I actually helped the motherfucker. Everything I did to keep Nora alive kept the baby alive, too. Things go a little screwy, Jack and whatnot, but he handled it all pretty well, I have to admit."

"Very well," Kendrick agreed.

"All of them," David said, "everyone who died, he just channeled that energy through himself, sucked it up, just to stay alive long enough so that Nora could finally deliver her baby and he could slide into it, separate his healthy soul from his sick body. He puts the disease in the little girl. How long will she live? A week? But he comes back in the healthy baby boy. Jesus . . ." He pounded his hand a couple of times against the window frame.

"So he will indeed come back," Kendrick said.

"Yeah. They'll raise him and haul him back over here in ten years or so, set him up in business again. The old road to glory and power. Land of opportunity. Land of fucking people over."

"At least by that time," Mrs. Daugherty said, "I'll be somewhere he'll never find me. Get away from him and—"

She glanced at Joel's corpse, looked away again.

David was still staring out the window, thinking. He said out loud, "But he fucked up once, at least. He fucked up one thing." He looked at Father Kendrick. "Me."

"True."

"That gives me an edge, doesn't it? That means that there must be something I can do to get him, to—"

"David, face it. He's won."

"Mr. Trevisan," Iva Daugherty told him, "your tenacity is admirable, but Stefan Dragomir has wisdom—"

"I understand that, I know that! But this is me! I promised Nora and I promised myself that I was going to nail his ass to the wall! This is me now! Nobody else!"

He stared at them hotly, Father Kendrick and Mrs. Daugherty, and growled in his throat and clenched his fists, refusing to give up.

"He's overlooked something," David said. "He must have. Damn it, it's not possible for—"

He stopped.

The snow.

Outside the window.

Snow drifting down, snow coming down.

He turned and looked at Father Kendrick. "I've got it."

"Got—"

Snow, and his blue wall, and all the screams, and the blood raining down—

"I've got him, he's dead, he's mine, he's dead."

39

"Blood tests," he said to Mrs. Daugherty. "All babies have blood tests."

"Of course they do."

"Phone the hospital lab. I want the blood that was taken from the baby boy."

"Dear God!"

"Is there someone you trust? In the lab?"

"Carla."

"Are you sure?"

"She has nothing to do with Dragomir—I'm confident of that."

"Because we have to be certain."

"I'm certain, Mr. Trevisan."

"Okay, call her. Call her right now!"

"Dear God," Father Kendrick said.

"Call! Now!"

They had taken the baby across the river into Kentucky, into Bellevue, a small house there, another house owned by Stefan Dragomir.

The basement had been prepared for Eric Mortimer's arrival—the windows painted black, and a great wooden table set up in the center of the floor, and the walls painted black, as well, and covered with drapes, with hanging tapestries done beautifully by hand.

Tapestries that were centuries old.

Tapestries that depicted events in the life of Eric Mortimer, the life of Stefan Dragomir, the life of this evil soul through many centuries.

Eric, Stefan, dozens of other names, being burned at the stake, being beheaded, sitting on a throne, copying books in a scriptorium—

The soul, the black dark soul, soul of evil, thousands of years old, born and reborn, the soul dragged shrieking from the bloody wombs of women sacrificed time after time throughout history.

He went around the library, pushing and shoving things out of the way, chairs, the loveseat, the big library tables—

"Father, could I ask you to go out to the car—"

"Yes, yes."

"—get into the trunk, get the stuff I brought."

"Yes, right now."

David dug into his coat pocket and threw him the keys.

"Hurry, hurry, please,"

"Yes—"

There were six of them.

The baby was in a basket.

They placed the basket on top of the table and put dozens of black candles around it, then lit them.

The baby, Eric Mortimer, the thing, watched them do it from his basket, watched them with his black eyes, the eyes of his reborn soul.

Mrs. Daugherty put down the phone and said to David, "There are blood samples from both babies—"

"We only need the boy's."

"I understand that, I know. Because they were premature and because labor was induced, they take blood samples regularly."

"What're we talking? Like a small test tube? However much that is?"

"That's what Carla said, yes."

"They sending the boy's blood over here?"

"Yes."

THE EYES OF NIGHT

"Mrs. Daugherty—can we trust this woman? Carla, whoever's going to send the blood?"

"Implicitly."

"Dragomir has people all over the map."

"But he doesn't own everyone, Mr. Trevisan. He doesn't own Carla. He doesn't own a lot of people. His . . . followers are no doubt all gone now, anyway. Why would they stay at the hospital now? The police are there, Nora's been murdered—"

"Just so this is the baby boy's blood."

"It is. It will be, I'm certain of that."

"Okay then." Carefully, "Okay then."

"Mr. Trevisan, I don't know if it's possible for me to hate him as much as you do, and to want him dead as much as you do, but I do hate him, and I do want to see him dead."

David smiled at her. "Help me with this, can you? I'm going to need some space, here on the floor. . . ."

One by one they filed past the baby, took its small pink right hand and kissed it, looked into its eyes, the eyes as black and dead as glass, as marbles, as stones, and moved on, taking positions around the table, lifting their hands, praying, praising the baby, Eric Mortimer, the thing.

David drew a wide chalk circle on the bare wooden floor of Iva Daugherty's library, drew it around a small antique table, which he covered with a blanket and used as his altar.

He set candles and his bowl of incense and his sword on the table, his altar, and waited.

The car pulled up in front of the house and Mrs. Daugherty, who'd been watching from the window, ran out in one of her expensive furs and hurried down into the drive to take the package from the driver.

"Carla!"

"I decided to bring it myself."

"Thank-you, thank-you, Carla. And, please, remember—"

"I was never here, Mrs. D."

"Carla, whatever can I do to repay you?"

She laughed and said, "Let me think about that one!"

They prayed to it, as they would to their god, their evil god, this ageless spirit that had come down to them through time for their care, to be protected by them, for them to die for, for them to scream and shriek and lust and die for.

They chanted to it.

Chanted a chant, a great ancient prayer, deep and ancient and cold as the sky, as the winter, as death, a prayer to keep it alive, this ancient soul—

Keep it alive, give it strength, so that it would live, reborn now, so that it would live—

The first of them, a young man, picked up a razor with his right hand and slit the palm of his left. The blood ran down his arm and he licked the blood, smeared it over his face, then offered it to the baby, to the thing, to the ageless soul, so that it might drink and live, live.

Mrs. Daugherty ran inside, ran down the hallway, ran into the library to give the package to David, and he tore it open, brown paper and tape—

Test tube of blood.

There was a sticker on it, a label.

BABY BOY MORTIMER

"Over there, please," he told Iva Daugherty and Father Kendrick.

She stood in the shadows, in a corner, her back to the furniture that had been pushed out of the way, and she watched David Trevisan light red candles, watched him pass his hands over a brass bowl he had, watched him cross his arms on his chest and then raise his arms and look up at the ceiling and chant words she'd never heard before....

"Dear God," Iva Daugherty whispered.

"That's precisely what this is," Father Kendrick told her.

* * *

THE EYES OF NIGHT

The second put the razor to her hand, the palm of her hand, sliced and brought up the blood, licked it and smeared it over her lips and over her face, then offered it to the black eyes, to the baby surrounded by black candles, so that it might drink and live.

And she continued the chant to it, a heartbeat sound, they all did, the six of them, the throbbing pulse of a heartbeat, the chant, beating, beating. . . .

He wet his fingers with water and touched his forehead and his mouth and his heart, crossed his arms over his heart and bowed.

"In nomine Agla Elohim Sabaoth. Elion. Amathia. On."

"It isn't what you do. It's what you are."

He lifted his sword, raised it above his head.

"Defende me in proelio contra spiritus malignos."

"They're all contaminated."

He poured incense into his brass bowl, lit a long wooden match, and set fire to the incense.

"Veni neco mea inimicus. Veni, Agla Sabaoth."

"So you. Are the young. Man. Who killed. Theodore. Fry."

The smoke from the incense poured upward in a cloud, reached to the ceiling, and David breathed it in, lifted his arms, and stared into the hot burning coals of incense.

"Interficis hic animus."

"You're out of your league, Mr. Trevisan."

He lifted his hands to the elementals and spirits that guarded him and followed him and carried his sorcery out upon the currents in moving waves of power to do or undo according to his will.

"Interficis hic animus. Veni, Agla Sabaoth."

"I've got him, he's dead, he's mine, he's dead."

They prayed, they chanted, the third cut his hand and drank the blood and offered the blood to the baby, and it with its black eyes leered and sucked and watched, watched these slaves bleed in the candlelight and pray to him, as they had done before and before and before, over the thousands of years of all the times of fire magic and blood worship.

"Interficis hic animus," and he opened the test tube, poured the blood into the bowl of burning incense, and yelled, *"Aeior!"*

The baby with black eyes, covered with blood, staring, watching the six as they moved around it, praying to it, chanting—
The baby began to cry.

"Aeior!"

It shrieked.
The flames of the candles wobbled.
The air moved, a wind grew, *wind* in the basement—
"That smell! I smell—what is it?"
"It's crying, why is it—"
"It's incense! *Incense!*"

"Aeior!"
David threw his arms out, held his arms out, and howled.
"You're mine, you son of a bitch!"

It was crying and shrieking, screaming, waving its arms and legs in the basket.
"It'll knock over the candles!"
"Who's doing this?" one of the women screamed. *"Who is doing this?"* To the ceiling, to someone she couldn't see, *"Who are you?"*

Thunder boomed, the glass in Mrs. Daugherty's tall windows rattled, and the stark, piercing odor of blood, sharp and metallic, came into the library.
"You're dead, you son of a bitch! You're mine and you're dead!"
And now, as if carried on the thunder, a great wind rolled in, and the flames of the candles did not go out but grew

brighter, and the smoke of the incense seemed to boil up and fill the room like a black fog . . .

It was screaming and shrieking as blood popped from its nose and ears and ran down out of its eyes in long red sheets. It was gurgling and hissing and trying to escape—

"Who is doing this?" one of the women continued to scream.

"Chant, chant for it, *give it strength!*"

"*They're killing him! How can they kill him?*"

A black mist formed around it as its body, turning fiery, burned the blood that poured from it, burned the blood as the flesh began to steam and crackle—

Great veins appeared on its head and exploded.

Great burning welts appeared on its skin as it kicked its legs and waved its arms and shrieked, shrieked as thunder boomed, as all of them there screamed—

"*He's dying, he's dying, he's dying, he can't die!*"

Burning candles fell off the table, the basket caught on fire, and one of the six, her clothes, her robe caught on fire.

"*He can't die! Help me! I'm—!*"

Father Kendrick and Mrs. Daugherty fell to their knees as the wind roared through the room, as the flames of the candles lit up the entire library—

"My God, my God!"

"I can *hear* him! Where is he? *I can hear him!*"

It screamed as it died. Screamed, the baby, the ageless thing, the undying soul.

As the woman, one of the six, died on the floor, shrieking, "I'm burning, *I'm on fire!*" and as the others tried to save her and save it.

Screamed, roared, roared, as the blood poured out from it and the flames of the burning basket wrapped around it—

—roared, not in its baby's voice—

"*Aeior!*"

* * *

—but in Stefan Dragomir's voice, in the hoarse, dying, masculine roar of an ancient Stefan Dragomir, howling, howling like an animal, roaring because it was killed, it was dying, it had been killed—

The roar boomed and echoed in Mrs. Daugherty's library like the pounding thunder outside, bounced back and forth between the walls as David laughed at it, laughed at it, laughed at Stefan Dragomir, his soul, his dying soul, his roaring, howling, dying voice, as it echoed and faded away...

Faded...

Faded...

The smoke in the room.

The smell of incense, the sharpness of burning blood.

The wind, dying, etheric wind, sorcerous wind.

David, panting, leaning on his table, looking at the burning incense, the blood, Dragomir's blood...

As it echoed and faded...

And David laughed.

His voice was hoarse, his voice was a whisper, but he looked out the window at the night sky, stared at the moon and the clouds, breathed, breathed the incense and the blood and felt the sorcery as Stefan Dragomir's roar of death died out, and crossed his arms over his chest, bowed and smiled and said, "I ad infernum."

Go to hell.

DAVID C. SMITH is the author of eighteen novels. *The Eyes of Night* features characters introduced in *The Fair Rules of Evil*, which was published by Avon Books. Smith lives in Akron, Ohio.

Avon Books presents your worst nightmares—

...haunted houses

ADDISON HOUSE   75587-4/$4.50 US/$5.95 Can
Clare McNally

THE ARCHITECTURE OF FEAR
                        70553-2/$3.95 US/$4.95 Can
edited by Kathryn Cramer & Peter D. Pautz

...unspeakable evil

HAUNTING WOMEN   89881-0/$3.95 US/$4.95 Can
edited by Alan Ryan

TROPICAL CHILLS   75500-9/$3.95 US/$4.95 Can
edited by Tim Sullivan

...blood lust

THE HUNGER   70441-2/$4.50 US/$5.95 Can
THE WOLFEN   70440-4/$4.50 US/$5.95 Can
Whitley Strieber

Buy these books at your local bookstore or use this coupon for ordering:

Mail to: Avon Books, Dept BP, Box 767, Rte 2, Dresden, TN 38225
Please send me the book(s) I have checked above.
☐ My check or money order—no cash or CODs please—for $_____ is enclosed
(please add $1.00 to cover postage and handling for each book ordered to a maximum of three dollars).
☐ Charge my VISA/MC Acct#_____Exp Date_____
Phone No _____ I am ordering a minimum of two books (please add postage and handling charge of $2.00 plus 50 cents per title after the first two books to a maximum of six dollars). For faster service, call 1-800-762-0779. Residents of Tennessee, please call 1-800-633-1607. Prices and numbers are subject to change without notice. Please allow six to eight weeks for delivery.

Name _____

Address _____

City _____ State/Zip _____

NIT 0489

WHITLEY STRIEBER

The world will never be the same...
TRANSFORMATION
70535-4/$4.95 US/$5.95 Can

THE #1 BESTSELLER
COMMUNION
70388-2/$4.95 US/$5.95 Can

A NOVEL OF TERROR BEYOND YOUR IMAGINING
THE WOLFEN
70440-4/$4.50 US/$5.95 Can

THE ULTIMATE NOVEL OF EROTIC HORROR
THE HUNGER
70441-2/$4.50 US/$5.95 Can

Buy these books at your local bookstore or use this coupon for ordering:

Mail to: Avon Books, Dept BP, Box 767, Rte 2, Dresden, TN 38225
Please send me the book(s) I have checked above.
☐ My check or money order—no cash or CODs please—for $_____ is enclosed (please add $1.00 to cover postage and handling for each book ordered to a maximum of three dollars).
☐ Charge my VISA/MC Acct# _____ Exp Date _____
Phone No _____ I am ordering a minimum of two books (please add postage and handling charge of $2.00 plus 50 cents per title after the first two books to a maximum of six dollars). For faster service, call 1-800-762-0779. Residents of Tennessee, please call 1-800-633-1607. Prices and numbers are subject to change without notice. Please allow six to eight weeks for delivery.

Name _____
Address _____
City _____ State/Zip _____

STR 0589

CREATED TO SERVE, NOW THEY'RE DEDICATED TO DESTROY HUMANKIND

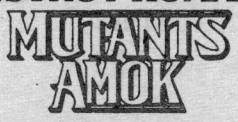

MUTANTS AMOK

by Mark Grant

MUTANTS AMOK 76047-9/$2.95 US/$3.50 Can

They had been bred as the perfect killing machines—vicious, fearless warriors genetically designed to triumph on the battlefields of the 21st century. But the mutant servants have revolted and a small band of human rebels—their one-time masters—are the last hope of a besieged planet.

MUTANTS AMOK #2: MUTANT HELL
76048-7/$2.95 US/$3.50 Can

An attempted revolt by a brave but foolhardy band of *Homo sapiens* guerrillas has been crushed. Their captive leader, Max Turkel, is faced with a grim and terrible choice: either slow, agonizing death at the hands of his inhuman enemies... or collaboration.

MUTANTS AMOK #3: REBEL ATTACK
76191-2/$2.95 US/$3.50 Can

The savage mutants have captured the beautiful lover of Jack Bender—leader of the courageous band of human rebels—spiriting her off to Hollywood to star in a grisly mutant "snuff" film.

Buy these books at your local bookstore or use this coupon for ordering:

Mail to: Avon Books, Dept BP, Box 767, Rte 2, Dresden, TN 38225
Please send me the book(s) I have checked above.
☐ My check or money order—no cash or CODs please—for $_____ is enclosed (please add $1.00 to cover postage and handling for each book ordered to a maximum of three dollars).
☐ Charge my VISA/MC Acct#_____ Exp Date_____
Phone No _____ I am ordering a minimum of two books (please add postage and handling charge of $2.00 plus 50 cents per title after the first two books to a maximum of six dollars). For faster service, call 1-800-762-0779. Residents of Tennessee, please call 1-800-633-1607. Prices and numbers are subject to change without notice. Please allow six to eight weeks for delivery.

Name_____

Address_____

City_____ State/Zip_____